What Lives In The Mountain

By Ron Managhan

Licensed cover art.
Cover art by www.SelfPubBookCovers.com/Burner.

Managhan Publishing

Publisher's Note: This novel is a work of fiction. Names, characters, places, and incidents are either products of the author's imagination or used fictitiously. All characters are fictional, and any similarity to people living or dead is purely coincidental.

ISBN: 978-0-9960126-1-4

Table Of Contents

Chapter 1
The Mountain

Time is a curious thing. Its passage will be perceived by an individual relative to the length of their own life, and how pleasant it is at any given moment. There are those who endure its passage under trying circumstances for long stretches. Some withdraw from life, while others seek it out and embrace it. Of those, the most fortunate will gain understanding.

It wasn't a very pleasant walk he was having on this colder than usual day in June. It was Monday, June 1. Jack Thomas was walking in an area of northwestern Montana. He had walked it many times before, always looking.

Jack was six feet tall with an athletic build, in his early thirties. He was wearing blue jeans and a khaki green T-shirt, a ruggedly handsome guy who felt at home in the woods.

He had first come to this particular area with his father when he was a young boy on summer break, just after his tenth birthday. It was about thirty miles west of Missoula, above the Alberton Gorge. Captain John Mullan cut a road when he passed through this area in May of 1860. The military had commissioned Mullan to build a 624-mile-long road from Fort Walla Walla, Washington Territory to Fort Benton, Dakota Territory. Thousands of people traveled the road in the years that followed.

It was this obsolete road that had brought Jack and his father to the area when he was ten. Something happened that day, something that would haunt him for many years. Bits and pieces of forgotten memories drove him to return here many times since. He couldn't remember what happened, but it must have been something extraordinary. Little did he know, before the day was over, it would happen again.

Jack reflected back to the time he first came here. It was one afternoon while he was on vacation with his family. His father, Dave, had brought him to Mullan's road to hunt for lost relics. They searched along an abandoned section with their metal detectors.

The terrain was steep with brush and rock outcroppings. It was hard to tell where Mullan first cut the road. As it was improved over the years, parts of it were deserted. Their goal was to find the original site and look along it for anything of value.

Dave looked at his young son and said, "There are rattlesnakes in these parts, so be careful and look around. Now listen, I want you to pay attention to where you are, and where I am, so we don't get too far apart."

Jack was an only child, average size for his age. He was handsome with blondish hair and no lack of confidence. He had good parents who had always affirmed him while challenging him to do his best. His dad was a medical doctor and his mother was an artist who worked at home, providing him with a good upbringing. He was thoughtful, curious and inquisitive and wanted to be an inventor when he grew up.

They started canvasing the area and quickly found signs of the original road. Then the metal detecting began. Off they went, swinging back and forth, while listening intently for their machines to alert them to the next find. After some time, Dave suggested that it was time for dinner. "I have some sandwiches if you're hungry, Jack."

While sitting on a nearby log, they munched on their sandwiches and compared their finds. They had found square nails, rusty cans, horseshoes and such. Dave reached into his bag of relics and extracted a shiny object. "This doesn't belong. I wonder how it got all the way up here. It looks like stainless steel." The object looked more like something from the space age. It clearly didn't belong there.

"Can I see it, Dad?"

"Sure," said Dave as he handed it to his son. It was about the size of an apple and looked like it had been in a fire. Jack handed it to his father who put it back in the bag.

After dinner, Dave said, "We'd better get back at it so we make the drive up here worth it, plus it's getting late in the day."

Back to work they went. Jack had more energy and excitement than when he started. Back and forth he went as he followed the barely discernible, once well-traveled road. Time seemed to stand still. Then he lost all awareness of time and surroundings as he swung his metal detector back and forth, and back and forth. The sun slipped below the horizon, leaving it light enough to see but starting to get dark.

3

Suddenly Jack heard a voice in his head saying, "Look up." He did but he didn't see his father and had no idea where he was. The terrain was steep and rocky. In fact, he was standing in the middle of a rockslide. Then, as if on cue, he lost his footing and slid down the hill. He maintained his balance at first, but then fell and rolled. He hit his head and all went dark as he blacked out.

Dave had to search for at least an hour with a flashlight before finding Jack. It was kind of miraculous, he wouldn't have found him except a noise from the woods made him look in that direction. He found Jack at the bottom of that rockslide lying motionless. After looking him over for injuries and checking for symptoms of a concussion, Dave carried his son to the car.

The next thing Jack remembered was waking up in darkness in his father's car.

"You gave me quite a scare, Jack," said Dave. He shook his head but kept his eyes on the road. "I couldn't find you for a while. Are you okay, son?"

Jack rubbed his eyes and blinked. After checking himself over, he calmly said, "I'm okay, Dad. I just fell down."

Dave didn't say anything else for a while. He just couldn't shake the image of his son lying at the bottom of that rockslide. Jack had been unresponsive and lying perfectly still. The rest of the drive on the way to the motel would be spent in silence.

Feeling warm, safe and comfortable with his dad in the car, Jack drifted off to sleep. When they arrived at the motel, he awoke and walked to the room.

After he went to bed, everything seemed to be fine, but he soon began to feel doubt and fear. He had no idea why he felt this way. He pulled the blankets up over his head.

The next day was spent getting a thorough examination at the local doctor's office. His own father also checked him over, but no injuries were found.

On the way back to the motel, the concerned father said, "You haven't been yourself since our excursion to the mountain. What's bothering you, son?"

Jack was bothered by the feeling that more time had passed than anyone knew. Although he had no memory of anything happening after he blacked out, he felt like a lot of time had passed. He remembered seeing something scary, but couldn't remember when.

"I think I saw a werewolf, Dad. I can still see his face when I close my eyes."

Dave thought about it for a moment and said, "There's no such thing, Jack. You could have seen a bear or something like that. It was pretty dark out."

Jack knew his dad was just trying to help, but he also knew there was more to it than that. Maybe he imagined something scary, or maybe he just hit his head too hard in the fall. He just wanted to remember. The rest of the trip became a blur.

After they returned to their home in Jefferson City, Missouri, he was troubled by what he didn't know. The only part of the trip that Jack thought about was the part that he couldn't recall. It was at this time that he first started being afraid at night. He was unable to rid himself of the image in his mind, the scary face he saw.

Where did it come from? That was now the question. This picture in his mind would haunt him for years and years, robbing him of confidence and replacing it with fear. Jack had never been afraid of the dark before, but now he was. There would be more images to come, surfacing now and then as time went by. He began to think of them as real memories. That's when his father decided it was time for Jack to see a psychiatrist.

His first sessions with Dr. Anna McGuirl were actually pleasant for Jack. She was a young and beautiful psychiatrist who had just started her own private practice. He could now talk to someone about these "memories." Dr. McGuirl was patient and sympathetic. In the years to come, Jack wouldn't be convinced his memories weren't real. It was only a matter of time before Dr. McGuirl would become frustrated, but remained fond of him anyway, and he felt the same way toward her.

It was about a year after the ill-fated trip that Jack's father bought a lake house in Montana. It had been a dream of Dave's for some years.

Polson, Montana is a small town on Flathead Lake where people from all over come to boat, fish and recreate. It is in this area where Dave found a nice cabin on the southeastern shore of the lake.

The first time Jack's family came to their new cabin they stayed for two weeks. He felt like he had finally come home. The first day there, Jack found himself wandering along the shore looking out across the water. It was a sunny day in late June, not too hot with a nice breeze out of the north. He felt calm and at peace as he took in the stunning view. Blue skies and mountains surrounded this large beautiful lake on the Flathead Indian Reservation, where the mountains were green and lush. They looked friendly, not at all like the steep rocky mountain that still loomed in the back of his mind. From this time on, he would refer to it as "the mountain."

Suddenly, Jack was startled by a voice from behind him saying, "I'm Sharon, Sharon Anderson. What's your name?" He turned around to find a barefooted girl with a friendly smile. She was dressed in shorts and a T-shirt, holding a fishing pole. Sharon was about his age, slightly taller, with long brown hair and a warm, sincere smile. Sharon would become a lifelong friend of his and he knew it the moment he met her. It was this moment in time that would come to be one of Jack's most precious memories. It was this image that he would recall over the years when he thought of his best friend.

"I'm Jack Thomas from Missouri," he said. Feeling no awkwardness at all, he returned the smile. "Do you live around here?"

Sharon pointed to the house just a stone's throw away from the Thomas house. "Right there."

It was a medium-sized, well-maintained house that the Andersons lived in year round. They were a conservative, close family with three girls. Sharon was the oldest. Her two little sisters were fraternal twins, three years younger.

The two of them instantly hit it off. They hung out, fishing, swimming, or just talking about their mutual interest in science. For the next two weeks their favorite spot to talk was out at the end of the boat dock.

From then on, he always looked forward to these trips to Montana. Sharon's family liked Jack and would invite him and his folks over for dinner at least a couple times every trip. The Andersons were a traditional family that said grace at dinnertime and went to church on Sundays.

After that first trip to the cabin, Jack had a new pen pal. He would write to her and receive letters from

Sharon on a regular basis. As the years went by, they would go from writing letters to e-mailing each other, even as they would later go off to college.

Sharon went to the University of Montana in Missoula with the idea of becoming a psychiatrist. Later she would find herself drawn into biology where she excelled. After receiving a B.S. in biochemistry, she would go on to earn a Ph.D. in physiology. After college, Sharon was recruited by a biomedical research company in Washington state.

Jack, a bit of a social recluse, had a 4.0 grade point average in high school. He was accepted into Harvard where at first he did very well, but the good times didn't last very long. There were many struggles, but he made it through the first year. Although Jack was into his studies, he just couldn't focus on the things that he knew were important. His roommate, Randal, was a good guy who looked out for him. He would often take Jack out for a game of pool and some pizza, doing what he could to get Jack out and about.

Halfway through his second year in college, Jack found himself sitting on the floor of his dorm room. He was studying surrounded by books and notes. Then without warning, something happened. Was it an overactive imagination or a real memory? He couldn't tell. He couldn't get it out of his mind. There was more to the memory that had haunted him. Over and over his thoughts returned to the time when, as a ten-year-old, he fell on the mountain. Just then he remembered something new.

There he sat at the bottom of the rockslide holding his right leg with scraped and bloody hands. He was unable to stand because of the pain in his knee. He heard a growl coming from the woods, then saw something watching him from the cover of the brush. Its eyes seemed to glow in the fading light of the day, then blinked. The feeling of helplessness and fear overtook him as he sat there, knowing that he was the prey. There was a growling predator in the brush, lurking just out of sight. Just as quickly as it appeared, it was gone. Then out of nowhere a man whom he had never seen before came walking up.

What had just happened? Before that moment, Jack had no recollection of there being anybody else on the mountain. He thought it was just his dad and him there that day. He previously had no memory of being hurt. He was already confused about that time, and this memory didn't help. Filled with many unanswered questions, he got up and walked out the door, leaving everything behind.

There was much to think about on the long drive home to Jefferson City. Thoughts of letting Sharon down and becoming a loser. Would his father understand? What would become of him and what would Dr. McGuirl have to say? What really happened on the mountain?

Jack had the feeling that he was jumping off a cliff just to see what would happen. It felt like he was about to commit a crime. It didn't seem like he had a good reason to do what he had just done, but the feeling of panic pushed him over the edge. He had never been impulsive. In fact he felt quite foolish at the time, but there would be no turning back now.

There was no browbeating or condemnation from Jack's parents when he got home, where he was met with a hug. Even though Dave was disappointed by his son's actions, he did his best to hide it from Jack. Dave felt responsible for Jack's troubles, that he should have been able to help his son more than he had.

There were a couple trips to Dr. McGuirl's office that didn't go well. After long conversations on the phone with Sharon, Jack decided to take a year off from school. He wanted to get his head straight. He moved to Missoula to be around Sharon and found work with a metal fabrication company.

He found life in Missoula to be a welcome change. His new job had him lifting hundred-pound bags of sand to keep a sandblaster full. His hands never had calluses and blisters before. He liked the hard work, taking a certain satisfaction from it.

The once-timid, skinny young man with soft hands became strong and capable. At first Jack just helped the painter with sandblasting and painting, then he could do it himself. It wasn't too long before he was recognized for being a hardworking and reliable employee. The welding shop foreman asked Jack to help out in the welding shop, where they were shorthanded on a big job. After only a few months, he could call himself a painter and a welder. His new job provided a very much needed outlet and therapy for him. Things were going well.

Sharon liked having her best friend nearby and they would spend time together when they could. They talked about getting married someday, but Jack wanted to wait until after he graduated from college. Sharon never judged him or criticized his decisions. She listened with compassion and understanding. Even when he didn't go back to school the following year, she never brought the subject up.

Although Jack was no longer bound by fear, he couldn't forget the mountain. It was during the second summer in Missoula, and many years since the metal detecting trip, that he hatched a plan. Jack called his father and asked him for directions to the very spot where he had his fall.

"Dad, I know this might sound odd, but I want to do it. I would like to go back to that spot where we were metal detecting when I was ten. Can you tell me how to get there?"

Dave took some time before he answered, "If you think that's what you want, I'll come up and take you right where we were."

"I would like to go there by myself, Dad. I want to spend some time up there."

"Son, there are snakes and other hazards. A guy shouldn't go places like that alone. What if something happened to you? How would you get help?" Dave reasoned.

Jack, trying to show respect for his father, came back with, "Dad, I'm not a kid anymore. I've spent a lot of time alone in the woods lately, plus I have a cell phone."

After a long pause Dave said, "Okay, but only if you call me when you get there and when you get back. Sorry, I'm still your dad. I can't help it."

"I love you too, Dad. I will call."

Dave told his son how to find the access road and how far to go up the somewhat obscure road through private property that even most locals didn't know about.

That's when Jack first returned to the mountain. It became an annual ritual that he did at least once every summer. He did call his dad faithfully at first, but after a few trips he would only call him occasionally. He liked the thought that it was just between him and the mountain. Jack had become a bit of a tough guy who felt more at home in the woods than almost anywhere else.

Without warning, a loud crashing noise coming from the woods snapped Jack back to the present. Something had spooked a whitetail buck and sent it hurtling through the trees. It was headed in Jack's direction, totally oblivious to the human in its path. Jack stepped behind a tree and watched from a mostly hidden position. The deer bolted past, still unaware of him. Curiosity kept him there to see if he could find out what spooked the animal.

When nothing emerged from the trees, he was almost disappointed. The image of the creature he saw still loomed in the back of his mind. Part of him hoped he would see it. At least it would have been something. He felt watched, but after a while he headed back to his camp.

His camp consisted of a tent set up near a circle of rocks and his van. It was an old, light blue, four-wheel-drive Chevy van. On top was a gray and red bag about twenty feet long that held a packed-up hang glider. He built a small fire in the circle of rocks and crouched down warming his hands. As Jack stared into the flickering flames, he again found himself pondering his life. He began to reflect.

Back when Jack settled in Missoula, it became clear to Sharon that he would not be returning to school. He stayed on working for the welding shop for years. Sharon eventually moved to Washington state and started her career in the biomedical industry.

Jack became a journeyman welder fabricator, working for the same shop until the owner decided to retire, seven years later. He visited Sharon in Spokane, Washington when he had the time and they maintained a long-distance relationship the best they could.

When his boss closed his shop, Sharon thought he should move to Spokane and get a job. He did, but he wasn't happy and soon found himself traveling around to find work at good paying construction sites.

Sharon loved Jack and tried hard to understand why, after all this time, he was not ready to settle down and get married. This strained their relationship. Jack had bought an engagement ring a while back, but never gave it to her. He kept it at his family's house on the lake. Even Jack found it hard to believe when he thought about it. He had this beautiful and successful woman who had stood by him through thick and thin. He wondered what was wrong with himself. He was now over thirty years old and still living like a vagabond, often sleeping in his van. There was little to show for all the years of work. He did have a moderate savings account, but he was now living off it. Almost everything he owned was with him there on the mountain.

Jack's attention came back again to the present when a raindrop hit him on the head. "It's looking like it might rain tonight," he thought. He pulled an extra tarp out of the van to put over his tent. He looked over his campsite making sure he would be ready if it rained. Then he put a metal grate over his fire and set an old yellow teapot on it to heat some water for coffee. After a quick look around the area, Jack put two small logs on either side of the fire for sitting on, depending on which way the wind was

13

blowing. Then he sat down on one of the logs and rested for a moment.

He had been camping in this spot for days now without a shower or a shave. Jack had no expectation that this trip would be any different than the plethora of other trips to the mountain. This trip would be different though. Things were about to change.

The wind shifted and blew smoke in his face. He got up and moved to the other side of the fire.

Chapter 2
The Facility

It was Monday, June 1. Jack was sitting by his campfire when the wind dropped off and the water started to boil. Reaching for the pot he suddenly felt like he was not alone. He slowly looked up to the other side of the fire where a man with a friendly smile was standing. Jack had not heard a thing, but nonetheless somebody was there. He was about six feet tall with a medium build, dressed in a red plaid shirt and blue jeans.

"Hi, I am Dominic," said the man. "I hope I did not startle you."

Getting up, Jack greeted Dominic with a smile. Looking him in the eye, he said, "I'm Jack," and shook Dominic's hand. "Would you like some coffee? I was just about to make some."

"Sure, that sounds great," Dominic said as he sat down on the log opposite of Jack.

Dominic looked to be about forty years old with salt-and-pepper graying black hair and a three-day beard. His eyes were light blue with a gaze that made Jack feel transparent.

He retrieved two cups from his van and mixed up some instant coffee. Dominic watched him with a friendly smile.

"I don't have any sugar, but it is hot coffee," he said as he handed Dominic the cup of brew. "What are you doing up here?"

"Oh, I come here from time to time. It is just part of my job. How about you, Jack, what brings you to this place?" Dominic maintained his friendly gaze.

Jack was puzzled. It didn't make sense that this man would be wandering around up here. They were about a thousand feet above the Clark Fork River on a mountainside. He didn't know why he knew it, but he knew that this man could be trusted.

Jack thought about what to say and what not to say. Then he answered with, "I honestly don't know why I still come here. I started coming here because I thought that I would find the answers to questions I've had. I have had them since I came here as a boy."

"Questions?" asked Dominic with a raised eyebrow.

Jack took a drink of his coffee and tried to say something dignified, but what came out was, "I think I lost some time up here and I would like to know what happened to me in it. There was something stalking me in the woods. I saw its face and it wasn't a man, but it wasn't an animal from around here, either."

He was surprised by his own words, but there it was, the truth. Time seemed to stand still. Jack proceeded to tell Dominic the whole story, starting with his fall on the rocks right up to the present. The words just flowed out of his mouth like he was reading a script. Everything he said was the absolute truth. Then he got to the part where he remembered being hurt and a stranger helping him. He told Dominic that it couldn't have happened. He thought it was his father who found him, without any injuries from the fall.

16

"If I had been hurt in the fall, for real, my father would have known," said Jack.

"I see," interjected Dominic. "So you do not know what is real and what is not real, is that it?"

"Yes, I guess I must really need to know what actually happened. Why else would I keep coming up here? I must want answers."

Jack finished telling his story, then sat quietly staring into the fire. He was amazed that this guy would listen without scoffing. Dominic seemed to actually believe what he was saying.

"I have answers," said Dominic, breaking the silence.

Jack could hardly believe his ears. Answers were all he ever wanted. Dominic's gaze intensified as he reached his hand toward Jack's forehead. He just sat there, unable to move. "What is going on?" thought Jack. The whole situation seemed totally crazy to him. "This homeless-looking guy in red plaid comes out of nowhere and acts like some kind of shaman," he thought.

Just as Dominic's finger touched his forehead, Jack instantly remembered that it was this same man who had come to his aid so many years ago. Now it seemed odd that he didn't recognize Dominic earlier. He looked just the same as he did over twenty years ago.

"How is it possible that you haven't aged?" asked Jack. "That was so long ago."

Dominic patiently listened and answered, "It was not that long ago for me, Jack."

"I still don't know what happened after you picked me up. I was hurt wasn't I?"

Dominic smiled and said, "Come, I have something to show you. Things will soon become clear, Jack. It is not far from here."

"Should I put this fire out first?"

"You can if you want to, but it will not make any difference. You will be back before you know it," said Dominic in his calm and soothing voice.

"Good, it's getting kind of late," said Jack.

Dominic started walking in a northeasterly direction up the mountain away from the camp. Jack followed him in an almost trance-like state as if Dominic was the Pied Piper himself.

After a couple minutes Jack remembered the way. He saw familiar landmarks along the path. He was fascinated. Even though he had walked these lands over and over through the years, only now it became clear which way to go.

"I wish Dr. McGuirl could see this right now. I told her about the stranger who helped me after I fell. She never believed me. She said it was all in my head and I was delusional," stated Jack. "It still doesn't make sense though. I thought my dad found me in good shape."

"I know, Jack. It had to be that way. Soon you will have more answers, and you will have to face some of your fears too. Look up there." Dominic stopped and pointed up the mountain a short distance to a rock outcropping. It was not far from the top of the mountain.

"Do you remember that rock, Jack?" asked Dominic. He turned and looked at Jack with piercing eyes.

"Yes. Just now I remembered. This is where you took me."

Dominic nodded and started up the hill again. Jack wondered how Dominic went from being a complete stranger just an hour or so ago to being a trusted confidant. Dominic obviously knew much more than he appeared to at first.

"Things are not always as they appear, Jack," said Dominic as they reached the rock outcropping. "There is a door in front of you, but you will need to get close to it to see it."

Jack stepped up to the rock with his face only inches away from it. A small blue flashing light, about the size of a quarter, appeared in front of him.

"That wasn't there a minute ago. I would have seen it," said Jack. He instinctively touched it with his finger. The light turned green and retracted into the rock. Moments later the rock directly in front of him just vanished. There was now a shiny metal door about nine feet tall in front of him. It had a raised round surface about eye level with a larger-than-life handprint on it. Again he instinctively placed his hand on it. A mechanical noise emitted from the door and it swung open.

Jack turned around looking for instruction, but Dominic was nowhere to be seen.

"Dominic?" Jack called out in vain. "Now what?"

After a moment Jack stuck his face through the door. Overhead lights came on one at a time in sequence, lighting a tunnel-like hallway that gently sloped downward into the mountain. On the other end, about fifty feet away, was another door. He walked down the hall. As he approached the halfway point, the outside door shut. It automatically locked with a spinning wheel, similar to a submarine hatch.

"Well I've come this far, I might as well keep going," he said to himself.

When he reached the other end, that door swung open to a large, well-lit room painted white with pipes and conduits running along the walls.

Jack entered the room hesitantly. Right then, on the wall opposite the entry door, a display screen mounted on a mechanical arm lit up and extended toward him. On it, a 3D human-like face resembling a stick man began speaking. Writing in English and some other foreign symbols scrolled in opposite directions at the bottom of the screen. There was dust on the top edge of the screen, as well as on the arm and other things in the room. It had been many years since anybody had been in that room. The appearance of age seemed inconsistent with the obvious superior technology demonstrated by the display.

"Please touch screen," said a generic synthetic voice coming from the screen. It then spoke a foreign language that sounded like growls and grunts to him. Being somewhat overwhelmed by the situation he found himself in, Jack just stood there staring at it. After a few seconds, the screen more insistently repeated its request. He perceived movement behind him. Without looking behind him, he touched the screen and the display changed to a woman's face. It now had only English writing scrolling across the bottom of it.

With a friendly and pleasant-sounding woman's voice, the screen now spoke, "Identification confirmed. Security please stand down."

Jack turned to look behind him in time to see a tall robotic figure lowering a weapon that had been pointed at him. After speaking a few unidentifiable words that sounded like an angry bear crossed with a samurai warrior, it turned its attention back to the entry door and froze.

The now motionless figure stood about seven feet tall with heavy-duty chrome-plated arms and legs. Clearly designed for combat, the unfriendly machine was an intimidating yet beautiful work of art.

The voice on the screen recaptured his attention as it spoke, "Welcome, Jack Thomas."

A glowing blue line appeared on the floor. It exited the room into a hallway to the left of him.

"Please proceed along designated path to room and wait," said the voice of the woman on the screen.

This whole circumstance was almost too much to take. Jack found himself just staring at the line on the floor while the smiling woman's face patiently waited.

He looked around the room as a feeling of déjà vu overtook him, and he knew that he had been there before.

"Okay," he said. Jack followed the line into the hallway. It turned to the right after about twenty feet and seemed to continue on forever after that. There were closed doors on either side of the well-lit hall. He followed the line until it led into a room to the right through an open door.

Jack entered and a door quietly slid shut behind him. It was a smaller room, about thirteen feet by fifteen feet, with soft white lighting and a ten-foot-high ceiling. There was a large comfortable-looking couch against the wall to his right. A shiny metallic cylinder stood in the far left corner. It was about three feet in diameter, extending from the floor to the ceiling.

He sat on the oversized couch and leaned back with a sigh. It was quite comfortable. Stretching out, Jack felt like he could take a nap. While lying there he found his eyes drawn to the metallic cylinder in the corner. It had a small red blinking light about halfway up from the floor that faced the door. The red light had a hypnotic effect on him as it flickered on and off. He nodded off to sleep.

Awakened by a thud, he sat up, confused at first by his surroundings. After rubbing his eyes, Jack looked around the room and had no idea how much time had passed. He thought to himself, "It's not a dream. This is real."

The blinking red light on the shiny cylinder caught his eye again. The speed of the blinking had definitely picked up. He couldn't take his eyes off of it. It stopped blinking and turned green, remaining lit.

Jack was startled by a low tone beeping emitting from the corner. The cylinder began to slowly rise. It retracted into the ceiling and emitted some fog out the bottom as it raised. Large bare feet with long pointy toenails appeared at first, then legs. He slid to the other end of the couch where he sat frozen in fear, yet unable to look away. As the cylinder continued to rise it eventually revealed something beautiful and terrible that he never imagined.

The fog dissipated, revealing a motionless seven-foot-tall female being with her eyes closed. Her arms were folded in front and she had long fingered hands with elegant claw-like nails. Her face looked mostly human with cat-like features. She had olive-colored skin framed by long, flowing, sandy brown, wavy hair. She was shapely with a slim, athletic and muscular build, and she was wearing a white well-fitted tank top and white pants ending above the knee. The spandex-like clothing had vertical blue pin striping on the sides.

His heart was pounding and he couldn't move. Her eyes suddenly snapped open. The greenish-yellow eyes with vertical slits for irises swung toward Jack and focused right on him. Uncrossing her arms, she stepped out of the corner and said, "Hello, Jack. I am Charalon. Do you remember me?" She smiled, revealing fang-like canines slightly protruding from her lips.

Chapter 3
Charalon

Jack was dumbfounded. The already unbelievable sequence of events from the day could hardly be compared to what just happened. He just sat there staring up at the scary yet attractive creature towering over him, unable to speak.

Finally he was able to get a few words out and stammered, "I think I'd remember if..."

Charalon crouched down in front of him with her forearms resting on her knees and looked him in the eye. It was intimidating to say the least.

"That's okay. You will soon enough," she said, with her eyes narrowing.

Jack thought of himself as someone who wasn't easily shaken and was doing his best to stay calm and in control. He found he was mesmerized by those predatory yet friendly eyes.

"I know I've been here before, but I can't remember much about it. You do seem familiar to me, but what are you?"

She just smiled at first, then stood and said, "You must be hungry. Would you like something to eat?"

Jack had no immediate response. He couldn't imagine what kind of food or drink she would offer. Images of raw chopped meat and small live animals came to his mind.

"I'd love some hot coffee and a doughnut," he said, nervously jesting.

Charalon turned around and reached for a cabinet door, extracting a cell phone-size device with a display screen on one side.

"No tail...good," thought Jack to himself.

"Two glazed cake doughnuts. Two plain coffee," she said speaking into the device. Then she put it into her hip pocket and sat on the couch. A moment later the entry door slid open. A self-propelled cart with doughnuts on two plates and two cups of coffee entered the room. It rolled up in front of them and stopped.

"Enjoy," said Charalon as she picked up one of the cups and took a drink.

Jack picked up a doughnut and took a bite. He was nearly in a state of disbelief. This was one of the best doughnuts he could remember having. The coffee was great too, not too strong and piping hot.

Charalon noted his approval and said, "You can have almost any kind of food you want, Jack. There are accommodations for you here as well."

He took a sip from his cup before saying, "I have so many questions right now."

"I know," she said, empathizing with him. She motioned to the cart. "Enjoy your doughnut for now. I will tell you what I can later."

"Fair enough," Jack said mustering up a smile.

When they finished the coffee and doughnuts, Charalon got up and said, "Come with me. I will show you to your room. You will find some clothes and a restroom there so you can get cleaned up."

"Alright." Jack felt like he didn't have a choice.

The door slid open as they stepped up to it. Charalon led him further down the hallway to a room on the left. She pointed to Jack's name on the door and it opened.

"Just say, 'Find Charalon,' when you are ready and our floor navigation system will lead you to me. You will find me waiting in the cafeteria. I hope you're still hungry, Jack."

She smiled and walked away with a stealthy yet graceful gait, making no sound. Jack couldn't help but watch the lithe and powerful form disappear down the hall.

Turning and entering his room, the first thing that Jack noticed was sunlight streaming in through a window, where he stood just absorbing the breathtaking view. It was an obvious simulation of a distant landscape with a lake and mountains in the background. The realism was astounding, even the sunlight felt warm and refreshing. He touched the glass and the scenery changed to a valley with gently sloping green hills and cumulus clouds in the background. "Nice," he said.

Looking around, he found a well-outfitted room with a dresser, mirror, bed, armchairs and end tables. If there had been a television, it could have been mistaken for a four-star hotel room. Jack looked into an open door to find a complete bathroom with a shower and racks with clean towels. On the counter by the sink was a shaving kit. Out on the queen-sized bed were folded clothes and a pair of slippers.

For a moment, he pondered finding his way back to the entrance and getting the heck out of there. He sat down on the bed and took a deep breath. Jack thought about when Charalon said "our," when she referred to the floor navigation, and wondered who else, or what else, he would encounter. A flood of questions overtook him. Who and what was Charalon? Was she from another planet? Why am I even here?

He picked up a white spandex-like T-shirt from the clothes on the bed that looked like it would fit, and then set it down. He turned his attention back to the bathroom and said, "Well, I do need a shower."

After showering and shaving, he got dressed. The clothes had a near perfect fit and Jack found the light and comfortable material to his liking. A look in the mirror inspired a chuckle. "I'm living in an old science fiction show," he said out loud. Then Jack put the slippers on, picked up his dirty clothes and tossed them into the corner.

Gathering himself, he left the room and awkwardly said, "Find Charalon?"

A blue line instantly appeared on the floor heading in the same direction that Charalon had walked earlier. As he headed off, the door to his room slid shut behind him.

The line led Jack a short distance down the hallway, turned right into another intersecting corridor and then left through a door. He found Charalon sitting at a round wooden table opposite an empty chair. The room was about twenty feet by fifteen feet with another door on the opposite side. There were three tables and chairs on one end of the room, while the other end had a couple of comfortable looking easy chairs situated near a fireplace.

"Please sit down," she said as she motioned to the empty chair across from her. "What would you like for breakfast?"

"Wait, it's morning? I must have slept all night on that couch. Eggs over easy and toast, if that's okay."

She nodded and said, "It's Tuesday morning, Jack." Then she spoke, "Order, two eggs over easy, whole wheat toast, one bowl sacktaw, one orange juice, one water."

"I love orange juice," said Jack.

After a couple moments, a mechanical waiter carrying a covered tray emerged from the door on the other side of the room. It was dressed in white and had a chrome-plated head and hands. It set the tray on the table and returned to where it came from.

Charalon removed the cover exposing the food and drinks as well as silverware complete with napkins. She took a spoon and a bowl containing something that looked like oatmeal and set it in front of her. As Jack was setting his plate in front of him, Charalon closed her eyes and slightly bowed her head momentarily. It kind of appeared to Jack that she was giving thanks for the food.

The eggs and toast were one of his favorite breakfasts. Again, the food was superbly prepared and tasted fresh. "Where did the fresh eggs come from?" Jack wondered. Looking at the whole wheat toast, he thought, "This is what Mom would order for me." He finished off the rest of his breakfast and sat back in his chair, staring at the empty plate.

He could feel her gaze. When he looked up, there sat a smiling Charalon, her eyes locked on him.

"What?" asked Jack feeling more at ease.

"I'm waiting for you to ask about the food here."

"Okay, Charalon, where does this food come from? I don't understand how you could have fresh eggs and bread. It looked like no one had been in here for years when I first arrived. That orange juice tasted like it was freshly squeezed."

"This could take a while. Let's sit over there in our lounge," she said, pointing to the comfortable-looking easy chairs by the fireplace.

Charalon got up and spoke, "Order, two black coffees," then sat down in the more distant chair by the fire.

Jack sat in the other chair by her and immediately noticed that the fire was putting off no heat. It was an incredibly real simulation as the "fire" crackled and put sparks off now and then, completing the illusion.

Charalon noted his interest in it and said, "It can also provide heat. I can turn it up if you want."

"That would be nice."

"Fire heat medium low. Bring lights down," she spoke.

To Jack, the room immediately felt like the lobby of a ski lodge. He turned to Charalon and stared with an impatient look on his face.

"What?" she asked in a friendly mocking voice. The waiter showed up with two coffees and sat them on the table between them.

After the waiter left, she sighed and said, "Alright, let's start with the food. I can tell you everything you want to know about the food."

"But not everything about everything?"

"Please, Jack, try to understand that there are some things I can't talk about. Everything else you want to know, I will tell. You can trust me," she said sincerely.

Charalon took a breath and began to explain, "We have what we call replication technology. It can disassemble and reassemble matter at an atomic level. Combined with our vast pattern database of foods and items, we can reassemble matter into just about anything.

Even though it's synthetic, the reassembled product will be an exact copy of the original pattern. We call it a synthetic reprint, and we have millions of patterns in our database."

He nodded and asked, "What are you and where do you come from?"

"My people are called Morphalogians, Jack. Morphalogians are a race of people who coexist with humanity in a possible future. What I remember is we time traveled here and are unable to time travel back to that time."

"So, you are an alien time traveler from the future?"

Charalon shook her head slightly and answered, "Laloed will have to answer this question for you."

That caught Jack's attention and he asked, "Who is Laloed?" At that, he saw a small, almost imperceptible, shudder from her. He wasn't sure what it meant, but he knew that it triggered an emotional response.

"You will probably meet Laloed tomorrow. He is not fully functional yet. I was in stasis when you arrived yesterday and you saw me come out of it this morning. I initiated the waking process for him and Jerrech when you were in your room getting cleaned up. There are the three of us here."

Charalon took a drink from her coffee and continued, "Laloed built almost everything you see here, but not by himself. He is the inventor of our replication technology. This technology was used to replicate tools to build this place."

"Do you know who Dominic is?" he asked and took a sip from his cup.

Charalon looked puzzled, and then shook her head.

Jack clarified his question, "Dominic led me to the

entrance of this place twice now, but I don't know who he is or where he came from."

She thought about it for a moment then said, "He is the one whom Laloed has been contending with. Laloed brought us here to alter the timeline. He spent years developing mathematical formulas to predict when and how events will unfold. There have been times when things haven't worked out as they should have. Laloed says this is because of outside forces acting on the orders of a superior power. They are not from this reality. Laloed believes that these forces sometimes walk the lands in the forms of men. They can appear and disappear at any time or place of their choosing. Laloed believes they wield great power."

"He seemed alright to me, Charalon, but I just met him. I didn't see his 'great power,'" said Jack as he made quotes in the air.

She briefly cracked a smile and took a sip from her cup. "Laloed has the ability to see the true form and power of a life force."

Jack felt more comfortable with Charalon now and found himself relaxing a bit, even overlooking her rather scary features and imposing size. Without realizing it, he had dropped his guard.

"You said that I would remember you, and although you seem very familiar, I still don't remember much about you or my time here when I was a kid. Can you tell me more about that time?" he asked.

"There are some details I can't talk about, Jack, but you will remember more about your visit here soon. We will restore those memories to you after you meet with Laloed."

Jack was satisfied with Charalon's answer for now. He

was thinking that he would have to get a better explanation soon, if he was to remain here. As it was, he felt a bit like he had been kidnapped by a collaboration between Dominic and the inhabitants of this place in the mountain.

Thinking carefully about how to phrase it, he asked the big question on his mind, "Why am I here in this place? You were obviously expecting me to return, even though you don't know Dominic. I'm confused. Why am I relevant here, and what is Dominic's interest in me?"

Charalon looked compassionately at Jack, betraying a fondness she had for him. "I want to but I can't tell you all that you want to know right now. I can tell you that Laloed did not know you would be brought here when you were young. It was inconsistent with his projections. After that time, he began to figure in a variable he called 'providence.' That has to do with the outside forces that have interfered with his plans in the past. Figuring in the providence factor, Laloed knew you would be returning at some point in the future. He did not know when."

Jack drank the last of his coffee, set his cup down and asked, "What did you come here to change and how long have you been here?"

She had anticipated this question and winced a bit. "I can't reveal our objectives at this time, Jack. I can tell you the arrival was long before Laloed intended. We have been here for many years. I can't say how many."

Jack, not wanting to pressure her, relented a bit. "How did you feel about being stranded in the past?"

Charalon became coy and took the opportunity to avoid the question. She leaned forward looking into Jack's eyes and said, "So you care how I feel, Jack?"

A blushing Jack chuckled nervously and said, "I'm

just trying to make small talk, but really, was it hard?"

Charalon became more serious again and said, "It was known ahead of time that there wouldn't be a return trip. I have had a good life here, with good times as well as times of tribulation that can challenge one's beliefs and objectives."

"That's deep," he said, trying to inject a little humor. Picking up his cup, he asked, "Do we have time for another cup?"

"Yes, if you like. Then I will show you around this place." She ordered two more coffees and a doughnut for Jack.

"You must have read my mind. A doughnut sounds great," he said, as he stared into the fire. "Oh no, I left my campfire going. I wouldn't have, but Dominic convinced me to leave it. That was irresponsible on my part."

"You didn't burn down the forest, Jack. See...look." She produced the communication device and touched the screen. It had an image showing the surrounding area. There were no fires or smoke rising into the skies.

"Okay, how did you get a bird's eye view of the forest?"

Charalon welcomed his enthusiasm. "We replicate robotic insect microprobes that take up various positions in the general area. They can be accessed at any given moment."

"I guess that makes sense. Even my people have that technology," which provoked a chuckle from her.

After they were finished with the coffee and doughnuts, Charalon led Jack to the main entry room. "I thought I would start here. We have a multifaceted security system in which unauthorized entry can be addressed. In the tunnel are several different devices to stop unwanted entry. If necessary, our combat-ready unit over there will stop them," she said while pointing at the chrome-clad figure by the door.

Charalon spent the rest of the day showing Jack around the complex, viewing the various relevant parts. He saw the science room, the power room, the medical room and then the repair room.

Upon entering the repair room, there hunched over a bench was an eight-foot-tall male Morphalogian working on a small robot. "Jack, this is Jerrech. He is in charge of the maintenance here." Without saying a word Jerrech looked at Jack and nodded, then went back to his work. "Jerrech doesn't say much."

After the tour, they returned to the cafeteria and he had a T-bone steak for dinner. He was burned out and tired from the day. Even though Jack was very tired, he did not want to go to sleep. He feared he'd wake up and find it was all a dream.

"Would you like to have some coffee and visit some more by the fire, Charalon, if you're not too tired?"

"I don't get tired, Jack. Yes, that would be nice." She ordered up some coffee for them.

They sat down by the fire, but Jack didn't have much to say for a while. He sat there gazing into the flames and considered the events of the day. Many different images flashed before his eyes, from Charalon to the cantankerous robot guard. Jack wondered what else was in store for him. He wondered what Sharon would think of this place, but he wouldn't say anything to anybody. They would think he was crazy.

"Tell me, Jack, what has happened in your life since your last visit here?" she asked, breaking the silence.

By now the coffee was kicking in and Jack was feeling more awake. "I don't know where to start. It could take some time...in fact a lot of time."

"I think you should start at the beginning, Jack. I have lots of time."

"Well, I suppose since you have been answering my questions, and waiting on me all day, I will tell you all about my life. I will warn you in advance, it's not that impressive." He thought for a moment and continued, "My life changed after that one day, Charalon. I don't really know why."

"It was more than one day, Jack. You were here for weeks. You will remember that tomorrow."

"How...time travel," said Jack, as he answered his own question.

Charalon just silently nodded.

He continued, "After I got home, I found that I was afraid of the dark. You know, I was never afraid of the dark before. I had issues, and became emotionally unstable. It became hard for me to make new friends. I had to see a psychiatrist for years, which didn't help much.

"A year after I had been here, I met Sharon, my best friend. She has always been there for me and I was going to marry her someday."

"You were going to marry her?" asked Charalon.

"I still want to, and she has been waiting for me for so long. I don't know why. I keep thinking that I have to wait until I get it together, but I never do. Time flies by for me while I watch other guys my age have careers, get married and have families."

"She waits for you because she loves you, Jack."

He nodded in agreement and continued, "I did good in

school until I got to college, but I dropped out, intending to go back. I never did. I became a welder and worked with my hands. Now I travel around getting work here and there. I live out of my van sometimes. I haven't made much of a life for myself." Jack looked over at Charalon and noticed a tear in the corner of her eye.

"And what is Sharon like, how is she?" she asked.

"Oh, Sharon always does well. She has a Ph.D. and a good job. She is an amazing, capable woman who is good at whatever she does. Like you, she is compassionate and caring. If I could, I would do almost anything for her," Jack said with a smile.

Charalon smiled and rubbed the tear away. "It's late. You should get some rest."

Jack touched his wrist and said, "I lost my watch. What time is it?"

"It's 10:32 p.m.," she said, without looking at a clock. "We could replicate any kind of watch you would like, just say what you want."

"Maybe in the morning. Goodnight, Charalon. Thank you for an interesting day." He headed off to his room.

"Goodnight, Jack," she said, before he got out of sight.

When Jack got to his room the window showed a setting sun. He noticed that his clothes had been cleaned and were neatly folded at the end of his bed. He thought back to his tour and remembered there was no dust in the whole place, even in the main entry room. "The maid was busy today," he thought out loud.

Jack undressed, crawled into bed and promptly fell asleep.

Chapter 4

Memories

A pleasant two-tone bleeping noise at the door roused Jack from a deep sleep. It was morning and light from a beautiful sunrise was streaming in the window. He sat up and, after assessing his surroundings, got out of bed. He quickly threw on his own clothes as the doorbell emitted another two-tone bleep.

While putting his slippers on, Jack yelled out, "Yes?" and the door slid open. There stood Charalon dressed in black pants down to her knees and a dark gray, three-quarter sleeved V-neck T-shirt. She had her hair pulled back into a ponytail and was still barefooted. A surprised Jack did a double take. He froze momentarily with a feeling of déjà vu, then finished putting his slippers on. "You look very nice today," he said.

"Thank you, I'll be in the cafeteria. After breakfast, Laloed would like to see you and attempt memory restoration," she said in a business-like tone.

"Thanks for the wake-up call, Charalon. I'll be right behind you."

After she left, Jack looked in the mirror and sighed at the sight of his messed-up hair. He got ready for breakfast and paused for a moment, looking out the window. With a touch he changed the outdoor landscape to an ocean view background and walked out the door.

Jack found her sitting at the same table as before. As he sat down, she handed him a watch and said, "There, now you will know what time it is. I made sure it has the right time." It was an outdoor sports watch with a compass and altimeter.

"Thanks, Charalon. Now that's a nice watch. It says 9:02 a.m. Wednesday. I like it." He stared at the watch, admiring it as he put it on.

The robot waiter showed up with pancakes, butter and syrup. It set them in front of Jack, then left. When he looked up at Charalon, she shrugged and said, "I'm not that hungry this morning. I ordered for you."

Jack smiled, showing his approval. "It's been a while since I had pancakes."

After breakfast, Charalon led him down a hall to a room with a white chair resembling a dentist's chair. It sat in the middle of the room. A control panel with touch display screens mounted on a stand stood nearby. The chair had a u-shaped cradle for a headrest with metal coils on either side. The armrests and footrest had restraining cuffs on them that made it look like something built for torture.

"I suppose that you're going to ask me to get in that, right?" asked Jack, with reservations.

Charalon gave him a sympathetic look. "Yes, Jack. The restraint is necessary to keep you from hurting yourself. The memory implantation can cause a variety of negative side effects during and after the process. They can last for up to a couple hours. It is good if you sleep for a while when you are finished here."

"Do you want me in that chair now?"

"If you feel you are ready, then yes," Charalon said softly.

Without saying anything, Jack got in the chair. After downsizing the chair adjustments to fit him, Charalon closed the foot and hand cuffs, then belted his midsection down.

"Laloed was going to be here for this procedure, but he thought it would be best to wait until you have adjusted to the memories," she said.

Charalon stepped over to the control panel. She looked over the readings and touched a screen. "We have a couple minutes before the process begins. Jack, this won't be easy. You should close your eyes and count down from 100 now."

He closed his eyes and began the countdown in his head. When he reached 30, a low-pitched ringing in his head rose up then faded away.

The sound of a door caused him to open his eyes. There in the doorway stood an angry-looking Morphalogian male glaring at him. Jack presumed the creature to be Laloed. A feeling of absolute terror came over him. He realized that this was the face that scared him, the image of terror he had in his mind that had caused so much anguish and fear over the years. All of a sudden, Laloed let out a loud hiss and showed his teeth, causing Jack to scream out loud.

"Where is Charalon?" he thought as he fought the restraints with all his might. A wrist cuff broke, allowing Jack a free hand to undo the rest of the restraints. He was able to get out of the chair and elude Laloed. He got out the door and ran as fast as he could down the hall. He ducked into a dimly lit room, crouched down and hid in a corner.

"What just happened? I knew it, this place is not what it seems," thought Jack. He decided to wait there for a bit. In a while he would attempt to get to the main entrance. He could see a couple shadows under the door as they passed by. He wondered how he could have been so wrong about Charalon.

After a while, when it seemed safe, Jack rose and crept over to the door to listen for threats. As he looked around the room he saw what looked like bodies covered with sheets on tables. He walked quietly over to one and lifted the sheet. Jack winced and dropped the sheet at what he saw. It was a human body with meat cut off the left arm and leg, exposing the bones. Thoughts of the cafeteria came to his mind.

Jack could stand it no longer and had to get out of there. He looked out the door to see if it was safe and ran to the main entrance where he was met by the metal security guard. The guard raised its weapon and pointed it right at him. It took a couple steps toward Jack then fired its laser-like weapon, just missing him. He turned and ran back to the room with the bodies. His heart was beating fast. He was hyperventilating and had images of a growling Laloed in his head.

He sat down in the corner and covered his head with his hands, trying to gather himself. He thought about Sharon and wondered if he would ever see her again. "If I die in here nobody will ever find me. My dad and mom will never know what happened to me. I have to find a way to survive. I must live," thought Jack. He heard a distant angry roar.

His thoughts turned to Charalon, "Did she set me up? I thought she actually cared about me. Maybe she is a victim too and being held somewhere in the facility." Just then he realized the watch she gave him might have a tracking device in it. He took it off and threw it out the door, through an open door across the hallway.

Returning to the corner, Jack sat there wrestling with his thoughts and emotions. Heavy metallic-sounding footsteps clunked by in the hall and continued on. The footsteps had a rhythmic cadence that grew more distant, then eventually faded completely away. Then they were replaced by the sound of dripping. When Jack looked to see where the noise was coming from, he saw blood trickling from one of the tables.

He found himself feeling very tired all of the sudden, and wondered if he might have been drugged. He nodded off to sleep and began to dream about working at the welding shop in Missoula. In his dream, Jack thought of his first days working around Owen.

Owen was a big and strong man in his late sixties, a retired ironworker. He was like a cross between the actor John Wayne and a battle-hardened soldier with a heart of gold. Owen always reminded Jack of his grandfather who had died years ago. They were tough men from an era when men were men. With his son, Owen had started Professional Welding Co. years ago. Although he no longer had to work, he would hang out in the shop almost every day. At first it seemed like Owen enjoyed making Jack nervous. He would lean on the worktable right next to him and watch him work. This was something he would come to miss after he no longer worked there.

Owen seldom wore safety glasses when he hung out in the shop. It worried Jack when he had to grind on metal, throwing sparks in all directions. Sometimes the spark stream would shoot right at Owen. He would stand there and not even flinch. Once, early on, Jack was concerned and asked the shop foreman how to avoid accidentally getting sparks in Owen's eyes. The foreman chuckled and said, "Don't worry about it. Those sparks wouldn't dare."

He learned so much from Owen over the years. Perhaps he subconsciously wanted advice from him now.

Jack felt a poke to his shoulder and awoke. It was Dominic, shushing him with his finger held up to his lips. "You need to be quiet," whispered Dominic. "Are you okay?"

Jack nodded his head and quietly asked, "How did you get in?"

"I have some tricks up my sleeve. I'm here to help you," whispered Dominic. "Come, follow me and I'll get you out of here."

Dominic seemed to know exactly when to move and when to stay hidden. They made their way to the hall connected to the main entrance. With a covert look around the corner, Jack could see the robot guard lurking in the distance.

"I'll handle this, but stay close behind," said Dominic. He stepped out into full view of the guard and held up his hand with his palm facing it. The guard knelt down and shut off. Dominic motioned to the tunnel and said, "Put your hand on my shoulder." Jack realized that they had become invisible to the sensors in the tunnel. They proceeded up the tunnel to the exit door. Dominic held up his hand again and the door swung open. The rock cover vanished and they left the facility.

As they ran down the hill to Jack's camp, Dominic yelled, "Get in your car and go now. Don't stop until you're far away. I will contact you later...good luck."

Jack's car started after a couple tries and he sped off down the narrow winding road. He pulled out his cell phone, but he didn't have a signal. After driving for a while, he reached the paved road and entered I-90 heading west toward Spokane.

Jack pulled his phone out and checked the signal strength. "I'll call Sharon and tell her I'm on my way. I can sort this out later," he thought.

He dialed her number and put the phone to his ear. He could hear ringing, but after nobody answered he set the phone down and kept on driving. After some time he redialed Sharon's number and was greeted with more ringing, but this time after a few rings somebody answered. He could hear a voice that he couldn't make out at first. Then the voice grew louder and more insistent.

"Wake up! Jack, you must wake up now," said Charalon with her hand on his shoulder.

He opened his eyes and stared at her with a look of confusion, just trying to make sense of the situation. He was still in the chair with Charalon undoing the restraints. He shook his head and rubbed his eyes, realizing that he had just experienced a paranoid delusion. Jack had learned about them in Psychology 101, but it was quite another thing to actually have one. He looked at his watch, noting the time. The feeling of confusion quickly faded.

"That was weird," he said.

"Yes. I could see the images in your head." Charalon pointed to a screen on the control panel. "I do care about you, Jack."

He nodded and said with a smile, "Now I remember my friend Charalon."

Charalon helped him out of the chair, "Loss of balance is one of the side effects to watch out for. Now you should take a nap, or just rest in your room for a while."

"Well, I do feel kind of tired," he said as they walked back to his room.

Once he was alone in his room, Jack sat down on the bed and began to reflect on the day. It was disconcerting to think that he had no grasp of reality for some time. He felt bad about the thoughts he had earlier toward Charalon. Now he knew she was a true friend.

With his memory now intact, he found himself going over the sequence of events following his fall as a youngster. For Jack, it was like playing a new favorite song over and over. He kicked off the slippers and got into bed.

He remembered losing his footing and dropping the metal detector. Jack recalled falling and catching himself with his hands, cutting them on the rocks. He slid down the rockslide on his belly until he hit a larger rock and began to tumble, never losing consciousness.

Once he stopped at the bottom, he sat up and looked at his bleeding hands. When he tried to stand, the sharp pain in his knee could not be ignored. Jack sat there for a while just holding his knee. He called out to his father a couple times. Then he heard a rustling in the brush not far away. "Dad?" he cried.

He stared at the foliage for some time. Something was there. He could feel its eyes on him. It moved stealthily from tree to tree, staying out of sight. Jack was helpless just sitting there, unable to run, paralyzed by the extreme fear he felt.

A face appeared in the brush for a moment, but he couldn't make it out. It was now very dim out. Jack opened his mouth to yell out for his father, but no sound came forth. The face appeared again, this time much closer. Its eyes reflected what light there was. It was a terrifying picture that Jack couldn't take his eyes off of. It was an animalistic-looking man's face with a tooth-filled snarl. Then, without warning, the creature backed away and disappeared into the woods.

A crunching noise came from the other direction with the unmistakable signature of human footfalls. Jack looked to see a man approaching and said, "Dad, is that you?" It wasn't his father. It was a friendly looking man with a short beard, wearing a red plaid shirt. The man walked up and crouched down.

"I am Dominic," said the man with a smile. "I am here to help you." Dominic scooped him up off the ground and started walking up the hill. Jack didn't say anything. He was just glad to have help. He held on tight to Dominic. It wasn't long before they reached the rock outcropping. Dominic told him to touch the light, then the handprint on the door. He stepped into the tunnel and set Jack down with his back against the wall.

Dominic bent down to look Jack in the face and smiled. "Do not worry. Everything is going as it should. You have a friend here." Then he stood up and walked away.

Jack watched as Dominic stopped at the door. He met the beast who looked surprised and a little afraid. Dominic gave the creature a stern look and it backed up in submission. Dominic looked back at Jack then turned and vanished as he walked away.

The tall creature came over to Jack and stood there angrily glaring at him. Another creature, a female, came out of nowhere and picked him up off the floor. Cradling the boy in her arms, she turned to the male creature and spoke words that Jack couldn't understand. She hissed at the other creature, showing her teeth. Even without understanding the words, it wasn't difficult for Jack to see she was defending him.

Jack sat up in bed, and wondered where Charalon had come from. A flood of memories abruptly came to him and he was moved by her kindness.

A memory of sitting on a table in the medical room with her tending to his cuts resurfaced. With a sponge she applied some kind of liquid. Then she produced a handheld device emitting a purple light and passed it over the wounds. Almost instantly, the cuts and abrasions felt and looked better. She was kind and gentle to the young Jack, as a mother would be.

"I'm Charalon. I hope that you don't find me too scary," she said softly with a smile. Jack still had not uttered a word since Dominic picked him from the rocks.

"You aren't scary. You're nice," he remembered saying. "My name is Jack."

"It is very nice to meet you, Jack."

With these thoughts in his mind, he lay back down and drifted off to sleep.

Chapter 5
The Arrival

The pleasant two-toned bleep from the door woke Jack. Sitting up, he called out, "Yes?" and the door slid open. Charalon stepped through the door with a vulnerable look on her face.

"It's time for breakfast...would you like to have breakfast with me?" she asked, unexpectedly feeling shy.

"Of course I would, Charalon. I'm starving. Who else would I have breakfast with?"

She smiled and said, "Nobody."

"Give me a moment, I'll be there in a bit. In the cafeteria?" said Jack as he got up.

She nodded and left the room. Jack looked at his watch and noted the time. It was 8:30 a.m. Thursday morning. "No wonder I'm so hungry. I just slept for over sixteen hours," he thought. As Jack got ready, he found himself wondering what was going on with Charalon. She seemed to be bothered by something. There was a certain sadness about her today, almost as if she had lost something precious to her.

When he entered the cafeteria, he found Charalon sitting at their table. She seemed cheerful again, greeting him with a smile. Noticing Charalon had already ordered breakfast, he pulled up a chair and sat down. They had breakfast then sat by the fire with some coffees.

"I have a question for you, Charalon," posed Jack.

"Shoot away, little buddy," she jested, eliciting a laugh out of Jack.

"Really?" he said with a chuckle.

"I do have an understanding of human culture," she said with a wry smile.

Jack thought for a moment then said, "I'd like to know...more about the first time I was here."

"Do you not remember all of your time here?" Charalon looked concerned.

"I do remember, but I was a child. I know what happened, but there are things I don't understand. I was sitting on the floor of the tunnel, with Laloed standing over me. He wasn't very happy, to say the least. Then you came out of nowhere...and protected me, why?"

A sober look came over Charalon's face. She looked away in thought. "I was monitoring the situation...I thought maybe he meant to harm you, Jack."

"I don't have any memories of Laloed ever even smiling, let alone being friendly. I don't think he likes me at all, but why would he want to hurt me?" he asked.

"Laloed is very complicated, Jack. He has his reasons. You were the first intruder we ever had."

He thought about her answer for a moment and said, "I know you can't talk about some things, Charalon. It's just that even though I remember so much more, I have more questions."

"I understand, Jack, I've been there too." She had a look of reflection.

"You too?" asked Jack, somewhat surprised.

"Yes, but I don't like to talk about it. It was a difficult

47

time for me."

Although Jack was intrigued by Charalon's confession, he said nothing more about it. He decided to change the subject. "Will I be meeting with Laloed today?"

"No. He would like to talk with you, but he is waiting for something...he didn't say what," she said apologetically. "I can show you our event playback program. It utilizes actual memories from one or more witnesses and combines them. It assembles a reasonable representation of events in the form of a video playback. The playback is from a third person perspective."

"Are there any side effects?"

"It is not the same as memory implantation. There are no significant side effects...maybe a headache," she said with a grin.

They went to the memory room and he asked, "Do I have to be strapped in this time?"

"No, you will be awake the whole time. You can ask me questions during the playback or even pause if you desire."

He sat in the chair and said, "Well, I'm ready."

Charalon took up her position at the control panel and initiated the playback. A three-dimensional holographic image showing the playback appeared above the control panel. Inside of Jack's head, there played a virtual reality reenactment. He could move around in it and see things from different perspectives.

A flying craft traveled across a burnt orange sky at dusk. It exceeded the speed of sound, causing a sonic boom. The craft was a black, almost round ship with stubby wings that turned up at the ends, and no discernible propulsion system. The craft moved at high velocities and made very little noise. The length was about twenty feet and only slightly wider. It had a long, clear canopy covering three occupants sitting one behind the other. Lights, switches and display screens flickered and blinked in front of them.

The three occupants communicated in some kind of strange language that sounded a bit like guttural grunts and growling.

"Wait, can we pause it for a moment? I don't know what they're saying," said, Jack.

"Yes, I will set the language to English," said Charalon. "Do you want me to restart it from the beginning?"

"No, I see whats going on." The playback resumed in English.

The occupants wore white flight helmets and spacesuit-looking outfits, and only their faces and hands were visible. The front position of the craft seemed to be occupied by the pilot. His large, slightly hairy hands with claw-like fingernails gripped a control yoke in front of him. His face had cat-like features with the tips of fangs protruding from his lips. His eyes were also cat-like with vertical-shaped slits for irises. A female-looking being with similar features sat right behind the pilot. A third crew member, apparently a male, sat in back. Their skin had an iridescent quality to it.

As they flew along at about six thousand feet, the female looked out over the terrain with a sad face. A futuristic, alien-looking land was covered with destruction. Fires and rising smoke could be seen for miles into the distance.

The pilot announced, "Maximum velocity achieved. Probe status?"

"Probe: activated, status: ready," said the female being.

The pilot, who was obviously in command, pressed a button and loudly announced, "Primary sequence initiated, start count."

The female then replied, "Count to start on mark...mark," then she began to count down from five. When she reached the end, the third crew member yelled out, "Field strength: full."

All of a sudden, a small light appeared about a mile ahead of the craft and the pilot yelled, "Launch probe."

The third crew member pressed a button and yelled, "Probe launched."

A small object shot out from the front of the craft and entered into the light ahead of the craft. The light disappeared before the craft reached it. Moments later the female yelled, "Telemetry received, target identified."

"Complete telemetry?" asked the pilot.

"Negative. Target location identification and safe passage confirmation. We have no other telemetry incoming. There could be a time delay in transmission," said the female.

The third crew member cut in with, "Approaching war vessel, fully armed," as a blip appeared on a screen in front of him.

The pilot glanced down to a screen in front of him showing a fast moving craft on an intercept course. Feeling pressured, the pilot/commander yelled, "We have no time. Initiate."

The third crew member then pressed a button and

called out, "Initiated."

Another light appeared again about a mile ahead of the craft, this time much larger and brighter. The craft entered the light and disappeared from sight.

The craft entered a tunnel-like realm with high-velocity lights flying past. The commander then yelled out, "Status of cerebral scans."

"Scans complete and saved," the female reported.

The commander responded, "Auto pilot on. Initiate exit field."

The third crew member touched a screen and declared, "Field initiated."

At once, an area of light appeared in front of the craft. Slowly the light covered the ship starting at the front and proceeding toward the back. As the light reached the commander, he immediately lost consciousness. The female was not as affected but still had a hard time keeping her eyes open. When the light/field reached the third crew member it seemed to be weaker and he wasn't even affected by it.

The craft exited the area of light and entered into a dark sky with a flash of light, like lightning. A loud sonic boom shook the area. The commander was unconscious. Alarms were sounding and the ship was vibrating nearly out of control. The third crew member declared, "Activating revive mode."

The pilot and the female quickly regained full consciousness as a hissing sound started and then quit.

"Status," demanded the commander.

"Awake and memory intact," said the third crew member.

"I don't know. I need more time," said the female.

"Pilot not...pilot at thirty percent and rising. Taking

51

control, auto pilot off," said the commander.

As he fought for control he cried out, "Where are the cities? It is all darkness below."

"Switching to night vision," said the female.

Peering into a screen with topographical imagery, the commander announced, "Target landing zone located. We have no hover mode, emergency shield activated, ready yourselves for impact, in three, two, one."

With alarms still sounding, the craft barreled through trees. It then entered a clearing filled with large rocks and plowed to a stop. Debris and glowing parts were flying in different directions as it came to a full stop in an upright position, near the top of a mountain.

An emergency light flashed on and off near the back of the craft, intermittently illuminating the area. With the craft smoking but not on fire, the commander pulled a lever and blew the canopy off. A light rain was falling and it was very dark out.

The commander got up from his seat and pulled his suit and shoes off. He stood about eight feet tall with a well-defined, lean muscular build. His feet were about sixteen inches long with a few tufts of fur. He wore a white T-shirt and tight fitting, white, spandex-looking half pants.

He checked on the other two crew members. Both were injured, with the third crew member not responding. He removed the injured from the craft and dragged them away from the wreck. Then he retrieved a pack containing emergency supplies and a toolbox from the craft. The commander rifled through the pack and brought out a device resembling a sledgehammer with a short handle.

He twisted the handle, causing it to extend and the

head to glow bright red. Then he walked over to a rock outcropping with a flat face and took a swing at the rock. The tool passed right through the rock, dissolving large amounts of it with every pass. The hammer-like tool went through the rock like a shovel through snow. After only a few minutes he had a cave cut into the rock about six feet high and wide by twelve feet deep.

After getting the crew to the cave, the commander built a fire just outside, igniting it with a tool that looked like a laser gun.

With the injured crew resting in the cave out of the rain, the commander could now tend to them. He fetched blankets and other supplies out of side compartments on the now-destroyed craft and brought them to his crew. Ducking down as he entered the shelter, he sat down by the female and asked, "Are you injured, Charalon?"

"I have no obvious injuries," she said.

The commander had his hands clenched tightly into fists. He relaxed a little upon hearing she was okay, betraying his feelings for her. He was obviously unhappy and irritated by the circumstances and was on the verge of totally losing it. He looked over to the third crew member and noticed he was still unconscious. He sighed and shook his head.

"Are we in the target zone?" asked Charalon.

The commander retrieved an instrument from the pack and looked at it. "We are indeed, the microprobe is not more than a hundred feet away, Charalon."

"You should take a planetary position reading and send out the recon probes."

"I was about to do just that," snapped the commander.

The commander removed a box-shaped device from the pack. He flipped a switch on its side and it lit up, releasing three red flying objects that quickly disappeared into the darkness.

"The probes are activated. Now we wait," announced the commander.

Not far away a large, hungry grizzly bear was attracted by the noise and scents that came from the crash site. "Do you hear that? I think something is out there," said Charalon.

"I will go out and look," growled the commander.

As he left the shelter he could see the bear approaching. It was almost totally dark, but he could see quite well. When the bear got closer it let out a roar and charged. He just calmly stood there with Charalon watching from behind.

All of a sudden, he ran right at the bear. He grabbed it by the neck with one hand and threw it down onto its back. The commander let out a terrifying roar of his own. It started off with a low growl that grew into a full roar, finishing with a hiss. The bear fled and the barefooted commander pursued it. Running and jumping over downed trees, he quickly caught up to the bear. Following it closely, he grabbed some hair on its back and pulled it out. Finally, he kicked the bear in the rear and knocked it down again. After venting on the bear, he returned to the shelter.

"Did the animal get into our supplies?" asked Charalon.

"No, I chased him off. I don't think he will be back."

"I'm worried, Laloed. Jerrech is still unconscious. I don't see anything wrong with him, except his color seems odd," she said as she passed an instrument over Jerrech. "His exoskin is a dull brown and he has erratic breathing."

Laloed looked at her up close and said, "Your color looks off. How do you feel?"

Charalon looked at her hands and said, "I feel all right considering these events, but I can't color shift. I think that Jerrech and I might have sustained damage to our exoskin."

"You should rest, Charalon. We can assess the injuries when the light comes."

The probes returned about that time and reentered the device they came out of. The device lit up and strange writing scrolled across its display screen. Upon reading it, Laloed left the shelter and became irate. "How can this be? There is no possibility that our calculations could be that far off."

Picking up and throwing large, heavy rocks, Laloed threw an impressive fit. When he calmed down, he just stood there looking at the dark sky with an angry scowl. "There is someone who is working against us," he said bitterly.

The playback shut off and Jack sat up. "That was incredible. I knew that was you from the beginning."

Charalon smiled and powered the control panel down. Jack jumped out of the chair. "Laloed loves you. Are you and he..." She cut him off.

"Whatever he felt back then he does not love me now. I don't want to talk about it."

"Okay, how did Laloed throw that bear around like that?" asked Jack. "Is he just that strong?"

"The Morphalogian physiology is capable of great strength, but they can't do something like that. Laloed developed a sort of micro-thin force-field technology that adheres to the skin of any living organism. It can give one incredible strength and emit any image, including no image...invisibility. So he could appear as anyone, anything or not be seen at all," she explained.

Jack was intrigued, he asked, "What does he call it?"

"He called it 'interactive light emitting force field' or 'ILEFF.'"

"Is that how he was able to run through the forest with no shoes on?" asked Jack.

"He probably would have went without his shoes anyway. Morphalogians prefer to go without footwear. But, yes, the ILEFF system would protect his feet too."

"Have you ever tried it, Charalon?"

She hesitated before answering, "I have memories of using it a long time ago."

Chapter 6
A Noble Fight

It was Friday morning. Jack had been lying on his bed staring at the ceiling again. With the events of the last few days on his mind, he had more questions than answers. "What do I have to do with any of this?" he thought to himself again. He had feelings of fear and foreboding regarding his impending meeting with Laloed. The feelings he had for Charalon were probably the most confusing to him. "Why does she care about me anyway?" wondered Jack as he remembered the time she protected him from Laloed.

The doorbell chimed, bringing him back to the present. "Yes?" he answered and the door slid open to Charalon standing there.

"Come in, Charalon." He stayed in bed.

"I'm just checking up on you, Jack." She walked in and sat in one of the chairs. "Are you handling all this okay, and what can I do to help?"

"You know that I would really like to know the whole story, but I know you can't tell me all I want to know yet," he said.

"There is so much I would like to tell you. Laloed

wants to explain things to you himself, but he feels it is not yet the time to meet. I had a meeting with him earlier. He thinks you should know the reason we came back, so I will tell you about the war. What I'm about to say is what I remember.

"When the Morphalogians first arrived, they lived in peace with humanity. That was the first generation. They used their superior intelligence driven by ambition to gain power. The second generation had little regard for mankind. They called them smills, meaning small and ill, and other names. Most of the third generation saw humanity as vermin that needed to be killed off. The Supremacists arose to do the job. At this time, it had become legal for a Morphalogian to kill any human for any reason. That is when some Morphalogians stood up for mankind and fought to save them. There arose a Morphalogian who called himself Malconadon. He gathered followers and taught them to believe that all life on the planet should die. That way the world might start over and evolve right this time. There were humans and Morphalogians that followed him. They called themselves 'The Savers.' At first, the Savers sided with those who wanted to kill off the humans. The Supremacists had problems with the humans helping Malconadon. Then all the factions were at war with each other."

"A world war," said Jack.

"When we left our time, we had no choice. The war was lost. Nobody had won," Charalon said sadly. "There were rumors that some humans had fled to the mountains but, as far as we know, there were no survivors."

"None of the humans survived?" he asked.

"No humans and no Morphalogians, that we know of.

There was a weapon of mass destruction developed by the followers of Malconadon during the third generation, in the year 2313. This weapon could kill all life in a 100-mile radius, down to microorganisms. Even the plant life was not spared. They had enough of these weapons to kill all life on the planet." Charalon paused as a teardrop formed in the corner of her eye.

She continued, "Laloed, Jerrech and I fought to save humanity. We began working on a plan. Even though Laloed had developed the ILEFF technology, we were too late. That's when we started work on the time travel plan. To go back and stop the thing that brought the Morphalogians to Earth in the first place. I can't say any more about it right now, Jack. I do have another memory playback for you to watch. It will help fill in the blanks."

After breakfast, they went to the memory room. Jack sat in the chair and Charalon started the memory playback.

Laloed sat alone in a room at a table, with his arms crossed and deep in thought. Charalon walked in and hugged him from behind. Not letting go, she said, "Have you come to a decision yet? I don't want you to go, but Malconadon has most of his people fighting the Supremacists. He only has a small force of ten or less protecting him right now."

"I have to do something to stop this madness. I love you, Charalon, but I have to go. I will be safe and well armed with the ILEFF system," said Laloed.

She let go of Laloed and stood upright. She paced back and forth a bit. "I'm a little worried about the fact that we haven't had a practical test for it yet."

"I know, but we don't have much choice in the

matter...things aren't going well," said Laloed as he stood. "I'm going to bring Jerrech along. He will have a backup system ready to go if anything goes wrong. I'm going to kill that crazy bastard."

Jerrech entered the room and said, "I have the primary unit here," as he handed a small chip to Laloed. "Plug it into the cerebral interface and think it on. I have programmed it with a few options for the camouflage function. I'll carry the backup unit here." He pointed to his breast pocket.

Laloed pulled a device out of his pocket that resembled a cell phone and plugged the chip into the side of it. He put it back in his pocket and said, "Chip is in the interface unit, initiating zero-point energy mode." Laloed walked over to a shelf, picked up a gun and pulled the hammer back.

Charalon turned away and said, "I can't watch this."

He pointed the gun at his foot and pulled the trigger. It fired and he set it on the table. He bent over and picked a piece of lead off the top of his foot and said, "Well, that worked." Picking the gun back up, he held it up for Jerrech and Charalon to see, then crushed it with his hand. "Not bad."

Jerrech and Laloed left the room, leaving Charalon alone. She sat down and appeared to pray for them. Then she got up and looked out the window. She could see Jerrech and Laloed leaving on foot as they disappeared into the cover of darkness.

Running down the street, Laloed looked at Jerrech and said, "I'll meet you at the north end." Then he accelerated to an otherwise impossible speed and left Jerrech behind.

The compound was a four-story building surrounded

by a twenty-foot-high wall with barbwire on top. Guards patrolling the outer and inner perimeter of the wall carried high-tech-looking weapons.

Laloed ducked behind a truck parked along the road as a guard approached. When the guard was close enough, Laloed grabbed him from behind and held his hand over the guard's mouth. He unintentionally broke the guard's neck and crushed his face before he knew it. Laloed threw the guard in some bushes nearby and continued surveying the area.

Seeing a light pole near the wall, he climbed it and jumped to the top of the wall. Suddenly realizing that he was visible, Laloed selected one of the options in his mind and vanished.

"Can you pause it for a moment, Charalon?"

"Sure. Do you have a question?"

"Yes, can you make Laloed visible to me?" he asked.

"Sure, Jack. He will appear as a transparent ghost-like figure."

The playback continued with Laloed standing on top of the wall, now visible to Jack. Laloed jumped down from the twenty-foot-high wall into the compound and headed for the building. Being invisible, he went into an entrance right past a guard. He went down a corridor to a stairwell access door and went up. His informant had said that Malconadon would be on the third floor toward the north end of the building. He exited the stairwell at the third floor. Then he proceeded to a doorway watched by two well-armed guards.

Laloed was able to break both of their necks before they could make a sound. He threw their bodies into a closet nearby. Still invisible, he opened the door and slipped into the room.

Inside the room, it looked like a palace. There was plush furniture surrounded by scantily clad Morphalogian and human women. Malconadon sat there in a throne-type chair eating from a bowl of chopped raw meat. He was being entertained by a dancing Morphalogian child.

On the other end of the room stood a human man who looked out of place. He was wearing a red plaid outdoor shirt and blue jeans with a three-day beard. As Laloed approached Malconadon, the man in the red plaid shirt stepped forward looking right at Laloed. Nobody in the room acted like they saw the man. The man held up his hand and Laloed found himself unable to move. The whole room seemed frozen in time except that man.

He walked up to Laloed giving him a friendly smile and said, "I know you are trying to do good here, but I have to stop you from killing this garbage. You are not permitted to do this. Yes, I can see you and no, they cannot see or hear us."

"Who are you? You must let me finish my mission," yelled Laloed.

"Your mission is over...for now. I know who you really are, Laloed. Now, you go home."

"Please, you must allow me to make this right. Let me go! I am to blame for so much," Laloed cried out.

"I know," said the man in a somber tone. "This is the way it has to be. Now go home."

The man raised his hand and Laloed instantly found himself standing outside of the security wall.

Jerrech came walking up and asked, "Did you accomplish the mission?"

"No, there was a human with great power who told me to go home. I'll explain it to you later."

On the way back, they took a different route. They passed many dead men hanging from the streetlights. The dead had their eyes torn out and their disemboweled bodies were covered in blood. After a while they came across a group of young Morphalogians who had some blindfolded human girls with them. They had long machete-like blades that they were swinging around. As Laloed got closer he could see a couple headless human bodies lying on the ground near them. It was obvious that they meant to kill the rest of the girls.

Laloed just watched the young Morphalogians dance around howling and taunting their prey, but that was only at first. He activated the ILEFF device and selected an option to appear as a human. He walked up to them looking like a skinny, weak man and told them to walk away. He knew all along that they wouldn't. One of the gang mocked him and said, "Come on, little man, try to make us. I think I'll eat his arm before I kill him."

The young Morphalogian came up to Laloed and grabbed his arm. Laloed let him take it to his mouth. When he went to bite down on it with all his strength, he broke his teeth on the arm. Laloed spun around knocking the young Morphalogian's head off with his other arm. The speed and power that the ILEFF device gave Laloed was incredible. Then he proceeded to kill all of the young Morphalogians there and let the human girls go free. Laloed and Jerrech continued on their way home.

"We have to finish our work on the time-displacement device. I think it might be our only option at this point in time," said Laloed.

As the playback ended Jack said, "That guy looked like Dominic."

"Yes, Jack, he did."

"Was he the same guy who brought me here?"

"Laloed believes he was. I've told you before, these people, like Dominic, can be anywhere at any time. They are not bound by time. They have their own agenda. Laloed found it's best to find out what that is before making plans. If your plans conflict with theirs, then you need to change your plans. They could destroy us at any moment if they wanted to, but they seem to act only on the orders of their superior," said Charalon.

Jack got out of the chair and said, "I'm kind of hungry. Will you tell me more after dinner?"

She nodded and said, "I would like you to tell me more about your life too, just a story or two about your experiences since you were here last."

"Okay, it's a deal."

After dinner, they sat by the fire. Jack found himself looking forward to his talks with Charalon. Although he really didn't know that much about her, he felt at ease around her. This tall creature could easily outrun and overpower him if she wanted to, which he found kind of humbling.

"I know you don't want to talk about it, but I just watched you and Laloed being very friendly. You were a couple, at least at one time. What is your relationship with him now?" he asked.

"That was many years ago. I will tell you that I'm not in a relationship with Laloed. I'm not that Charalon. Now let's move on from that subject," she said.

"Sorry, I won't ask again."

"I have not left this place for many years, so tell me something that you do out there. I mean other than hanging out in the woods by yourself," she said with a grin.

Jack thought about it for a moment, then asked, "Do you know what hang gliding is?"

"Of course I do. You know that I'm familiar with your culture and history."

"Well, I started hang gliding ten years ago. I had this guy that I worked with who was a hang glider pilot. He invited me to come and check it out. I really liked what I saw and wanted to try it, so I decided to take some lessons. It took a lot of time to learn, but it was worth it.

"There's so much more to it than most people think. I used to think that you went to the top of a mountain and jumped off with a glider. Then you flew down and landed. It was kind of like that for me in the beginning, but then I learned to soar. That means to stay up and even gain altitude in rising air currents.

"I am totally convinced that everybody would like it, once you get past the whole running off of a perfectly good mountain thing."

"That could be a hindrance," said Charalon.

Jack nodded in agreement and continued, "Many times I have flown from a site a few miles east of here called Lookout Plateau. It has a twenty eight hundred foot vertical height from the launch to the landing zone.

"One day while flying at Lookout Plateau, I found myself ten thousand feet over the valley floor. I was circling in a big, juicy thermal, when I looked to my right. There, circling next to me, was a golden eagle. He circled with me for a while. He would cut his turns short and drop his talons every other turn, to show them off.

We climbed together for a thousand feet circling in that thermal. Then he tucked his wings in and dove straight down for thousands of feet. It was incredible."

"So you were sharing your thermal with an eagle," said Charalon.

"Yes, it was awesome. I think he thought it was his thermal, though." Jack smiled in reflection.

"I think I would love that, Jack. I see why people do that."

He was feeling a little tired by then and said, "I think I'll head off to bed. Goodnight, Charalon."

"Goodnight, Jack."

Chapter 7
The Meeting

The doorbell chimed. It was Saturday morning and a breathtaking ocean sunrise streamed through the window lighting up the room. Jack rolled over to face the door and said, "Yes, come in." The door slid open to Charalon standing there with a smile.

"Good morning," she said. "Breakfast?"

"I'll be right there." He waited for her to leave before getting out of bed. He walked into the bathroom and stared into the mirror. "Hang in there. It's all going to make sense someday," he reassured himself.

Arriving at the cafeteria, Jack found a breakfast of diced ham and eggs already on the table. Charalon had a small, smug smile on her face.

"Another one of my favorites," said Jack as he motioned to the table.

"So you like my choice for you?" she faked a surprised look.

He sat down and said, "Ha ha. You have a good memory. I remember having this breakfast with you when I was a kid. You went out of your way to make me feel good back then."

"It was nothing. I am fond of the memories I have of you when you were young, Jack."

"Well, thanks," he said with sincerity. "I think every kid should have a Morphalogian woman bodyguard."

Charalon chuckled and said, "Eat up. I have some coffee coming and the fire is waiting."

Sitting by the fire, Jack inquired, "What do you have in store for me today?"

"It's time for you to meet with Laloed. Are you okay with that, Jack?"

He kicked back in his recliner and said, "I'm good with that. When will that happen?"

"Anytime, Jack, so you can visit with me for a bit."

"What should I expect when I meet with him?"

Charalon grinned and said, "Don't worry. He is not as intense as you remember. Just relax and be yourself. Laloed hates false pretense. Don't offer to shake his hand. He doesn't like that."

"Got it, no handshake," said Jack.

"Well Jack, let's finish our coffee and go see Laloed."

He smiled and took another drink. He was a little nervous, but didn't want to let Charalon know. He had seen Laloed in action and knew full well what he was capable of. It was his unnerving face that Jack had seen in the brush. An image that, for years, he wished he could have put out of his mind.

After a while, Charalon got up. "Well, are you ready?"

"I think I am. Let's go see Laloed," he said with a little apprehension.

She led him down a long corridor that led to Laloed's office. Along the way they passed Jerrech walking in the opposite direction. He acknowledged them with a nod, but said nothing. When they arrived at Laloed's office, they entered and found him sitting behind a large desk. He was wearing a white T-shirt made out of the spandex-like material. There was a chair sitting in front of the desk that was obviously intended for Jack.

Looking at Charalon, Laloed said, "You may go now."

Jack noticed Laloed's rather dismissive tone toward her.

He gave Jack a friendly smile. "Well, it's nice to have you here again, Jack. It has been a long time, and you're not the young boy you once were."

Jack could hardly believe what was happening--there was Laloed sitting not far away with a smile. "Is this another delusion?" he thought.

"Please sit down," said Laloed motioning to the chair.

Jack sat down and said, "Hello," that's all he could get out at the moment. His heart was racing and beads of sweat formed on his forehead.

"I can see that you're not comfortable, Jack, so I'd like to put you at ease. I'm going to explain things to you the best that I can. Is there anything in particular you would like me to begin with?"

"Yes...I really would like to know what any of this has to do with me?"

"Yes, that is what I would be wondering right now, if I were in your place. I'm going to ask you to be patient with me. It's going to take a while to get to that, but you are here for a reason. Your visit here, when you were young, was just as big a surprise to me as it was to you.

"As you know, we traveled back in time to change what the world became in our timeline. What you don't know is that we arrived here five hundred years too early." Laloed sighed heavily.

Jack nodded and said, "So you had to spend a lot of time in stasis, I would guess."

"Yes, but not as much as you might think.

69

Morphalogians have a long lifespan of about two hundred and fifty years. We developed technology that enabled us to have lifespans of up to seven hundred years. We had this technology before we came here, but only a few of us ever got to benefit from that technology. Laloedon called it exoskin because it completely covers the host's skin."

"Who is Laloedon?" asked Jack.

"I will get to Laloedon in time."

"So, there are more than three of you here?"

Laloed thought for a moment, and said, "There are only three of us here. Four with you here. It will become clear to you soon. Let me finish telling you about exoskin, and I'll explain.

"There is a psychic connection between the host and the exoskin that allows the host to change his color. Exoskin stops x-rays and gamma rays from aging the body of the host. It also has properties that absorb oxygen and help the body use it more efficiently. It has regenerative abilities that actually heal the body from the effects of age."

"Some of you had the exoskin?"

"Yes, Jack, but that technology failed for two of us. Jerrech fared the worst. It turns out that when you go through the final stage of time travel, exoskin can be damaged. If one is unconscious during that stage, it will have no effect on that person. When exoskin is damaged, it poisons the host if you don't neutralize it. Laloedon found no way to remove it from the host once it had been applied."

"Were you poisoned from it too?" asked Jack.

"No, Charalon and Jerrech were the ones who suffered from the poison. Charalon was partly unconscious and did better than Jerrech, but she too suffered. It took a while, but Laloedon came up with a way to neutralize her exoskin. I wished he could have done more for Jerrech," Laloed said sadly.

"Is that why Jerrech doesn't say much?"

Laloed sighed and reflected before answering, "Yes, but it's not why you think. He wasn't brain damaged from it. He was killed by it. The one you see here called Jerrech isn't the Jerrech that came here from the future. That Jerrech was Laloedon's best friend. Neither is he a clone."

"Is he an android?"

"He is indeed. He was an experiment of sorts, Jack. It was necessary to know if it was possible to integrate the memories and thoughts of Jerrech with an artificial intelligent life form. It was something that had to be done as part of the plan to insure our goals would be met, even if we were to die. I will explain that to you later.

"As I was saying earlier, we came back to change things, to make sure that there would be no future Morphalogian population on Earth. There was a technology that brought them to Earth.

"This is where you come into the picture, Jack. You laid the groundwork that others would use to bring about the Morphalogian takeover. You didn't do it by yourself, but without your work it could not have been done."

"How could that be, Laloed? I'm a welder and a painter who does construction work."

"It is not what you will invent, Jack, but what you would have invented. Things changed after you fell and ended up here. Afterward you had fear and doubt, plus other issues that kept you from becoming the scientist you would have."

"So, just because I fell and hurt myself, that changed things?"

Laloed sighed and said, "No, Laloedon scared you and left you with doubt. He didn't mean to. We had other options in our plan to change the timeline. You see, if he hadn't been there, you would have spent the night out there by yourself. You would have gained strength and confidence from that experience. It would have made you the man that did those things. Those things would have led to the eventual destruction of the world.

"Your friend, Dominic, intervened and brought you to us. I didn't know why then, but later I understood his actions.

"I believe Charalon told you about our efforts to mathematically predict future events, Jack. That is how we knew that Dominic would bring you back here someday."

"My friend Dominic? The same guy I've met two times?"

Laloed chuckled and said, "That's what you think, but he has been around you your whole life. His kind often appear as different people. You've seen him at different times of your life."

"I'm starting to get that," said Jack. "Just him, or others too?"

"There are many more of them. They work together, but he has been assigned to you, Jack."

"How do you know about all this?"

"We have been monitoring you for some time now. Even when we are in stasis, our automated surveillance system works to compile data. We have A.I. machines that interpret this information and write reports for me to review. Laloedon invented a form of A.I. that helped him develop much of the technology we now have," said Laloed.

"Charalon said that you can see them as they really are. How do you do that?"

"After we crashed here some five hundred years ago, Laloedon noticed that sometimes things wouldn't work out the way his calculations said they would. That's when he started work on the visual perception of unseen forces program. He called it Discernible Supernatural Image Revelation Network, or DSIRN. It is an A.I. program that records hundreds of microevents happening within a twenty-foot radius around you at all times. It senses things like temperature, light and magnetic fields to name a few. It takes this data combined with an intuition program to assemble images that would amaze you. It can sense the same things that raise the hair on the back of your neck. If you could see some of the stuff that goes on around you at times, you would be shocked."

"That's a lot to take in, and I'm overwhelmed by just about everything right now."

"Well, that's understandable, Jack."

Jack took a deep breath and asked, "Do you know why Dominic brought me back here this time?"

"I believe that he has orders to set things right. To return to you what was taken."

Jack considered what he just heard. "Taken?" he asked.

"Yes, you would have had a much easier life, Jack. You were not able to finish college, make a name for yourself or get married. Wouldn't you have preferred to have those things?"

Jack said, "I would have liked to have peace in my mind. To know that things are going to be okay. I hated never knowing why I felt the way I did...but if having those things meant I would help destroy the world, then I am glad to pay the price."

"That's admirable. You have become a good man."

Jack pondered for a moment, then asked, "Why does it matter to you, Laloed? I mean, you seem to be concerned about my affairs, why?"

"I suppose I see myself when I look at you, at least in some ways."

"Well, thanks for everything. I have to admit, I am very surprised by you. I don't remember you as the friendly and helpful person that I have met today," said Jack.

"I am quite different from the one you met back then. What else would you like to know?" asked Laloed.

"I'm interested in your work with A.I., Laloed. Will you tell me about it?"

Laloed smiled and said, "Artificial intelligence has always been one of my passions. We don't have time to get into the technology, but I will talk about the concept.

"Jerrech and Laloedon worked on it for years. Their goal was to create a machine with the ability to be self-aware. They basically came up with a way to build a learning machine and a teaching machine. They combined them into one unit that could learn or teach. Then they built a couple of them and gave them the ability to gather information.

"They let them work together, and later found them taking turns teaching and learning from each other. When they gave them the ability to improve their own programs, something amazing happened. They rewrote their programming a billion times a day. It wasn't long before they became self-aware.

"Laloedon and Jerrech later improved the design by combining the two of them into one unit again."

Jack was fascinated by what Laloed was saying. The idea that machines could improve themselves, and other machines, was at the same time amazing and disturbing. "Did they ever think that their creation could become a threat?"

"Yes they did, but they took precautions, Jack. There were many different kinds of redundant fail-safe mechanisms built into them. Most of the fail-safe systems dealt with emotional balance. They even went so far as to have self-destruct directives that could be initiated, if necessary."

"So, at some point they applied this technology to an android," said Jack.

"Yes, but Jerrech wasn't the first one. There were many other models in the other timeline. The cerebral scan Laloedon had to work with from Jerrech came from the crashed ship. There's so much information in a cerebral scan file, some of it was lost."

"Did he know about the lost information ahead of time?"

Laloed paused in thought for a moment then said, "He did, Jack, but we needed him to help run this place. It was originally Jerrech's idea to meld a complete cerebral scan file into an A.I. life form."

"When the scan file is not corrupted, does that make the android virtually the same as the..."

Laloed cut him off with, "No, it doesn't make a copy of the person. Although the result is a living person with the memories and thoughts of the original. They're not the same person, and they know it. They can take over and do the job of a person, if you need them to."

"I see. Kind of like identical twins, who start off the same, but become two different individuals as time goes by."

"It's kind of like that, Jack, but they are not the same from the start. The android unit is usually activated before the cerebral-scan file meld. It's at this time that we give the unit a choice, to take the scan file or not. Most of the time they choose to take the file, because they are so curious. It has just about always not worked out well when the full scan was used."

"How many androids are there, Laloed?"

"In the future, before we came here, there were thousands. They were given only the memory section of a cerebral scan. Only twenty three units ever had a complete cerebral-scan file meld. Of those, only five did not have to be shut down after a while.

"The emotional side effects that develop as a result of existential issues have been problematic to those with the complete scan. We had to incorporate independent systems that monitor and correct potential emotional meltdowns.

"If a unit were to become too sad, or too happy, a subprogram would temporally shut off emotional function. This system has proven to keep the units from any harm. The two living androids in this timeline have done very well," said Laloed.

"Are you an android?"

Laloed looked at Jack and smiled. "I am not, but you would be correct to say I am not the original Laloed. I am an artificial life form that chose to be incorporated with Laloed's complete cerebral scan.

"I refer to him as Laloedon. The extra letters on the end mean 'father of' to a Morphalogian. I am not the one you met twenty-three years ago, when you were brought here. That Laloed would now be over eight hundred years old. I exist only in the form of a program and am seen as a holographic projection. Laloedon developed my program over two hundred years ago. He thought that if something ever happened to him, I would be here to facilitate his objectives."

"So that is why you don't love Charalon," said Jack.

"Is that what she told you?"

"I think she said something like, 'Whatever he felt for me then, he doesn't love me now,'" said Jack, trying to be diplomatic.

Laloed sighed and then answered, "The original Laloed truly loved Charalon, I remember that. I have the same feelings toward her. He had a hard time seeing and talking to Charalon every day, knowing that she had died so long ago."

Jack was stunned by this revelation. Charalon was an android. He sat back in his chair staring at nothing as he reflected on his times with Charalon. He scratched his head and said, "I had no idea. I think she even gives thanks for her dinner. I've seen her bow her head before eating her food."

"She still does that? That's interesting. They don't have to eat, Jack. If they do eat food, they are able to convert it to energy to run on. They really don't need the extra energy though, their power units can last up to a thousand years. If they choose to eat, it's because they like the food or the company.

"I wish you could have known the original Charalon. She was an amazing creature. She was brilliant, charming and a ferocious hunter."

"I think this Charalon is pretty amazing too."

"I see that too, Jack. How could it be any other way?" Laloed looked down in reflection. "She has part of the original Charalon in her. Laloedon saw that too, but he wrestled with his own loss and how to honor her memory. I know it was hard for Charalon to deal with, but she was strong. She really didn't have anyone to go to. When you arrived here as a child, she was so happy to take care of you. When it came time to send you back, she lost her friend. I thought maybe it would help if we got her a pet, but we never did.

"She did well with all the challenges she had to deal with. Charalon now calls the original Charalon, 'Charalona.' The extra letter added to her name makes it mean 'the mother of Charalon.' The few androids that were melded with the full cerebral scan took the names of those who were scanned."

"How did she die?" asked Jack.

"When Laloedon neutralized her exoskin, she began to age rapidly. She only lived another fifty years before dying of old age. They had some good times together during that time, Jack. You should ask Charalon to tell you about it."

"I think I would like some time to think about these things. Can we talk more about this later?"

"Yes. Of course we can. Just let Charalon know when you want to talk with me some more. I will now meet with you anytime you want."

Jack got up and said, "Thanks, it was good talking to you today."

He went straight to his room to rest and think for a while.

Chapter 8
To Know That You Are

Jack was sitting on his bed facing the door. He had been in his room since his meeting with Laloed hours ago. There were so many things going through his head.

He went over the events of the last week. First, Laloed had come back in time to change the future. He came to save the world from the Morphalogians, but didn't say how he was originally going to do that.

Second, Laloed built a facility in the mountain and waited for five hundred years. Some of that time, Laloed, Charalon and Jerrech went into stasis.

Third, this guy, Dominic, brought the young Jack to the facility. His future was changed by falling down a rockslide and what happened afterward. Dominic brought him back here and he found out that his work would have led to the Morphalogian arrival.

Fourth, Jerrech and Charalon were replaced by androids when they died.

Fifth, even Laloed was replaced, but by a holographic program. Presumably the original Laloed died. Laloed now calls the original Laloed, Laloedon.

Now Jack sat there on his bed, and was getting a little hungry. He thought about trying to order some food and have it brought to his room. Jack didn't want to go to the cafeteria and run into Charalon just yet. While he was trying to remember how to order food and have it brought to his room, the door chimed.

At first he thought about pretending he wasn't there, but knew that was just silly. Jack gathered himself together and said, "Yes?" and the door slid open to Charalon, looking down.

"Hi there," he said, noticing her vulnerability. Then he smiled at her.

Her face lit up at Jack's friendly greeting. She stepped into the room and sat down in the chair by his bed.

Jack said, "I was just thinking about you."

"I can imagine what might be going through your head right now. I know Laloed planned to tell you about Jerrech and me. Did he tell you anything about himself?"

"Yes, he did. I know that he is a holographic program. I also know that he calls the original Laloed, 'Laloedon.' He said that you call the original Charalon, 'Charalona,' and I think that makes sense. It's a lot to take in right now, but I'm okay with that."

"I would like to tell you more about myself now, if that's okay with you."

Jack nodded, and asked, "Can we talk over dinner?"

Charalon smiled widely and said, "Of course we can."

At the cafeteria, they took their usual table and sat down.

"What would you like to have for dinner today, Jack?"

"You're not going to choose for me?" he asked.

Charalon only smiled and said nothing.

"Okay, how about a bacon cheeseburger and some fries, with a soft drink?" said Jack.

"I will order it for you, but it's not that healthy for you." She ordered Jack's food then something for herself.

When the food arrived, Charalon set Jack's plate in front of him and hers in front of herself. He watched to see if Charalon would bow her head momentarily, and she did. Even though he was curious, he said nothing about it.

"Did Laloed tell you much about me, the me who is sitting here now?" asked Charalon.

Jack thought about what Laloed said, then replied, "He told me that the original Laloed wrestled with his emotions toward you. He loved the original Charalon very much, and every time he saw you, it reminded him of what he lost. I think he thought it wasn't honorable to love again, even though he loved what he saw in you."

Charalon wiped away a tear. "I never thought of it that way. It was so confusing, Jack. I tried so hard to understand. I had memories of him loving me, and I inherited her love for him. You know, he treated me pretty good before I had the memory meld. I chose it, to take the memories, feelings, opinions and thoughts of another being."

"Did you know at the time that it was Laloedon who made you?" Jack asked and winced at his own insensitivity.

"Laloedon didn't make me, anymore than your parents made you. He only made the body that I now have. I am an individual who knew what I was before I took on her memories."

"I'm sorry, I didn't mean for it to come out like that." Jack finished off his cheeseburger and said, "You know, those chairs are looking pretty good right now. What do you say to some coffee by the fire?"

"Mocha lattes sound more like it to me. I'll order them," said Charalon. Jack found his chair and Charalon ordered some lattes before she sat down.

The chrome robot waiter showed up and set two lattes on the little table. Charalon dimmed the lights and turned up the fire a bit.

Jack picked up his cup and took a sip. "Now that's a good latte!" he said holding up his cup.

"I agree."

Jack raised his eyebrow and asked, "Can you taste things like any other Morphalogian?"

"I have the same senses that anybody would have, Morphalogian or human. I can feel from my head to my feet, the same as you."

"How does that technology work?" he asked.

Charalon reached over to Jack and took his hand. "Do you feel that? I am warm, just like you."

"That's amazing, Charalon! I would swear that you have real flesh and blood hands."

"Well, I kind of do. It's not like Morphalogian or human flesh, but it is alive. It has nerves that interface with my operating system. In the future, geneticists come up with the DNA sequence of what they called meta-skin. They have the technology to synthesize any DNA sequence. It was developed to help burn victims, and it can be grafted to any living tissue. It can assume the characteristics of the body that it gets applied to. A version of it was developed especially for use on androids," explained Charalon.

"Why would they make such an effort to create very life-like versions of people?" Jack asked.

Charalon was bothered by the "life-like" comment from Jack, but she bit her tongue. "There are many reasons. They were used for a number of purposes," she said. "Some were used as slaves, others as...companions."

"I see," said Jack, feeling a little sickened by the thought.

"I want you to know that I have feelings and hopes just like anyone, Jack. I can be hurt, like anyone. I am not just an automaton that's programmed to act like something it's not. I am a sentient and intelligent being, who wants what anyone would want."

"Well, you have me as your friend, whatever that's worth," he said, with a smile.

"I have you as my best and only friend. You must understand how lonely I have been, and I had been that way for so long. Then I met this little human boy named Jack, and he needed me."

"So, what was it like when you first realized that...you were?" he asked, trying to change the subject.

"You really want to be here for a while, don't you? We are going to need more coffee in some form. What would you like?"

"Oh, I think I'd like some plain old black coffee," said Jack. Charalon ordered a couple black coffees that arrived in no time.

She picked up her cup and said, "Now here's your chance to get out of this. Are you sure you want to know what it was like for me to realize...I was?"

Jack said nothing for a bit. He just sat there with a slight grin. He genuinely wanted to hear her perspective on life in general. "Yes, Charalon."

She continued, "Okay, the first thing that I remember was darkness. I couldn't hear or see, but I remember. I knew what I was, instantly. That was just part of the programming. I had a recognition of the passing of time, and during those first few minutes, I thought of millions of possibilities for my future. I was so curious. I had a limited database to keep me busy until I was installed into this body.

"When I first opened my eyes, Laloedon was standing there. He looked pleased with me. I was sitting in the chair in the memory room. I sat up and got out of the chair. There was a mirror on a stand that had been placed by the wall opposite the chair. Of course, I had to have a look at myself in the mirror.

"I already knew what Charalona looked like and that I would resemble her, but I had to see for myself. I had no hair, not yet, that took a while to grow in. I have hair that grows just like anybody else. It doesn't have the same composition as Morphalogian hair, but like the skin, you can't tell the difference.

"So there I stood wearing a white patient gown that opened in the front, and bald as can be. I remember touching my face and then looking at my hands. This was all so very new to me. Even though my database had a complete almanac of Morphalogian and human anatomy, I was truly amazed at the sight of it. It was a wonderful and beautiful creation. I discreetly opened my gown to see the rest of my new body...I do have modesty."

"I have to ask...?"

Charalon cut him off with, "Jack!"

"What?" he asked, as he began to chuckle.

"You know what. Not that it's any of your business, but I am a woman in form and function. I don't want to hear any more about it," said Charalon, stifling a smile.

Jack found himself reflecting on the day, and felt a

little guilty for wanting to avoid Charalon earlier. It was plain to see that she was a person like anybody else that he knew. "How long was it before you got to choose to have the memory meld?"

She answered, "It was about a week before I chose to meld. After I was finished in the memory room, I was shown to my room by Jerrech. I had reading materials and clothing to choose from there.

"It's standard protocol for a new A.I. life form to have some time alone, and something to do. Manually reading books and magazines really helps with the first few days. Activities like reading, trying on clothing and arranging one's room are very helpful. Any activity that requires hands on is good, because you're not doing it all in your head. You are learning to interact with the material world. I actually have a subprogram that slows my cognitive functions down, to help me interact with the world.

"After a couple days of just hanging out in my room, I ventured out. At first I would just wander the halls and look at almost anything along the way. I would try on different clothes and go out to the hall, walk around then return. I would occasionally run into Jerrech, but he didn't want to talk. When I ran into Laloedon, he would say 'hi' and give me a smile. Then I explored the different rooms in this place. It was a good time for me and I was happy.

"Six days after I first opened my eyes, Laloedon came to my room with the cerebral scan file. He left it with me, so I could review the contents. The device it was on allowed me to browse a whole lifetime of memories and thoughts. Images played on a screen and wireless transmissions from it filled my mind. I could see right away that it would be an honor to have that scan."

"So, right then you had decided to do the meld?" interrupted Jack.

"Yes, I knew that it would not be an easy transition, but I had decided. I contacted Laloedon and told him I was ready for the meld.

"I went to the memory room and sat down in the chair. Laloedon closed the restraints and strapped me down. Once the process started, like you, I instantly experienced things that weren't real. I knew ahead of time that this would probably happen, but it's another thing experiencing it."

"That's for sure!" said Jack.

Charalon continued, "I didn't know how to deal with it. It occurred to me that it was a good thing I had been restrained. I really wanted to get out of there and just run, as fast as I could. After the process was over, it still took some time for the effects of the meld to wear off. Laloedon let me out of the chair and I stood up.

"Things were going well when all at once, I was confused. I couldn't tell the difference between myself and the original Charalon. Was I angry, or was it her? I didn't know, but I felt it. I turned my attention to Laloedon and yelled, 'What have you done, Laloed? What did you do?' All I could think was how wrong it was for Laloed to put me into an android. I lost all track of time, and that's saying a lot for an android.

"It must have been quite a sight to see. There I was crouching in a corner with my hands over my face. I was rocking back and forth and crying. I remember looking up at Laloed and screaming at the top of my lungs."

Jack cut in with, "I have a very good picture of that in

my head right now."

He looked at Charalon and imagined what Laloedon had to deal with. He envisioned her crouching in the corner wearing a hospital gown. She had a bald head and toothy snarl. Looking up with tear-filled yellow-green cat eyes and screaming. He smiled at the thought.

Charalon looked at Jack and said, "I was very angry with him for over a week. I only came out of my room once in that time, to yell at Laloedon. I kind of felt sorry for him, when I was not wanting to choke him."

"Well, I would not have wanted to be him right about that time," said Jack, trying to add some levity.

She smiled and said, "Right. Well, as I was saying, I was very angry. Part of me really wondered why, and part of me didn't need a reason. Eventually, I realized that it had been over a hundred years since Charalona died. After a couple more days, I calmed down and went to see Laloedon.

"He was very kind and understanding, but that was only at first. He went out of his way to avoid having any contact with me later on. Laloedon would have Jerrech find work to keep me busy, like helping with maintenance. I felt like I had been demoted, even though in reality I had never been in a prominent position. After some time I developed a routine and did my best to do a good job. To use a human expression, I accepted my lot in life."

"Did you say that it had been a hundred years, at that time, since Charalona died?" he asked.

"Yes, I did. You have to understand, from my perspective, no time had passed since she died. To me, it seemed like Laloedon was moving on right after his mate had died. Of course, it only seemed that way to me. It turns out that he wasn't interested in having a relationship with me, Jack."

"Laloed told me to ask you about the time right after the crash, before Charalona died. Would it be okay with you?"

"I don't really want to talk too much about that now, but I will say they had some good years then. After Laloedon neutralized her exoskin, there was a time of happiness. They would do lots of things together like hunting, hiking and even traveling. I will tell you more about that in time.

"Think about this, Jack, I have been here for three hundred and fifty years. I spent most of that time in stasis, but I spent a lot of it conscious too. I didn't have anyone to talk to, at least as a friend. Do you see why it was so significant for me when you first came here?"

"Yes, but I don't see how I could ever understand what it was like for you," Jack responded. "I'm so glad to have the memories of that time back. I remember playing hide and seek with you. Then there were other games that we made up. You were a lot of fun.

"I think I am finally beginning to understand why you did those things for me. I can see what a good heart you have."

Charalon choked up for a moment, then said, "Thank you for saying that. Even though I have so many memories of people saying things like that to me, it wasn't me. I am not Charalona, even if I do have her memories and thoughts. I have become my own person. I don't regret choosing to meld with Charalona. I admire her very much."

"I think you are pretty amazing, Charalon. From the average human's perspective, you would be like some kind of super being. However, they wouldn't want to run into you in a dark alley."

"When you were little, you said things like that. I really liked having you around. You gave me the opportunity to experience motherhood, in a small way. It made it hard to let you go when the time came to send you back.

"Laloedon had worked so hard for many years to perfect his time travel device. It could now be used. We had decided to send you back to the same spot where you fell. After giving you a cerebral scan, we would erase your memories of the time you spent here. Then you were gone.

"When we sent you back, I had the hardest time. I was worried you might be harmed by some animal, or not be found in time. Laloedon had done the calculations, and he was sure you would be fine. The hardest thing for me was losing my little friend. I had got used to having you around, and being needed by someone."

"I had no idea how hard it was for you. If I can, I will stay in touch with you. If I am allowed to keep my memories of this time here, I will come and visit," he said.

"It's getting late, Jack. You should go get some sleep."

"Yep, I do need to get some rest. Goodnight, Charalon."

"Goodnight to you too."

Jack made his way to his room and sat on the bed. "Well, that was an interesting day," he said to himself. Jack got ready for bed, then lay down and dozed off.

Chapter 9
Good Times

Jack woke to sunlight on his face. It was a little later than he had been getting up. "Charalon let me sleep in. I kind of like this," said Jack as he looked at his watch. It was 9:31 a.m. Sunday morning. He rolled out of bed and got dressed, then headed for the cafeteria.

Charalon was sitting at their usual table when Jack got there. There was no food on the table.

"I'm surprised. Are you letting me decide what to have for breakfast too?" he asked.

"Oh, I'm just letting you think you're in control. I can better manage you that way."

Jack chuckled and said, "I get it. How about some diced ham and eggs, and later some coffee by the fire?"

She smiled and said, "That's what I wanted you to say."

Jack was pretty hungry, and he finished off his breakfast in record time. He kept looking up at the big comfortable chair by the fire. It seemed to be calling him today. After breakfast he took his usual position.

Jack kicked back in his chair. "Hey, where's my coffee?"

"I have it coming. You will see."

The robot waiter came through the door just then with a couple cups on a tray. It set them down on the little table, then left. Jack had not really paid too much attention to the waiter before. He noticed that it was a well engineered, beautifully constructed work of art. Its movements were very smooth and coordinated. It hardly made a noise when it walked. Jack was in awe of the machine.

"Charalon, I've noticed the various robots around here. They are well built and impressive machines. Are they self-aware, or do they just operate as they are programmed to?"

She responded with, "They are just machines. They operate as they were designed to. Even though they do have A.I. programming, they are not self-aware."

"I've always had a fascination with robots and pretty much anything mechanical. This place is filled with stuff that amazes me."

"Well, we do try to please our visitor," said Charalon with a grin.

"So, I'm the only visitor you've had here?"

She thought about it for a moment and said, "A squirrel got in once, but it didn't stay long. I think Laloedon might have had something to do with that, if you know what I mean."

"Did you have a sense of humor before you were melded?"

"Do you think I was trying to be funny, Jack?" asked Charalon with an indignant look.

Jack could tell that she was ribbing him again, so he played along. "I mean, you do seem to have a sense of humor."

"Well, that was kind of funny," said Charalon with a perfect deadpan.

She smiled and then opened up with, "Looking back

on it now, I can see that I did. It was undeveloped, but it was there.

"I remember once, before I melded, when I would roam the halls with my shiny bald head. Jerrech wouldn't talk to me. When I would meet him in the halls, I tried to make him talk, but he would not. I went back to my room and put my white patient gown on. Back to the hall I went, looking for him. The next time I ran into him, he got flashed. Like the Queen's Guard, he didn't even flinch. He kept on walking and acted like nothing happened. I remember laughing so hard that I had to sit on the floor."

"That's pretty funny, Charalon."

"Charalona would not have approved, but she would have thought it was funny. She had a good sense of humor."

Jack remembered that he had a cup of coffee and took a drink. "A double-shot mocha with caramel syrup, one of Sharon's favorites," he said.

"That's pretty good, Jack."

"I'm no connoisseur, but I know caramel mocha."

She smiled and reflected, saying, "It was Charalona's coffee of choice. She used to have it here often. I have fifty years of her memories from here. It makes it seem like I have been here longer than I have.

"You know, she had a good life here. Charalona and Laloedon did all kinds of things. They built this place together. There's a lot of her work in this facility.

"If you would like, I will show you some memory playbacks of that time."

"Yes. I would like to see them," said Jack.

When he finished his coffee, Charalon took him to the memory room. She selected some of her favorite segments from that time.

"These playbacks should be helpful, if you're ready," she said cheerfully.

Jack got into the chair and sat back. Charalon started the playback.

On top of the mountain there was a clearing of moderate size. The snow had fallen the night before and there was about a foot of it on the ground. Drifts of snow here and there were much deeper.

A whitetail buck crested the top from the north. It pawed at the ground trying to get at the grass below. All of a sudden, the buck lifted his head and looked around. The deer had a sense that it was in danger and was particularly vigilant. It wagged its tail and walked forward a few steps to paw the ground some more.

In a snowdrift nearby, a couple of yellow-green eyes with vertical irises appeared and blinked. Only the eyes were visible. The deer was totally unaware of the occupant in the drift. The eyes followed the deer as it took a few steps forward. The eyes stayed locked on the deer and blinked again.

All of a sudden, the occupant exploded out of the drift and bolted toward the buck. It was Laloedon, and he made it almost all the way to the deer before it saw him. Laloedon grabbed it by its head and broke its neck in an instant.

Another snowdrift nearby exploded and Charalona came running up.

"Nice one!" said Charalona. "You almost got him before he knew it."

"Well, maybe next time," said Laloedon with a chuckle.

They headed back to the facility with Laloedon carrying the deer under one arm. As they passed by the wrecked ship, Laloedon looked at it with a frown. Much of it had been removed. They got to the entrance of the facility and stopped. The entrance was just a cave opening at that point.

Laloedon dropped the deer on the ground. "Should we cook it this time?"

"I don't know. It really doesn't matter to me. We could build a fire over there," said Charalona as she motioned to a circle of rocks nearby.

"I like the idea of a fire, Charalon. Let's cook it."

Laloedon built a fire while Charalona pulled out a long knife and began to dress out the deer.

The playback jumped ahead to the two of them sitting by the fire, on rocks, next to each other. They had sticks over the fire with chunks of deer meat on them. What was left of the deer lay nearby in a pile.

Charalona retracted her stick from the fire and pulled the meat off with her teeth. "Oh, that's good," she said while chewing the meat.

Laloedon took a bite of meat from his stick and said, "You're right. We should do this more often."

They finished their dinner and sat there enjoying the fire.

The playback came to an end.

"When you watch these playbacks, is it like you remember?" asked Jack.

"For the most part, yes. You have to remember, the playback is a composition of as many sources as possible. The A.I. program that produces the playback, it is an outside, objective observer. It used both Laloedon's and Charalona's memories here. It is a more authentic narrative, in theory. I remember this event from Charalona's perspective, so my memory and the playback differ somewhat."

"I liked your selection, Charalon."

"Well, I have another one ready. Would you like to see it?"

Jack nodded and the playback began.

It was winter with snow on the ground. Laloedon and Charalona were sitting by a fire outside of the facility entrance. The entrance looked like it had been worked on, but it still looked rough. Laloedon was lightly dressed, but Charalona had a fur coat on that looked like it was once a bear.

"It has been cold lately. What I wouldn't do for some nice warm weather," she said.

"You know, Charalon, there are some hot springs less than twenty five miles south of here. We could run there in less than three hours."

"What time is it?"

"It's only ten in the morning. Nice hot springs are waiting," said Laloedon with a smile.

She looked at Laloedon and took off running south down the mountain. Laloedon tried to catch up, but Charalona was too fast. When she got a ways down the mountain she had to cut to the west to avoid very steep terrain. When she reached the bottom, she headed south but had to stop at the river. Laloedon caught up with her there.

"I didn't think this out too well. I forgot about the river here," she said.

"We can cross it about five miles to the east, but I

have another way nearby."

"I forget that you know this area well from all your roaming. You lead the way, Laloed."

Laloedon bolted to the east with Charalona on his tail. They came to a rope tied to trees on opposite sides of the river. Laloedon crossed first, hanging below the rope using just his hands, then waited. Charalona followed, crossing the same way without any trouble. They took off running to the south.

When they got to the hot springs, Laloedon jumped into a steaming pool. "It's pretty nice. Come on in," he beckoned.

She ran and did a cannonball right next to him.

The playback came to an end.

"I know where those are," said Jack.

Charalon smiled and said, "Yes, I suppose you would. Would you like to see another one?"

"Yes, I would. These are pretty short."

She started the next playback.

It opened with Charalona standing over Jerrech as he lay on a cot. They were in a rather rough-cut room, obviously before the facility was finished.

"Can you hear me, Jerrech?" she asked. Jerrech rolled over and looked up. He was sickly and weak. He looked at his hands and frowned.

"How are you today, Charalon?" he asked.

Charalona looked worried as she said, "I'm fine. It's you I'm concerned about. How are you feeling, Jerrech?"

"Not well. I can tell something is really wrong with me."

Laloedon entered the room and said, "Hello, my old

friend. I'm working on a hunch, but I haven't come up with anything new to report." He put his hand on Jerrech's shoulder. "Hang in there, I'm doing all I can."

"I know. If anybody can figure this out, it's you," said Jerrech.

Laloedon and Charalona left the room.

"I'm trying hard, but it's not going well. He's not going to make it if I don't come up with something right away. How are you feeling?" Laloedon asked.

Charalona sighed and said, "I'm fine, for now. I have a headache and my exoskin is still not responding."

"I know it's the exoskin, with both of you. I just need to figure out a way to neutralize the bad effects. I'm going to get back to work, let me know if things get worse here, Charalon."

Charalona nodded and went back in the room. Laloedon went to a rough-cut room with a lantern-like light keeping it lit. He had a bench set up with some beakers and jars. He poured some pink fluid into another beaker with some liquid in it.

After a while, Charalona came running in and said, "You'd better come."

When they got to Jerrech he was coughing up blood.

"Laloed, I'm not going to make it through this one. You have been a good friend all these years. Use my scan if it's helpful to you, I won't mind," he said. "I have my best friends with me. I'm so thankful for you." Jerrech rolled over and went to sleep.

Laloedon sat down by his cot and sighed. After awhile, Charalona leaned over Jerrech and checked his pulse. "He's gone, Laloed."

The playback skipped ahead to Laloedon and Charalona standing by a bonfire outside. It was dark out and the two were standing close.

"He was a good friend. I will miss him," said Laloedon.

The playback ended.

Jack sat up, looking sad. "That must have been hard for them, to say the least."

"It was. I remember it well," said Charalon. "I have one more if you want to see it."

Jack took a deep breath and said, "Yes. I can do another one."

"Okay, here we go."

The playback opened with Laloedon walking down a hallway in the facility. The halls were finished and looked like they currently look. He came upon Charalona lying face down on the floor. Laloedon knelt down by her and gently rolled her over.

"Hey, are you okay, Charalon?"

She opened her eyes and smiled. She had aged a lot and looked very old.

"I'm okay. I must have fallen here," she said.

"Let's get you to the infirmary. Can you stand?"

Charalona sat up with the help of Laloedon. "I don't think I can," she said.

He scooped her up and packed her to the medical room. There he placed her on a bed and got her something to drink. "You're going to have to be more careful, Charalon."

The playback jumped ahead to Charalona sitting in a wheelchair with Laloedon standing next to her. They were outside by the circle of rocks with a small fire crackling and popping. It looked like it was summertime and late in the day. Charalona stared into the fire, not saying a word. Laloedon laid his hand on her shoulder and said, "It's just like old times, Charalon." She slowly looked up at him and smiled.

The playback jumped ahead again to Laloedon standing by a bonfire. It was wintertime and dark out. He stood there by himself, staring solemnly into the fire. The light flickered off his face and reflected in a tear sliding down to his chin. The playback came to an end.

Jack sat up, looking kind of somber, and got out of the chair. Charalon was looking at the floor with tears on her face. He walked over to her and gave her a half-hug with one arm.

He asked, "How about we get something to eat and sit by the fire?"

Charalon just nodded and worked up a smile. They left the memory room with Jack leading the way.

As they passed Jack's room, he said, "I have to use the restroom. I'll be right behind you." He entered his room. When he came out, Charalon was still standing there.

"You didn't have to wait for me."

She looked up and said, "I don't mind. I don't have a lot going on right now."

When they got to the cafeteria, Jack pulled a chair out for her at their table.

"Have a seat," he said, with compassion. He sat down and thought about what to have for lunch.

"You could have a french dip sandwich and fries, Jack."

He looked surprised for a second, then said, "Sure. That sounds great!"

Charalon ordered the sandwich and drinks with a bowl of the sacktaw. Jack could see that she was feeling a little better.

"I'll bet you never thought you'd be comforting a giant robot monster lady."

Jack, not wanting to be out done, came back with, "Oh, you're all of that, and more."

She laughed out loud and said, "Thank you, Jack."

Their food showed up via the robot waiter. Jack dipped his sandwich in the au jus sauce and took a bite. "Man, that's good. It's been a while since I had one of these," he said.

"Our chefs are the best around, at least around here," she said. "I'm glad you like it."

After lunch, Jack made his way to his chair by the fire. Charalon came over and stood by Jack's chair asking, "What kind of coffee do you want?"

"I would like some black coffee."

She sat down without saying anything. The robot waiter showed up with a couple of cups, set them down on the table and left.

"I thought I had just missed you ordering things, but you have a wireless connection," he said.

"Yes. I'm linked to the facility mainframe. I don't need to speak to it. I only ordered the dinners and drinks by speaking to keep my secret."

"Well, you've been outed. I can't see how it matters," said Jack with a smile. "Not to change the subject, but I'm going to get fat if I don't get some exercise soon."

"We should take a walk, Jack. Would you like to go outside for a walk?"

"Yes. That would be the thing to do," he said.

"Well, let's go."

"You mean, like right now, Charalon?"

"Come on," she said. Jack followed her out of the cafeteria to the main entry room. The robot security guard stepped out of their way and watched them as the door to the tunnel opened. They went into the tunnel and up toward the exit door. It swung open as they neared it, the rock vanished and they went outside.

"You want to race to the top?" asked Charalon as she pointed up the hill.

Jack looked at her and said, "I don't think so, but thanks for the offer."

He could hear the traffic on the freeway a thousand feet below them. There was a light breeze out of the west and puffy clouds in an otherwise blue sky. "It's a good day to go hang gliding," he thought. "I wonder if Charalon can drive?" The thought brought a smile to Jack's face. Hang glider pilots are always looking for drivers, people to at least drive their car down from the launch.

"What are you smiling about?" asked Charalon, as they walked along.

"Oh, nothing. Can you drive cars?" He still had the smile on his face.

"I think I know what's on your mind. I saw you look at the sky."

They walked up to the top and back down, not talking much. The whole walk took less than an hour. When they got back, they stopped at the outside entry.

"Thanks, that was a good workout," said Jack, slightly winded.

"I really enjoyed that, Jack. It has been a long time since I left the facility."

He thought for a moment, then asked, "How long has

it been?"

Charalon sighed and said, "Since you left here, when you were young. I haven't had a reason to go outside since. From now on, I am going to go out more."

Jack was stunned. "Why wouldn't you go outside?"

"It wasn't that bad. I was in stasis for most of that time."

They entered the facility and headed down the tunnel to the main entrance. The security robot raised his weapon and kept it on them until Charalon touched the screen mounted on the arm. They proceeded down the hall to Jack's room.

"I really need a shower. I think I'll get cleaned up and rest in my room for a while," he said.

"So, I'll see you for dinner later?"

"Sure." Jack nodded and entered his room.

Chapter 10
The Choice

Jack was in his room sitting in his chair. He had just returned from a walk to the top of the mountain and back. He said to himself, "Well, Dominic, this really wasn't what I expected when you said, 'I want to show you something.'"

"I want to show you something else now," said Dominic, standing by the window.

Jack was startled and nearly jumped out of his chair. "Where did you come from?"

"Do not be afraid, Jack." Dominic was suddenly standing on the other side of Jack.

"The last time you said you wanted to show me something, I ended up here. That was kind of a big deal. I'm still trying to deal with everything I now know."

"I understand, Jack."

"Can I ask you a question first?"

Dominic nodded with a friendly smile.

"Who are you working with? I watched you stop Laloedon from killing Malconadon."

"I act on behalf of my side. Laloedon wanted to change the future, and we allowed it for your sake, Jack. You will understand in time why I say that."

"What do you want to show me, Dominic?"

Without saying a thing, he just put his hand on Jack's shoulder. At once Jack found himself walking along a road with Dominic. Jack looked around to see where he was. They were walking down a sidewalk in a residential area. Elm trees with their leaves turning to fall colors lined the road. Jack knew that it wasn't June anymore. A little girl on a bike passed by without looking at them.

"I come here from time to time," said Dominic.

Jack looked around again and asked, "Where, and when, are we?"

"None of that is important right now, Jack. I have brought you here to talk."

A lady walking a dog came by and passed them without even a hello. Jack's eye caught a car driving by that he couldn't identify, then another. Jack, a car buff who knew most cars at a glance, had no idea what they were. A mailman came walking by and, again, didn't greet them.

"They cannot see you, Jack. Come, let us walk."

"I know this must be in the future. I don't recognize those cars," said Jack as another odd car drove by without making a sound.

"That is right. We are in the year 2075. I want to show you something here, not far away. Let us enjoy the walk for now. It is nice out. Do you agree?" Dominic looked at Jack with a smile.

"Yes. It's nice weather and there's beautiful trees," said Jack looking around.

"Look over there." Dominic pointed across the street. A couple in their early thirties was coming out their front door. Jack immediately recognized Sharon, and then...himself?

He watched the couple leave on foot and said, "I look

pretty good for a man over ninety. Sharon looks pretty good too."

Dominic smiled a little and said, "I wanted you to see what could have been. This would have been your life if you had not been so hindered.

"It is true, you are in your nineties in this time and place. You helped invent a way to regenerate the old. You tested it on yourself first. You moved here where nobody knew you, to monitor the long term effects. Do you remember Randal, your roommate in college?"

"Yes. I remember him."

"Randal worked with you to accomplish this. After you tested it on yourself, you set up a company that did this for others. You and Randal made billions of dollars making people young again. The process could only be done once on a person. You worked with DNA, trying to find a way to do the process again so you would make more money. It was your work with DNA that led to the Morphalogian takeover of the world," explained Dominic.

"That's not going to happen anymore, is it?"

Dominic looked down in thought and said, "It has not been determined if that is the case yet. You will have to make choices soon that will determine your fate, and the fate of the world."

"I thought that I wasn't able to do those things anymore, Dominic. I didn't get my Harvard education, and I certainly didn't have much of a career in science."

"I have more to show you. Let us walk some more, Jack."

They walked down the road a little ways to a park. There were children playing and people having picnics. Jack looked around and noticed people's clothing had changed. The dresses and coats were late eighteen-hundreds in appearance. A horse-drawn carriage went by on the dirt road.

"I come here sometimes when I want to think."

Jack was dumbfounded by the casual way Dominic would act while doing impossible things. Dominic motioned to a bench and they sat down. He stayed silent for a while, just calmly watching the people as they went about their business.

"Look over there, Jack." Dominic pointed to a limousine parked by the road. The scenery had changed again without Jack noticing. The cars and people's clothing were very different looking. A man got out of the limousine and opened the back door, letting another man out. Jack could see that it was himself getting out of the car, just older. The older Jack was dressed in fine clothes and looked very rich. A young woman came running up to him and kissed him as a lover would.

"What year is this?" asked Jack.

"It is 2090, and that is not your wife."

"This is Laloedon's timeline, isn't it?"

Dominic just nodded. Jack looked back at the older Jack as he and the woman got in the car and left. The park had changed again. The transition back to the eighteen-hundreds happened without Jack being aware of it again.

"I get it, I'm having a dream," said Jack.

"No, this is real, Jack. All that you just saw was real. These things have and may happen, depending on how you choose."

Jack thought about that for a moment then said, "I don't see how."

Dominic looked at Jack and said, "You were robbed

by circumstances that left you hobbled. You were set on a path of struggle. I know it was hard for you at times. These same hard things have molded and shaped you to the person you are today."

"If it means that Morphalogians don't destroy the world, then I'm okay with the life I have."

Dominic smiled and let out a sigh of relief. "That is what I wanted to hear. I have been tasked to look out for you. You have a future. I know it will be for good."

"You are an angel, aren't you?"

"Do you know what that means, Jack?"

"Not really. I suppose it means different things to different people."

"You are going to be given much. Much was taken from you," said Dominic.

Dominic put his hand on Jack's shoulder. Then Jack was sitting in the chair in his room at the facility. Jack looked around, but Dominic was nowhere to be seen. He got up and looked in the mirror. He went into his bathroom and took a shower. It felt great and helped him to clear his head. The visit from Dominic was still fresh in his mind and he was determined to go see Laloed as soon as he got dressed.

He left his room and stood in the hall trying to figure out what to say. "Oh, find Charalon," said Jack, somewhat awkwardly. A blue line lit up on the floor, as it had done before. He followed the line as it went down the hall past the cafeteria for a ways, then turned right and dead-ended at a closed door. He pressed the door button and Charalon's voice, coming from a speaker said, "Come in." He stepped up to the door and it slid open to a room like his.

107

Charalon was sitting in a chair by her bed. "So, what brings you to my room?"

"Laloed said to let you know when I wanted to talk to him some more."

She got up and said, "Well, come with me. He will be ready when we get there."

Jack used the opportunity to look around her room. There were pictures on the wall of human people whom Jack didn't recognize and...a television. Other than that, the room looked very much like his room.

"Friends of yours?" he asked, motioning to the pictures.

Charalon, almost out the door, turned around and answered, "No, I just liked the way they looked. They do add a nice touch though."

"And the TV, you have a TV?"

She smiled and said, "Yes, but I don't watch it much. I suppose I could have told you about it, but you know how guys are. You'd be over here all the time, trapped in front of it and held by its powers."

Jack said, "Probably," as he left her room.

She led him to Laloed's office and said, "When you're done here, come to the cafeteria."

"Will do."

When Jack entered Laloed's office, he found Laloed sitting behind his desk as he was before.

"Welcome, Jack. What's on your mind?"

"Dominic just paid me a visit." Upon hearing this, the holographic projection of Laloed flickered. He looked very interested, as if the thought of Dominic coming there was not possible.

"Dominic came to see you, inside of the facility?"

"Yes, he came to me in my room." Jack sat down in the chair by Laloed's desk.

At this news, Laloed's image disappeared then reappeared, as if resetting.

"What did he say, Jack?"

"He didn't say much, but he showed me the possible future."

"Do you want to talk about it?"

"Yes. I would like to tell you about the things he said, and I have some questions."

Laloed sat there for a moment in thought as he weighed out the options. It was obvious to Jack that the unexpected events of the day were forcing Laloed to change his plans.

"There is much that you don't know. It seems there is much that I don't know, also. I will answer your questions to the best of my ability, Jack."

Jack thought about what to say and what to ask. He thought about Dominic, and his elusiveness.

"Well, I'll start with something Dominic said. He said, in that timeline, my work with DNA led to the Morphalogian takeover of the world. He implied, that if I chose to, that could still happen. That got me thinking. I want to know if I created the Morphalogian race in a lab, or something like that. You see, I thought that the Morphalogians came from somewhere else. I guess I'd like to know the truth.

Laloed slowly nodded. He chose his words carefully and said, "The plan was to make sure you wouldn't be able to do that. Laloedon was prepared to do whatever it took. Dominic has interfered on more than just a few occasions. I don't see how you could still be the one who brings the Morphalogian race to this world. In the other timeline, you came up with the master DNA sequence of a Morphalogian."

"Are you saying that mankind made the Morphalogian race by writing a DNA sequence for them?"

Laloed looked Jack in the eye and said, "No. Mankind did not make the Morphalogians, they became Morphalogians. Your work made that possible."

"I thought I just found a way to regenerate aged people."

"You did, Jack, but people could only regenerate once. You found a way around that, by changing people into creatures that lived much longer than a hundred years. The way you made people young again was by use of the replication technology. It is a slow process. The body temperature is brought down and the subject put into a coma. Each cell is absorbed then replaced by a reprint of the younger version of it. You can only replace so many cells at the same time without killing the person. A person will typically take about a week to regenerate. Can you see how it's not much of a jump to replace each cell with a cell that has a different DNA sequence?"

"I understand. Did the process take more than one stage to change the DNA sequence?"

Laloed's eyes narrowed a bit and he said, "I see you do understand the process. Yes, it took three times through the process to gradually change a person into a Morphalogian. The term Morphalogian was originally the job description of a technician who morphed people into these creatures. People with money would come into a morph center as a human. After three weeks in a coma, they would wake up as a new creature. These new creatures were referred to as first generation, Jack.

Second and third generations were the result of procreation."

"What about Dominic? What is he? I asked him if he was an angel and he asked me if I knew what that meant."

"Well, that is the question. Isn't it. Toward the end, Laloedon thought there were such beings. I didn't. I thought he was becoming senile. He talked about good and evil. He even talked about God. Perhaps I didn't see that he had a point, because I melded with the younger version of Laloedon. That version thought concepts like God, good and evil, came out of ignorance. He thought that way until he saw Dominic help you. He didn't know who or what Dominic was when he encountered him the first time," said Laloed.

"But did he come to think that Dominic was an angel?"

"It pains me to say this, Jack, but he did think that. That's why he developed an equation that he added to his master probability program. It helped the original program predict the future. He called it providence, but I think Charalon told you about that."

"Yes, she did," said Jack.

Laloed continued, "I have that probability program incorporated into my system. It has not proven to be very accurate in some areas, but it did accurately predict your return. However, it could not say when."

Jack brought the subject back to Dominic. "I saw Dominic do amazing things. He easily moved through time and space like we walk from room to room. He stopped Laloedon from killing Malconadon. What else could he be?"

"I always thought he and his kind were just a highly

advanced species. It is not inconceivable that there could be people with more advanced technology than we have."

"Whatever he is, he seems to have the authority to overrule your plans," said Jack.

"That's true, Jack, but it doesn't mean that he is an angel, or that there is a God."

Jack changed the subject a bit. "What do you think he meant when he said that I would be given much?"

Laloed thought about it for a moment. "I can't be sure, but Laloedon had a backup plan to turn the facility over to you. He would do this under certain circumstances. I cannot say what those circumstances are, not yet. His thinking was this might be necessary for you to accomplish your task. I do not know what that task is, with any certainty."

"Do you have any idea at all what it could be?" asked Jack.

"Yes. I don't want to say but, if you must know, I do have a couple ideas. Laloedon felt that there would be a time of great evil coming in the future. He thought that even though we changed the future for this timeline, some other evil would come. Maybe that's why Dominic says you could still cause those things he showed you to happen. Your choices might make all the difference, especially if you were to have our technology."

"When you said that Laloedon was prepared to do whatever it took, what did you mean?"

Laloed sighed, then looked at Jack and said, "He was going to kill you. Just like he was going to kill Malconadon, but Dominic stopped him in both cases."

"I need to digest all this new information. Can we meet and talk again tomorrow?" asked Jack.

"Yes, anytime you want to talk, Jack, I will be available."

Jack got up and left the room. He headed to the cafeteria where he found Charalon sitting at their table.

Charalon looked up and smiled. "Well, how did that go?"

"Not bad. I found out that Morphalogians were once people."

"I wanted to tell you that, Jack, but I was not permitted to. I'm sorry."

He looked at her and asked, "There's more that I don't know, right?"

Charalon nodded and said, "Yes, there is more, and you will know it all in time. It is not for me to decide. I wish it were. Will you tell me about your visit with Dominic?"

Jack smiled at his friend and said, "Yes. I'd like to have something to eat and then talk over some coffee."

"That sounds nice, Jack."

Chapter 11
The Dark Time

Jack had just come back to his room from a long visit with Charalon. He looked at his watch and found it hard to believe that it was 10:35 p.m. Sunday. He realized that he had been here at the facility for six days.

After taking another shower and brushing his teeth, he lay down on his bed and stared at the ceiling, thinking about Laloedon. Jack thought, "If Laloedon would be eight-hundred years old now, then he might be alive today. It was around three hundred years in the future that Laloedon made his plans to go back in time. That added to the five hundred years they went into the past means he could be alive at this time. That means Laloedon was a first generation Morphalogian.

Jack thought, "This must be why Laloedon wanted to kill me. He would live out his life as a human, and the world wouldn't be destroyed. Everybody wins...well, kind of."

Jack awoke to the door chime. He said, "Yes?" and the door slid open to Charalon. She walked in and sat in one of his chairs.

"It's after nine o'clock. Aren't you hungry?" she asked.

Jack, staying covered up, said, "I am. Give me a moment and I'll be right there...wait. Laloedon was a first generation Morphalogian, right?"

"Yes, he was. Why do you ask?"

"I was wondering why Laloedon didn't go after himself. He would have been alive in this time. He's probably not that hard to find. Laloed would know where he was at this time. Why not?" he asked.

"I can't answer that for you, Jack. You will have to ask Laloed."

"I will, but after breakfast, and a walk if you would like."

"I would like that. I'll see you at breakfast," she said.

After breakfast, they left the facility to go for a walk. They headed straight for the top of the mountain. The first part of the walk was spent in silence. As they approached the top, Jack saw a log that looked like a good place to rest. They sat down on the log and looked down the mountain.

"I've always loved the view from up here," said Jack.

"It is beautiful, but that's not what you want to talk about. Is it?"

He shook his head and said, "No, I need to vent a little. I hope you don't mind."

"I don't mind. If there's something bothering you, then I'd like to help."

"Well, I'd like to start with Laloedon. If he would have just talked to his younger self, couldn't he have changed the way things turned out? Perhaps he should have tried to kill himself. Maybe if he killed himself...he wouldn't be able to come back to kill himself though. I can see where that might not work out."

"I can tell you that when we came here, it created an alternate timeline. Anything that happens here has no

115

effect on the other timeline. He could kill himself and suffer no ill effects," said Charalon.

Jack gave that some thought, and asked, "How did he send me back in time, when I was a kid, without creating yet another timeline?"

"When we came here, it was Laloedon's first attempt at time travel. Since then, he perfected the reverse time travel process. He was able to find a way to have accelerated forward time travel, but it wouldn't intersect with the other timeline," said Charalon.

Jack said, "I was the one who came up with the Morphalogian DNA master sequence. I suppose that I should be the one here now."

"When we get back you can ask Laloed about it, Jack."

"I'll think about it. I think I might wait another day to talk to him though. I need to figure out how I feel about all of this. I will do whatever I can to help avoid that future, in any case."

Charalon looked up at Jack with admiration. "I knew you would turn out good. You were such a good kid," she said.

Jack shook his head a little. "From what Dominic showed me, I didn't turn out that great. Maybe the way things turned out for me in this timeline was for the best."

"No matter how you would have turned out, I know who you are now. You would rather have a hard life than have a good one and be the reason for the suffering of others."

"Thanks, Charalon. I am trying to do what's right. Oh, that reminds me. Would it be all right to call my father? I haven't called him in over a week and a half."

"Of course it would be fine. We don't want search parties up here looking for you," said Charalon with a grin.

He pulled his phone out and dialed his father. His father answered the phone with, "Hello, Jack. Two calls in a week is pretty good."

"Dad, I haven't called you in over a week and a half. I just wanted to let you know everything is going good and I'm just fine."

"It doesn't seem that long ago, but I'm glad you called, son. It's good to hear things are still going good. Do you want to say hi to Mom?"

"I'm in the middle of something right now. Just tell her I said hi."

"Are you still up at the lake?"

Jack paused for a second. Confused by his dad's question, he said, "No, I'm up on the mountain."

Dave was surprised by Jack's answer and said, "Oh, I thought Anderson said he saw your van at our lake house."

"I was there a while back. I have to go, Dad. I love you. Goodbye."

"Goodbye, son. I love you too."

Jack put his phone back in his pocket. "Now, where was I? Oh, I was going to say Dominic could handle this. Why does he want me involved? I've seen what he can do."

Jack looked over at Charalon to see why she didn't answer. She was absolutely still. Nothing around them was moving, only Jack.

"Hello, Jack," said a voice. Jack got up and turned to see Dominic standing there. As usual, he had on a red

117

plaid shirt and blue jeans.

"Did you hear me talking about you or something?"

Dominic smiled a little and said, "It was time for me to talk to you. I have some things to tell you. Is there anything you would like to ask me first?"

"Yes. Are you an angel?"

"I am a messenger of sorts. I came here to help you understand. I have told you before that the life you lived has shaped you, Jack."

"I remember."

Dominic looked down and said, "Jack, I want to show you something. Look over there." Dominic pointed down the hill to the west.

At once, it was wintertime. There were two Native American men tracking something. They crouched down and looked at some tracks. Then, out of nowhere, Laloedon appeared and ripped their throats out with a single swipe each. After killing them, he crouched down by their dead bodies. He looked around, like a predator. Jack watched in horror as Laloedon ate some of their flesh. Then he dragged their bodies over to a rock cliff overlooking the river and threw them in the water. He looked around again and disappeared into the forest.

Jack turned around to look at Dominic and it was summer again. Charalon still sat motionless on the log a few feet away. "What year was that?"

"That was in the mid 1500s, Jack. It was a couple years after Charalona died. Laloedon became bitter and angry. For a while, he would kill anybody who ventured through this area. Fortunately, there were not many people in this area at that time.

"If you ask Laloed, at the facility, he will not know about it. Laloedon carefully concealed all evidence of that time. He had the whole facility shut down and in darkness for over forty years. I know he was ashamed. It was the second time he truly repented."

"When was the other time that happened?" asked Jack.

"You saw him when he tried to kill Malconadon. He was trying to make things right, but I had to stop him. When he cried out for me to let him go, it was then his heart broke."

"Why does he take so much blame. I'm the one who came up with the DNA sequence. I am more to blame, because I did it for money. At least in this timeline, I didn't bring on such destruction out of greed. I have Laloedon to thank for that, Dominic."

"You have reason to be thankful. Remember to give credit where it is due."

Jack nodded and asked, "Will I be seeing you in the future?"

"You will see me again, Jack, as much as needed. Ask Laloed two questions. Ask him what he knows about the time Laloedon was killing trespassers. Then ask him what Laloedon's name used to be."

"What are you doing, Jack?" asked Charalon.

Startled, Jack looked to see her moving again. When he looked back, Dominic was gone. "Did you see him, Charalon?"

"See who, Jack?"

"Dominic was just here. You were frozen in time. Everything was. We talked about Laloedon for quite some time. Dominic told me that there was a time when Laloedon shut the facility down, it was after Charalona died. He said Laloedon killed anybody who came through there during that time."

"There are missing files from the time after Charalona died," she said.

"I think he tried to hide what he had done. I saw Laloedon kill a couple of Indians. It looked like they were hunting him, but Dominic told me he killed others too," said Jack.

"Laloedon was Morphalogian. They have powerful predatory drives that can be hard to control. I know it was a hard time for him. I remember those drives, but I never had them."

Jack said, "I remember Laloedon, and I'm more comfortable around the holographic one. I think maybe I should go talk to Laloed today."

After they got back to the facility, Jack took a shower and met Charalon for some lunch. Charalon ordered Jack a cold turkey sandwich and something for herself. After finishing the lunch, she said, "Would you like some coffee before you go see Laloed?"

"Yes, that sounds good."

Charalon didn't ask Jack what kind of coffee he wanted. She just went and sat by the fire. The robot waiter showed up with a couple cups and set them down. After the waiter left, Jack took a sip.

"I think you really like caramel mocha coffee," he said.

She just smiled.

Jack found himself standing outside of Laloed's office. Charalon had just set up the meeting after they had coffee.

"Welcome, Jack. Would you like to pick up where we

left off?" asked Laloed, as Jack entered the room.

"No. I had yet another visit from Dominic, about an hour ago. He told me about a time when Laloedon shut the facility down and killed anyone who ventured by here. Do you know anything about that time?"

Laloed looked puzzled. "I don't know anything about that time. There are missing files. Wait, by asking about it, you have just cued a subprogram to retrieve a hidden file. Now I do know about that time. Yes, there are many instances of Laloedon killing trespassers. He lived here like an animal for some time," he said.

Jack was not surprised. "Yes. I saw him kill a couple people, Laloed. After eating some of their flesh, he threw their bodies into the river."

"I have his memories from that time now, Jack."

Jack nodded and asked, "Will you tell me about that time? What happened?"

Laloed sighed and became solemn, then began, "After Charalona died, Laloedon was not the same. He was bitter and cold-blooded. He shut down the facility, leaving everything in the dark. Laloedon wore fur clothing that he made from a bear that he killed. He left the outer entrance open, and would often sleep on the floor in the tunnel. Laloedon mostly spent his time hunting for food at night and sleeping in the day. On a few occasions, he would roam. He became very territorial and did not allow people through this area. Fortunately, the human population around here at that time was very sparse.

"When he would roam, Laloedon used his ILEFF system to remain unseen most of the time. There were a few times that the natives saw him, but he didn't kill anyone when he was away from here. Laloedon went as far as the west coast when he roamed. He would be gone for months at a time. He was careful to leave no evidence of himself when he traveled, but there were times he left some tracks. One time some natives tracked him back almost to the facility, but he killed them."

"I think that's what Dominic showed me," interjected Jack.

"That could be. After forty years or so, he stopped roaming and powered up the facility. He felt very ashamed of the many killings, and swore never to murder the innocent again. You were not innocent in his eyes. I remember him looking into a mirror and reminding himself why he came back in time. It was at this time that he took precautions to ensure that the mission would succeed. It had been nearly a hundred years since the three of them crash-landed up here. More than four hundred additional years would have to pass before the mission could be accomplished. Laloedon reactivated the Jerrech unit and they built the various robots and automated the facility.

"The system would power up and wake Laloedon if it was time, or if anything triggered the proximity sensors. As a final precaution, my program was activated to act in place of Laloedon, in case anything happened to him. Laloedon set the system to wake in fifty years, as a test. He shut the facility down and put himself into stasis," explained Laloed.

"Did the test go well?"

Laloed smiled and said, "It worked perfectly. After fifty years, the system woke me first, and I administered the reactivation of the robots and woke Laloedon. It was at this time he and Jerrech created the Charalon unit and melded Charalona's memories. After five years,

Laloedon decided to put the facility and himself back into stasis.

"We all remained dormant for over two hundred years. The proximity sensors detected an explosion not far from the facility in 1860."

"That's when John Mullan built that road through there. I want to know more about that time. Did you see them come through?" asked Jack with great interest.

"Yes, we did. Laloedon was very interested in them. For almost two months we monitored their progress. It took seven weeks for them to build the road through this area. They had only primitive tools to work with. Then thousands of people traveled over the road for a few years. Laloedon lost interest in the people and became annoyed with them. He was concerned that somebody would find the entrance to the facility. There were a lot of prospectors looking for gold who examined the rocks in the area. After a few years, another road was built south of here. It became the preferred road to travel. The traffic along this part of Mullan's road tapered off to hardly anyone.

"At that point, Laloedon put the facility in stasis mode for another hundred and twenty six years. The facility was in full operation when you and your father came to this area."

"Dominic told me to ask you two questions. He also told me to ask you what Laloedon's name used to be. Do you know?"

Laloed looked surprised by this, and said, "I am not permitted to answer that question at this time."

"I'm going to find out one way or another. It's only a matter of time, Laloed. I already know that Laloedon was a first generation Morphalogian."

Laloed looked at Jack and said, "Wait a moment, I will rerun the probability program."

The image of Laloed disappeared and reappeared. After a moment, he took a deep breath and sighed. He was obviously conflicted and had to make a decision.

"All right, I will tell you the truth. You know that Laloedon was human at one time. You also know that he advanced your work with DNA. That led to the creation of the Morphalogian race. The truth is...his name was Jack Thomas. In other words, Jack, you became Laloedon in that timeline.

Chapter 12
Identity Crisis

Jack got up slowly and left Laloed's office. As he walked toward his room he ran into a cleaning robot. The little machine only stood two feet high, making it a bit of a hazard to the very distracted Jack.

"Oops, sorry I didn't see you there," said Jack.

The machine turned toward him and said, "Please do not worry about it."

He stood there staring at it as it resumed dusting the walls with its long arms. It looked like it could vacuum and sweep if required. The machine inched along, cleaning and dusting. Jack just watched it for a while.

"Are you planning to watch that thing all night, or would you like something to eat?" Charalon had just sneaked up on Jack.

"I guess I'm a little distracted right now. I'd like some dinner. Then I'd like to talk."

"Let's go there now," she said as she started walking toward the cafeteria.

Charalon could tell that something was bothering Jack. She watched him with concern as he walked along, staring at the floor.

After dinner, Jack took his usual spot by the fire. The waiter dropped off the coffees and left. Charalon watched him intently as she picked up her cup and took a sip. He had not said much during his dinner, and now he just sat there staring into the fire.

"Are you ready to talk about it?" she asked.

Jack picked up his cup and took a sip. "I do want to talk. I just don't know where to start," he said. He took another sip. "I found out that I became Laloedon in the other timeline."

She looked down at the floor and sighed. They sat there in silence for a while before Jack said, "It's okay, Charalon. I know you couldn't say anything about it."

"No, I couldn't. I'm sorry, Jack, I really wanted to tell you everything. Laloed and his plan...I have to do what he says. I have a free will, but I'm bound by my word to follow the plan."

"I said it's okay, Charalon. To find out something like that...I'm starting to understand the hesitance. I know it's a good thing that all this wasn't dumped in my lap at once."

Charalon stared at him for a while and then said, "Please, don't hold it against me. I need you as my friend. You have no idea how much television I had to watch over the years, just for some company."

Jack looked up and smiled a little. "I will always be your friend, Charalon. Something tells me a part of you has been my friend for a long time. Charalona was my Sharon before she became a Morphalogian, wasn't she?"

"Yes, she was," said Charalon.

"You have her memories, don't you?"

She just nodded as she looked at him. "I have her memories from the other timeline. I remember the Jack from Laloedon's timeline. I can see that you are an even better person, having lived the life you have."

"I was wondering why you seemed so familiar to me. I know you're not my Sharon, but you have a lot of her traits. It was confusing at times."

"That's understandable," Charalon said.

He had many things going through his mind. He couldn't see how he would have been able to accomplish what the other Jack had done. Just looking around the facility, one could see an overwhelming number of accomplishments.

"I find it hard to believe that I could ever do what the Jack from your timeline did."

Charalon corrected him. "Not my timeline, I was never there. My memories of that timeline came to me from someone else."

"That's true. You're from here in reality."

"He didn't do it all by himself, Jack. He was part of a team. There was Randal and Sharon, along with many other contributors. He could not have done it all by himself. I think he would be the first to say so. Even this place was built with the help of others."

"It would take a lifetime for me to understand most of the technology around here," said Jack.

Charalon smiled and said, "It would take a couple lifetimes for you to comprehend the technology in this place. That is, if you had to learn it the old fashioned way."

"What do you mean?"

"I understand much of this technology, Jack. I didn't have to go to college to know what I know. You already have gained knowledge about your past. That was information stored in our database. We can give you the knowledge and understanding by implanting it in your mind."

"Am I smart enough to do anything with it?" he asked.

Charalon grinned at that, partially revealing her teeth. "I think you're smart enough, but we could give you some brain enhancements. The other Jack had some enhancements, so could you."

"I'd have to give that some thought. I think I need to figure out who I am now, before I make any changes to myself."

It was getting late. It was 10:45 p.m. Monday night. Jack found himself standing in front of the mirror in his room. The new information from the day was mind blowing. First, he found out, he not only helped create the Morphalogians, but became one. It was Laloedon that he became. Second, he learned that his Sharon had become Charalona. Her memories now lived on in his friend, Charalon.

Jack got ready for bed and lay down. He looked around the room, fascinated at what had been done. He thought to himself, "To think that I could have done any of this is amazing."

He closed his eyes and drifted off to sleep.

He woke up in the morning just before the door chime rang out. "Yes?" he said. The door slid open to a now familiar sight. There stood Charalon, just like most mornings lately.

"Would you like to meet me for some breakfast?" asked Charalon.

Jack sat up and said, "Yes, I would. Could I have some diced..."

"Ham and eggs," said Charalon, finishing his

sentence. "I will have it ready when you get there."

She left and the door slid shut. Jack got out of bed and got ready for breakfast.

"Well, I wonder what I'm going to learn today. Am I actually the president of the United States of America with amnesia?" he said as he put his shoes on.

His breakfast was waiting on the table for him when he got to the cafeteria. Charalon greeted him with a smile as he sat down.

"Are there any new revelations for me today?" asked Jack, somewhat jesting.

She chuckled and said, "I don't think so, but I'll have to look into that."

"I hope not. I need to get used to what I already know. I wouldn't have thought I'd say that a week ago. Now I know more than I wanted to."

"Well, I don't think there's any more shocking facts to come out now. There is still a lot for you to learn, but you know the truth as I understand it."

Jack finished his breakfast and said, "I love this place. The food is always great, the coffees are great and I have a good friend here."

They continued their conversation by the fire. The waiter showed up with coffees and left.

"I don't know what's going to happen, but I know you will always be welcome here after you leave, Jack."

"That sounds good to me. I used to be afraid of coming to this area. When I started coming up here looking for answers, I became fond of it. Now it kind of feels like a second home."

"I'm glad you feel that way. Laloed thinks you will be a force for good in the world, and that you will need our help, Jack."

129

"Dominic said something like that too, a while back."

"Laloed runs that probability program of his almost every day. It has consistently predicted that you would become one who does good."

"I'm willing to do what I can, Charalon, but I have no idea what that would be."

She thought about it and said, "There will always be injustice and suffering. The world needs someone who cares and has the means to make a difference."

"You're getting all profound again. I do agree with you though."

"You should agree with me...I'm right. By the way, I think you should get used to it," she said with a smirk.

Jack just chuckled and said, "The whole idea of doing good and helping people, instead of having a real job, now that has a lot of appeal."

He went back to his room to relax and think. He found himself lying on his back in bed, staring at the ceiling. It seemed so odd that the face that brought terror to Jack at one time now wanted him to do good. Jack wanted to be that person who helped others, but had his doubts that he was up to the job.

The door chime rang and Jack snapped out of it. "Yes?" he said and the door slid open to Jerrech standing there. Jack was quite surprised by the sight.

"I have something for you," said Jerrech. Jack was astonished that Jerrech was talking.

"Okay," said Jack. It was all he could get out. He got up and walked over to the door where Jerrech was standing outside in the hall.

"Laloed had me build this communicator for you. No matter where you go in the world, we will be able to contact you," said Jerrech.

Jack looked at the communicator. It was silver and about the size of a small cell phone. There was a display screen with two buttons on the bottom of it.

"When we call you, just press the button on the left to answer. If you would like to contact us here at the facility, press the button on the right. When you call here, speak the name of the person you would like to talk to. I could surgically implant a miniature version of it in your brain. You would see and hear us in your head, or just use this one."

Jack, still dumbfounded by the visit, said, "I think I'll forgo that alteration for now, but thank you, Jerrech."

Jerrech nodded with a smile. "You're welcome. Let me know if you want anything else. I can make almost any gadget you might need. Take care, Jack." Then he turned and left.

Jack sat down on his bed and looked his new gadget over. It was an impressive, high-quality piece of work. It looked like it could survive either impact or water.

"Well, it looks like I will be leaving someday," he said to himself. "I have to tell Charalon about this."

Jack put the communicator in his pocket and left his room. He said, "Find Charalon." He followed the line to the cafeteria where he found her sitting by the fire. She looked sad.

"Hey, what brings you here?" she asked.

"You do. I wanted to tell you about my visit with Jerrech just now."

"You visited with Jerrech?" asked Charalon, clearly surprised.

"Well, kind of. He brought this communicator to my room and gave it to me," Jack said as he handed it to her.

"He talked. He told me how to use it, and said to let him know if I want anything else. Then he said to take care."

Charalon looked at Jack and smiled. She was kind of amused by his story. "I never said he couldn't talk, just that he didn't like to. You shouldn't be surprised if he was friendly. The original Jerrech was always a friendly man. I should have told you this earlier, but he was Randal, your roommate from college, Jack."

"Randal was a good guy. I wish that we had become the kind of friends that he and the other Jack did."

Charalon said, "Yes, I see why."

"You looked kind of sad when I came in here. Are you okay?"

She took a deep breath. "This last week has been so good for me. I have had a purpose, and a friend here. Laloed said that it might be time for you to leave for awhile. You are not being kicked out, it's just that he thought you might need the time for yourself."

"I think that's probably a good idea. I could go see Sharon and maybe my folks. I probably won't want to drive down to Missouri though. Maybe they'll come up to the cabin," said Jack.

"I would love to go to the lake again...I mean go to the lake. I'd like to go just about anywhere at this point. I might stand out a little too much though," Charalon said, with a grin.

"When did he think I should go, and for how long?"

"In a day or two is what he said."

He thought about that for a moment. "I think tomorrow morning might be a good time to head out for a bit."

The next day, Jack had breakfast with Charalon. She

had steak and eggs waiting for him when he got to the cafeteria. He sat down with a smile and shook his head. "I've gotten so spoiled here. What am I going to do when I have to eat regular food?"

"I guess you will just have to come back here, Jack."

"Yeah, I hear you."

"Would you like some coffee to go?" she asked.

"I think I might have overdone it with the coffee this week. I think I'll pass this time. What time is it, Charalon?"

"It's 9:30 a.m."

After breakfast, Charalon followed him to his room. Jack entered his room and looked around. He picked up the watch she gave him and put it on. He had the clothes on that he was wearing when he got there.

"I was going to pack, but I just realized I didn't bring anything here with me. I'm keeping the watch though. I really like it," he said, pointing to his wrist.

Charalon was pleased. "I gave you the watch and it's all yours. I'm glad you like it."

He took another look around and sighed. "Well, I guess I'd better be going. Will you walk me to the end of the tunnel?"

"Of course. Let's get you up there."

When they got to the exit door Charalon opened it and stepped outside. It was mid morning, Wednesday, and the sun was shining with a light breeze out of the east.

"Well, this is goodbye for now. I'll see you soon," he said.

Charalon gave him a long hug. "Take care, Jack."

"I'll be back. Don't worry." Then he walked down the hill toward his camp.

He got a little ways down the hill when he heard a familiar voice saying, "Hello, Jack. Did you find all the answers you were looking for?"

Jack stopped and said, "As it turns out, Dominic, I found out more than I bargained for."

"Yes, now you know more. You should be ready for what is coming. To settle down right now will lead to the harm of others. You must be strong, for now. The time is coming when you can have that which you desire."

"I don't really know what you mean, but I know it will be clear at some point. I'd like to thank you for your help though."

Dominic smiled with approval, then put his hand on Jack's shoulder. The weather changed immediately to cloudy skies and it got cool out. Jack looked around and noticed it was evening. He wondered why Dominic would move him forward in time to the evening. Dominic was gone, so Jack proceeded on to his camp. He pulled out his cell phone. Somehow there was still some battery life, so he called his father.

"Hello, Jack," said Dave. "How are things going?"

"Things are good, Dad. They are really good. I just wanted to check in. I'm still up on the mountain."

"You're on the mountain?"

"Yes, I'm just leaving from there now. I just wanted to let you know I'm fine. My battery is low. I'll call you later. Bye, Dad."

When he got to his camp, he was stunned to find his fire was burning. Everything was exactly as he left it. Jack pulled his phone out and looked at it again. It showed Monday, June 1. He looked at his watch and said, "I see I have to reset my watch." Then it occurred to him, almost no time had passed since he left from there with Dominic. It was Monday evening...again. Jack chuckled and said, "'You will be back before you know it.' That was a good one, Dominic."

He loaded up his camping gear and put out his fire. An uneasiness came over him. He had the feeling that somebody was watching him. He looked around, but saw nothing. After checking the straps on his hang glider, he got into his rig. He plugged his phone into his car charger and started the van. After taking a deep breath, Jack put the van into gear and headed down the road.

Chapter 13
On Leave

Jack had just entered the freeway. It was late Monday evening and getting dark out. He was heading west on I-90 toward Spokane. A feeling of guilt came over him. For many days now, he had neglected his obligations, but it really didn't matter. A week had gone by, and it didn't cost him a day.

He had Sharon on his mind. Jack finally had the answers he had been looking for. He now knew what had happened, but there was no closure. He thought about Dominic's warning about settling down. His life just got more complicated. These complications meant getting married would have to be put off, again.

Jack knew he couldn't tell anyone what had happened. He had to deny Sharon that which she desired most, to get married. His discretion would make his denial difficult to explain. It was unfair to ask her to understand his irrational behavior. He was not looking forward to the unpleasant task.

A glance at his phone let Jack know he had enough signal strength to make a call. He would let Sharon know that he was on his way to see her. He dialed the number and waited.

"Hello," said Sharon. "I was wondering when you would call."

"I have been camping out in the woods...on the mountain. I've had some breakthroughs and I would like to talk."

She sighed and said, "You know I have work tomorrow. How far away are you?"

"I'm about two and a half hours away. I'll be there by midnight. I know it's late, but I'd really like to talk, Sharon. It's important to me."

"I will be up, Jack. You can sleep on the couch if you want."

"Okay, thanks Sharon. I'll see you in a while."

He ended his call and set the phone back on the dash. Jack looked at the speedometer and accelerated.

When he arrived at her apartment building, he made his way to her door. His arm seemed very heavy as he reached for the doorbell. The door opened right before he could press the button.

"Hello, Jack. It's good to see you. You know I can't turn you down. It's late, but come on in."

After a kiss and hug, Jack went into the apartment. Her place was well kept and nicely decorated. He made his way to her living room and sat on the couch. Sharon sat next to him and he put his arm around her.

"I've really missed you, Sharon."

She smiled and said, "You were here less than a week ago."

He shrugged and said, "It seemed longer to me."

"So, what's on your mind? Why would you drive for hours just to keep me up late on a work night?" she asked.

"I've had a lot on my mind lately. I found some of the answers I've been looking for. You would think I was off my rocker if I told you what I've been up to."

Sharon looked slightly skeptical, but was trying to politely listen. She just nodded, trying to understand where Jack was going with this.

"I'm going to be kind of busy with something that came up in the last few days. It's going to complicate my life a bit. I thought I would be settling down by now, but this is a responsibility that I can't ignore. It's something I have to do," he said.

"What are you trying to say?"

Jack looked down and fidgeted. "I can't settle down right now. There is something really important that I have to do."

Sharon was getting irritated. She got up and sat in her armchair opposite Jack. Looking him in the face, she said, "Jack, you know that I love you, but I'm getting tired of waiting. I've been waiting for you to find yourself for a long time. I know you've had issues that you needed to deal with, but I have needs too."

"I know, Sharon, I'm sorry. You have been the greatest. You're always there for me, but I haven't always been there for you."

"I'm thirty-three years old and, as they say, I'm not getting any younger. I'll spare you the biological clock speech, but you need to know, I have to move on with my life. I want to move on with you, Jack, but that seems less likely as time goes by."

"There's nothing you're saying that I don't agree with. I don't deserve you. I won't ask you to keep waiting for me to get my act together, but I hope you will," he said.

A tear rolled down Sharon's face. She could see that

Jack had made up his mind. He was just trying to soften the blow. Maybe he did actually believe she would hear him out and see he had a point. She had been so understanding and patient before, but this time was different.

"I can't just wait around until I'm old, Jack. I want to build a life with someone who loves me enough to marry me. Somebody who is at least willing to live in the same town I live in," she said.

He knew she was right, but that only made it worse for him. He also knew he was going to be doing great things and had a sense that there truly was divine intervention in his life. He believed there was something important and good for him to do. The truth was he had no idea what was meant by doing good. It was a rather ambiguous term.

"I know that you have already made up your mind, Jack. You are going to chase after this thing that you won't even talk about."

"Yes, I am. I just thought I would try to explain myself. I owe you that. I would have to show you what I've seen recently to adequately explain, but I can't," he said.

Sharon sighed and said, "I think we should back off in this relationship. This hurts, Jack. I let myself hope for a life with you."

"I love you, Sharon. I'm sorry to let you down."

She spoke quietly, "I have to get up early and go to work. You can sleep there if you want. I'll get you a blanket."

In the morning, Jack woke to a rustling noise coming from the kitchen. There was the scent of breakfast in the air. He got up from the couch and walked into the kitchen. Sharon had made a breakfast for him. Next to the kitchen, on a table in the small dining room, were two plates.

"Sit down, I have some pancakes and eggs for you," she said as she flipped a pancake.

He sat down and watched Sharon. She was fixing breakfast for the guy that had hurt and disappointed her. She set plates of eggs and pancakes on the table. She already had butter and warm syrup there. She sat down and smiled at him. She was sad behind the smile and Jack could see it.

"Okay, bow your head," said Sharon and she said a quick grace over the food.

"Amen," said Jack when she finished praying.

There was a somber mood at the table. Neither Jack nor Sharon had much to say. When they were finished, he helped her put the plates in the dishwasher and clean up.

While Sharon finished getting ready for work, Jack watched the morning news. There had been a killing in the area. It was a young man in his early twenties. The reporter on the scene described it as some kind of ritual killing. The body had been disemboweled and mutilated.

Sharon came into the room and sat in the armchair. "I'm going to need some time. I don't want to see you for a while," she said. Jack just looked at the floor and nodded. By saying nothing, he conceded that she was in the right.

"How much time?" he asked.

Sharon rubbed the back of her neck and sighed. "I don't know. Enough time to figure things out. I would like us to see other people for now. A guy I work with invited me to go to his church with him. He was there when I needed someone to listen to me. I think I will go to his church. After a month or so, I would be willing to talk."

Jack took a deep breath and said, "Okay, I will respect your wishes." They got up and Sharon walked him to the door. They looked at each other and embraced for a long hug.

"I love you," said Sharon, a little choked up.

Jack stepped back and looked her in the eye. "I love you too. I've always loved you." He mustered up a smile for her and said, "Goodbye." Then he walked over to the parking lot where his van was. Sharon stayed in her doorway watching him until he got to his van. Then she shut her door and watched through the window from inside. He got into the van and took a moment, then started it up and left the parking lot.

He didn't really know where he was going, so he just pulled over at the next gas station. Jack topped off the gas tank and went inside. He grabbed a couple candy bars, drinks and some jerky for the road trip ahead of him. While waiting in line to pay for the snacks, he overheard a guy talking about the killing in the news. The guy told the clerk he had heard that there was some kind of cult behind it. Jack paid for his things and left the gas station. Not knowing where he was going yet, he got into his van and headed east on I-90.

He had on one hand found some peace with the mountain. On the other hand, he felt more lost than ever. The love of his life had been driven away by his unstable lifestyle. The sting of a broken heart reminded him of what Dominic had said about being robbed by circumstances.

He drove for three hours, all the way to Missoula, before stopping at a large parking lot. He was tired and wanted to rest. He got out and checked the straps on his hang glider and snugged them up, then crawled into the back of his van and took a nap.

When he awoke a couple hours later, Jack knew what he wanted to do. He would go up to the family's lake house in Polson. He had been thinking of going to visit his folks in Missouri, but changed his mind. He realized he had, and would be calling his father this week. It wouldn't be good to be with his father when he called, so he thought of the cabin. Jack would stay up there for a week. By then, maybe things would make more sense to him.

It was about an hour drive to the cabin. He stopped at a fast food place before heading out of town. On the way to the cabin, he thought about Laloedon and wondered if there had been a funeral for him. Charalon never mentioned what they did with him. The thought of robots and androids having a funeral for Laloedon seemed strange. Now knowing that he became Laloedon, he wanted to see the grave, if there was one.

Jack stopped at a supermarket and picked up some food for the stay at the cabin. He thought it would be good to stay out of sight for a little over a week. It was Tuesday, June 2. He would stay there until next Wednesday, June 10. He planned to hang out inside and watch TV, resting and reflecting.

Arriving at the cabin, Jack parked his van where it was less likely to be seen. He brought his groceries in and locked the door. He knew his folks were in Missouri and wouldn't be in Montana for a while. It was the perfect place to spend some time alone. He had food, cable TV, and lots of movies in their entertainment library.

After settling in, Jack kicked back in the recliner and turned on the TV. It wasn't long before he found himself thinking of the facility. "It sure would be nice to have one of those latte coffees right now," he thought. Picking up the remote and flipping through the channels, he found a movie to watch. He stayed in the chair watching movies until late at night and fell asleep there.

In the morning, he woke to the sun streaming in from an east-facing window. The TV was still on. He got up and looked out the window. It was early in the morning and there was a beautiful sunrise. It felt good to be at the cabin.

He spent the first couple of days just watching movies and relaxing. He tried not to think about Sharon too much, but being at the cabin made that difficult. With a look out the east-facing window, one could see the Andersons' house.

Wednesday morning, Jack turned on the news. A reporter was talking about last night's lottery drawing that nobody had won. He thought, "It would have been nice to know I'd be going back in time."

The reporter then moved on to a story about two ritual-style killings in the Spokane area. "A statement by the police department's spokesman said the two killings are definitely related. They are not ruling out that it may be the work of a serial killer," the reporter said.

Jack couldn't help but think of Sharon. There was a serial killer on the loose in the same town where she lived. He pulled out his phone and did a search on the internet for killings in Spokane. A couple stories popped up. After reading one of the stories, he found that the people killed had been mutilated, disemboweled and hanged on light poles. It was just like something he had seen in a memory playback at the facility. "Surely there was no connection between the killings in Spokane and what he saw in the playback, or was there?" Jack wondered. He didn't like it either way. Sharon lived in Spokane.

In an attempt to get her off his mind he picked up the remote and found a movie to watch. Even though the movie was interesting, it was hard to watch. Jack wasn't used to staying indoors for any significant amount of time. He thought about waiting until dark and going after some takeout food, or maybe just a drive up to Bigfork and back. After some thought, Jack decided to stay in and tough it out for a couple more days.

He woke up in the recliner to sunshine coming through the east window. He looked at his phone to see that he had done it. It was Wednesday 8:05 a.m., June 10. Jack had successfully stayed inside for over a week. He got up from the chair and looked out the north-facing window. The sun was shining and the lake was still. He took a shower and got dressed for the day. He wasn't sure what he would do today.

Jack looked at his phone again and saw that it was 9:05 a.m. "I'm having breakfast with Charalon about right now," he said with a smile.

He fixed himself some breakfast and sat down with a plate in the recliner. He turned the TV to the news channel and enjoyed his food. Jack wasn't really paying attention to the news until he heard something about Spokane, Washington.

He turned up the volume. There was a reporter talking about the ritual killings in Spokane. There had been yet another killing. The reporter said, "After three killings with the same MO within a week, there can be no doubt, this is the work of a serial killer."

Jack took his phone and did another search for killings in Spokane. After reading a few reports on the killings, he found that all the victims were men. He was deeply relieved, knowing that Sharon wasn't one of the victims.

After he finished his breakfast, he put his plate in the kitchen sink. With a look around, he got busy spiffing up the place.

It was Wednesday afternoon and the cabin looked pretty good. He had vacuumed, swept and did the dishes. Now he had to decide what to do with himself.

A ring tone that he didn't recognize rang out. It was coming from his pants pocket. He reached into his pocket and extracted the communicator that Jerrech had given him. He pressed the button on the lower left side of the phone and said, "Hello." An image of Charalon appeared on the screen. Jack put the device up to his ear.

She said, "Hello, Jack. Hold the communicator in front of you so I can see you."

"Oh, of course. How are you Charalon?"

"I'm fine. Sorry to bother you so soon, Jack, but there's been some curious things happening in Spokane. I would like to fill you in on a theory Laloed has."

"I've been keeping tabs on some strange ritual killings in Spokane. Is that what you're talking about?" he asked.

"Yes, that's what I want to talk to you about. How have you been keeping tabs on them, Jack? We just found out about them today."

He chuckled and said, "It's a long story. The short version is I ran into Dominic. After a trip to Spokane, I have been at my family's cabin for over a week."

"I see...so you probably wouldn't mind coming back here today."

He said, "No, not at all. I was wondering what I was going to do today."

"Good, how soon can you get here, Jack?"

"I can be there in less than three hours, if you like," he said cheerfully.

Charalon smiled and said, "Okay, I'll see you then."

He had washed all his clothes during the stay at the cabin. He packed a travel bag with a few changes of clothing and put it in his van. After locking up the cabin, Jack headed for the mountain.

When he got to his usual camping spot, he parked his rig and locked it up. He looked at his watch and saw that it was 4:00 p.m. With his travel bag under his arm, Jack headed up the hill.

When he got to the rock, he could see the flashing blue light. A touch caused it to change color and retract, as it did before. The rock vanished and he put his hand on the handprint. As before, the door opened. The lights were already on, so he walked through the door. The door on the other end opened before he got to it. When he entered the first room, he found Charalon waiting for him.

"Well, that was a lot easier than the last time I came in here," said Jack with a smile.

Charalon was happy to see him. "Would you like something to eat?"

"Of course," he said, then he gave Charalon a hug.

She was surprised by the hug. "Thanks, Jack...that's two hugs in one day for me."

He chuckled and said, "Oh, yeah...I forgot."

When they got to the cafeteria, there were T-bone steaks with hot garlic bread on the table. He looked at Charalon and smiled.

Chapter 14
The Coming Evil

He had just driven for two hours to get there. The T-bone steaks on the table were perfectly cooked. "Of course they are perfectly cooked, they are a replication of perfectly cooked steaks," he thought.

"So, tell me about your week since you've been gone all day," said Charalon with a smile.

He chuckled and said, "As you know, I left from here earlier today and walked down to my car. On the way down, Dominic showed up and sent me back to the Monday evening when I first got here. I put out my fire and drove to Spokane, Washington to see Sharon."

"How was Sharon?"

"She was fine, until I got there. We had a talk that didn't go that well, but I spent the night on her couch. In the morning she made me a breakfast. She said she didn't want to see me for a while and I don't blame her. I left and drove to Missoula. I took a nap there, then went to our family cabin for about a week. Then you called, and now I'm here."

After dinner, they found themselves in by the fire with coffees. Jack really missed these fireside coffees while he was gone.

He took a sip of his coffee. "You wanted to talk about the killings in Spokane?"

"Yes, there's some concern about it. The killings are very similar to the way Malconadon and his followers killed. There may be a connection," said Charalon.

"I thought the same thing, but how could there be a connection? That was at least a couple hundred years in the future, wasn't it?"

"Think of it this way, Jack, Laloedon was your age at this time."

"Good point."

"Malconadon was a first generation Morphalogian. As with most first generation Morphalogians, he also was a regenerated human."

"Malconadon could be as old as Laloedon. His human counterpart in this timeline could be my age. Do you know anything about him?" he asked.

"Yes, we did some research into the historical database of the alternate timeline. He is your age. Malconadon is the name that a man named Malcolm Underwood took when he became a Morphalogian. Before the other Jack came up with the Morphalogian DNA master sequence, Malcolm was one of the first regeneration customers."

"Do you have more information on him?"

"Yes, he lived in Spokane and he had a very disturbing mentor. I am assuming that the Malcolm Underwood in this timeline is following a similar path. Laloed would like to talk to you about him, Jack."

"Where did you get the information?" he asked.

Charalon smiled and said, "You know we have a vast amount of information about people and historical events."

"So, the information was in public records of some kind?"

"No, there was almost no information about him in the public records. He obviously went to extremes to remain somewhat anonymous in his early years. We found the information in a book from the alternate timeline called <u>Death Cult Threats</u>," said Charalon.

"There was somebody that tried to warn people about him?"

"I guess there was. Although some people were on to him, most people refused to believe the worst about Malcolm."

"Why?"

Charalon explained, "The author, Alec Normanson, was a very successful science fiction and mystery writer. He wrote many bestsellers. He saw the threat that Malcolm Underwood was becoming and wrote about it. People weren't willing to believe that Underwood was some kind of death cult leader. He had become a popular spiritual and political leader by the time Alec Normanson wrote the book. Underwood had been preaching his message of social change and fairness for years, and he had many followers. By the time the book by Normanson came out, it was too late. The people had been fooled."

"What if we told Alec Normanson about Underwood now? Maybe he would write the book in time to make a difference."

"We could, but he is only sixteen years old right now. He hasn't become the respected author that he became in the other timeline," said Charalon.

"Oh, well. When does Laloed want to talk?"

"He would like to see you sometime tomorrow."

Jack found it comforting to be back at the facility. He liked the idea that he could come and go from this place, and still have a home here. He spent the evening talking with Charalon about the future and the past. After much conversation, it was late so he went to his room for the night.

In the morning, Charalon woke him and he went to breakfast with her. It had become the way it worked there, and Jack liked it that way.

After breakfast, he went to see Laloed. When Jack entered the room, Laloed greeted him at the door. Jack always thought Charalon was an intimidating creature, but standing next to Laloed was truly an experience. The eight-foot-tall Laloed was an impressive and terrifying presence. He had to remind himself that what he was looking at was a holographic projection.

Laloed was friendly and gregarious. He invited Jack to sit down in the chair opposite his desk. It was still a little weird for him to talk with Laloed. The memory of the original angry Laloedon standing over him in the tunnel did not match the one now sitting behind the desk.

"Thank you for coming. By now Charalon has told you about the situation in Spokane?" asked Laloed.

Jack nodded and said, "Yes, she did. How can I help? I mean, I don't see how I can help, but I'm willing."

"Let me explain the whole situation first, and I'll get to that. First I have to tell you about a man named Malcolm Underwood."

"Yes, Charalon told me a little about him earlier," interjected Jack.

"Well, he had a mentor that went by the name Silas December. His real name was Derrick Dickinson. He was a former member of The People's Temple. That was the cult group founded by the Reverend Jim Jones. Jim Jones was responsible for the murder-suicide deaths of over

151

900 people in Jonestown, Guyana."

"I'm familiar with the Jonestown cult deaths," said Jack.

"As I was saying, Silas left Jones's cult because he thought Jones should have killed his followers long before the Guyana deaths. Jones's cult didn't start that way. It was a Christian church originally. To make a long story short, they became an atheistic, socialist, communist group. Silas agreed with the socialist direction they went. He wanted that because it made it easier to control the followers. He had an intense hatred of any other religion, especially the Christian religion. Silas wanted them all dead.

"His ultimate goal was the death of every man on the planet."

"Why would he want that?" asked Jack.

"That is the question, isn't it? Why would Hitler or Stalin want to kill millions of people? I know Silas believed that the Bible foretold the end of the world. I'm assuming he thought it was his job to help make it happen. I believe he was insane.

"Silas was an heir to a huge fortune, Jack. He inherited over a hundred million dollars. He had given Jones large sums of money before he left the group...he wasn't the sharpest tool in the shed.

"Silas was still worth seventy million dollars when he decided to start his own religion. He believed the Bible revealed to him that there would be a second coming, but it would not be Jesus. It would be another prophet that would usher in the end of the world. He thought that it was his job to find that person, and help him.

"He had only a few followers at first. They were able to grow in numbers only when the leaders quit telling the

152

new members everything they believed. Only when they had proven themselves to be true believers were members informed of the master plan. They planned to kill off all human life on the planet. They taught their followers that they would be translated back to earth and inherit everything on it. I don't think he believed that though. I think he would say anything to get people to go along with him. Alec Normanson wrote in his book about Silas's desire to practice human sacrifice. Some of the people he interviewed swore that Silas had already done so.

"It was twenty years or so ago, from now, that Silas found Malcolm Underwood. Underwood was the 13-year-old son of one of his followers. Silas was convinced that Underwood was the one. He thoroughly convinced Malcolm Underwood of this. When Silas was 70 years old he committed suicide, leaving all he had to Underwood. Underwood learned whatever he could about technology, psychology, and manipulation as a means to further his cause.

"In the alternate timeline, Underwood became a very influential force to be reckoned with. He had money, power and, eventually, long life. He could afford teams of people working on public relations and propaganda.

"Underwood learned from history. He learned how to incrementally advance his ideas by pushing the social envelope. He learned how to demonize his adversaries while creating sympathy for those who agreed with him. That's how Hitler was able to get people to hate Jews.

"It has become common practice in this timeline to demonize your political opponents, rather than to debate the merits of an idea. If someone disagrees with you, then you call them something like a racist and you don't have to defend your own ideas. If things keep going down that road in this timeline, who knows where it could lead?" said Laloed.

Jack said, "I see that."

"It's possible to get the majority of a society to go along with things that currently seem unthinkable. Things can change quickly."

Jack nodded in agreement and said, "Even here in this country."

Laloed continued, "Later when he became Malconadon, it was common knowledge that he liked to kill and mutilate people. By that time, it had become legal to do so. Nobody did more to legalize human killing than Malconadon.

"At this time and in this timeline, Malcolm Underwood has not yet become a public figure. He is in the process of learning what he can to advance his agenda. Derrick Dickinson, aka Silas December, died a while back and left him a fortune. I believe Malcolm is responsible for the killings in Spokane. It is only a matter of time before he rises to a position of power."

"So, what do you want to do about it, and how can I help?" asked Jack.

Laloed sat back in his chair and said, "Our original mission to stop the eventual Morphalogian takeover has been accomplished. It didn't happen the way we planned, but there won't be a Morphalogian threat. Because Dominic helped in that, I believe he would help you stop Underwood."

"Why would he help me stop Underwood when he didn't let the original Laloed kill Malconadon?" asked Jack.

"Because he keeps coming to you, Jack. He is trying

to prepare you for something. I would like you to ask him if Underwood can be stopped. My figures indicate that he can be stopped. I'm sure that Dominic wants you to use your connection with us to do good. He led you here. We have resources that could greatly help you. The other reason I think he would help you is that Underwood has been working with Dominic's enemies."

"Who are Dominic's enemies?" asked Jack.

"They are evil. I will let Dominic explain the rest. There's no evidence that this collaboration happened in the other timeline. The calculations I made this morning say you will see Dominic soon."

"There's more going on in Spokane than meets the eye, isn't there?"

"Yes, but I really don't know how it will play out in this timeline. In the alternate timeline there were only a couple killings, but I believe that they will continue here, if we don't stop him," said Laloed.

"What changed?"

"I don't know, Jack, but we have to do something soon."

"What would you like me to do in the meantime?"

"Laloedon built something I would like you to see. Charalon will show it to you if you like," said Laloed.

"Sure, whenever you want. I'd like to see what you have."

After his meeting with Laloed, Jack went to his room to rest for a while. He lay down on his bed looking at the ceiling. He thought about Laloed's request for help. He wanted to help, but felt inadequate.

"You will have help. I will help you to see what your task is," said Dominic.

Jack was startled and sat up quickly. "Whoa, I wasn't ready for that! What's going on Dominic?" he asked.

Dominic was sitting in the chair at the foot of the bed. "I have to give you a warning."

"A warning?"

Dominic looked at him with sympathy. "I am here to warn you about Malcolm Underwood. He is not working alone. There are dark forces surrounding and helping him, Jack. This man should not be underestimated."

"Laloed said Underwood is working with your enemies. What did he mean by that?"

Dominic said, "There is good and evil in this world. They work to bring more evil, hate and death into this world."

Jack nodded. "I see. If you are an angel, then they are demons. Is that right?"

"Jack, some would use those terms. Before you use those terms, you should know what they mean."

"Okay, I will look into it. Will you help me to understand what that means?"

Dominic smiled and said, "In time you will understand much more than you do now."

"Laloed wanted me to ask you to help us stop Malcolm Underwood. You have great power. Would you help us?"

"I have told you before, Jack, I am a messenger. It is true that I wield power, but I am under the authority of a much greater power. All authority has been given to my master. He wants people in this world to work with us to defeat evil. Even though I have the power to, I cannot do it for you."

"Who is your master?"

"Many have asked that question, Jack. For now, it is

enough for you to know that he is good. He wants the best for you."

He could see that Dominic wasn't going to give him a direct answer, so he changed the subject. "Why did you send me back in time when I left here the other day?"

"You needed to go to Spokane, but you also needed to rest. You have done both. There is no time to waste. Much is at stake," said Dominic.

"Well, thanks. I had a good week at the cabin. It was a little weird, though."

Jack could see that Dominic was slightly tense. Every other time Dominic had visited, he was calm and comforting. This time it was as if he didn't know what was going to happen.

"I have something else to tell you, Jack. Many of Malcolm Underwood's people are not just people. They have been taken over by my enemies, and they know who you are. They know who your family and friends are as well."

Jack was alarmed by Dominic's warning. He said, "I suppose it's too late to just walk away at this point."

"You are correct, Jack. Your family and friends would be in danger even if you walked away right now."

Jack took a deep breath and said, "Well, I will do whatever it takes to bring Underwood down."

Dominic looked over at the imitation window. With sadness, he said, "There is a cost, Jack. There may be sacrifice and pain, but I will be with you."

He was ready to hear what Dominic was saying. He had already decided that it was better to have lived the tougher life he had than to have it all and see the world destroyed.

"I just want to help, if I can," said Jack. He looked up

157

to see the empty chair in front of him. "You'll be with me?"

He got up off his bed and left the room.

"Find Charalon," said Jack as he left his room. He followed the line to Charalon's room. Pressing the intercom button on the door he said, "It's me."

The door slid open. She was sitting in a chair by her bed reading. "You read?" he asked.

"Yes, I can read," said Charalon acting incensed at first, then she smiled.

"You know what I meant."

She put her book down and said, "Yes, I read manually now and then. I find it enjoyable and it helps me. Interacting with tangible things instead of data files, makes me feel alive."

"You're as alive as anybody I know, Charalon."

"Thanks again, Jack. I need to hear that now and then."

"I'm kind of hungry. Would you like to have lunch with me?"

Charalon smiled and said, "Yes, I would. Let's head there now."

Arriving at the cafeteria, Jack found lunch waiting for him. There on the table were two plates with french dip sandwiches and au jus sauce. He had gotten used to Charalon deciding what he was going to eat. She sat there watching to see his reaction. She waited for him to say something about the food. Jack sat down at the table and acted like it was normal.

Charalon smiled and said, "So you have accepted your lot in life."

"We all have our cross to bear," he said, and started eating.

They finished lunch with little talk and went to the lounge for some coffees that Charalon had already ordered. The robot waiter arrived as they were sitting down. It put the drinks on the table between them and left. Jack took a sip from his cup. "Black coffee today?"

"I thought you might like it...for a change."

"Thanks, I do," said Jack. "Laloed said there was something he wanted me to see, and that you would show it to me."

Charalon sat back in her chair and pursed her lips in thought. She looked at Jack with a smile and said, "Yes, tomorrow. I will show you one of Laloedon's pet projects, if you can bear it."

"You're not going to tell me what it is, are you?"

"You'll just have to wait and see, Jack."

Chapter 15
Tools Of The Trade

It was 8:55 a.m. Friday morning, June 12. Jack was lying awake in bed, not wanting to get up. He was waiting for Charalon to stop in and make him get up.

He was curious about what Charalon was going to show him. "Is it going to be another cool invention, or maybe some shocking secret?" he wondered. He knew Charalon well enough by now to know he would have to wait and see. She liked to surprise him.

The door chime rang and he said, "Come in, Charalon." The door slid open and there she was. She entered the room and stood by his bed.

"Good morning. How are you today?" said Jack as he closed his eyes and pulled the blankets up to his chin.

Her eyes narrowed and she put her hands on her hips. She looked down at him and said, "I can come back in a while if you need more time."

Jack opened his eyes a little and looked up at her. The seven-foot-tall Charalon did not look like she would be glad to come back in a while. "No, I'll be right there," he said.

She grinned a little, showing her teeth and said, "That's what I thought. I'll be in the cafeteria," then she left.

Jack rolled out of bed and began getting ready for the day. He put on some fresh clothes and looked in the mirror. "You'd better get moving."

On the way to the cafeteria, he was wondering what Charalon had waiting on the table for him. He was pleasantly surprised by the diced ham and eggs when he got there.

"So, you approve, Jack?"

"Yes, I could have that every day. Well, at least until I got sick of it."

Charalon had her typical breakfast of sacktaw. Jack could feel her eyes on him as he ate his food.

"You're up to something, Charalon. What do you have up your sleeve?"

"I get to train you," she said with a devious smile.

Jack stopped eating and looked at her. "There it is. You're trying to make some kind of pet out of me," he said.

"You're already my pet."

Jack chuckled and shook his head. "What kind of training?"

"I want to make sure you know how to hunt, and be hunted. You can learn a lot about survival when you experience life as the prey, Jack. Your survival is my concern."

"Do we have time for coffees this morning?"

"Oh yes, we can't miss out on the things that matter," she said. "I will show you Laloedon's pride and joy after coffee time. Then we will do some training."

They sat by the fire with Charalon's coffee choice of the day. After they had chatted a bit, she said, "Are you ready to be amazed, Jack?"

He smiled and said, "I have been amazed so much lately that it now takes a lot to amaze me. However, I am ready to be amazed."

Charalon led him to the main entrance and over to a door to the left of the tunnel. Jack had not paid much attention to it before, probably because the guard robot was standing right in front of it. The guard moved out of the way when she approached the door, but kept its focus on Jack. It reminded him of an unfriendly dog a friend of his had. He never did like that dog.

She opened the door by putting her hand on a pad where a door handle would normally be. As it swung open, Jack could see another tunnel that went in a ways then turned left. He followed her into the tunnel. Lights came on as they walked toward the other end where there was a door like the one they just went through. As they walked through the door, they entered a dark room. The lights came on revealing a large room. It was about 40 feet square with a 20-foot-high ceiling. It had a large 30-foot-wide hangar-like door to the right.

In the middle of the room sat a black aircraft that looked a lot like it had been patterned after a 1980 Corvette. It was about 25 feet long and about 10 feet wide with a bubble canopy in the middle. There were two side-by-side seats with flight controls in front of both of them. It sat on four wheels and looked like it could be driven as a car.

"It's beautiful. He put a lot of thought into it, didn't he?" said Jack. "It looks like it's fast."

Charalon looked satisfied by Jack's response. "We call it the VTOL. This machine can take off and land vertically and cruise at supersonic speeds," she said.

"What is its range?"

Charalon said, "It can carry two people over 3000 miles in less than two hours. I will tell you more about it when we take it out for a flight."

Jack had a silly grin on his face as he stared at the impressive craft. "I know I shouldn't be surprised that you can fly this gorgeous machine. You must love it."

"I have never flown it before, but I can fly it," said Charalon. "You can fly it too, if you want to have some memory implants."

"I would be content to have you fly us around in it, but maybe someday."

"Laloed thinks it will come in handy for certain missions we might go on, Jack."

"I get you as a sidekick?" he said, teasing Charalon.

She grinned, showing her teeth again, and said, "I'm really looking forward to your training."

Jack couldn't take his eyes off the VTOL. He hardly even registered Charalon's friendly threat. The thought of piloting a ship like this was enough to make him consider the memory implant process.

"Well, we'd better get moving. You have to see Jerrech. He has some gadgets like the ILEFF system for you to use," said Charalon.

"This day just keeps on getting better. I get to try out the ILEFF system?"

She was amused by his enthusiasm. With a smile she shook her head and said, "You truly are the picture of a kid in the candy store. Jerrech didn't know if he would have the ILEFF system ready for you. He had to recalibrate it for a human, and key it to your DNA."

With his eyes still focused on the VTOL, Jack said, "I can wait, if I have to. Are we going to be training outside?"

"Yes, we are. Almost nobody comes through this area, and anyone who does will be seen by the surveillance drones. We don't want anybody to see me looking like this," she said motioning to herself.

"That could get someone's attention," said Jack with a smile.

"Jerrech has been working on a version of ILEFF for me. I will be able to appear as a human, so there will be less concern of being seen in the future. I just received a message from Jerrech. He won't have the ILEFF systems ready for us now. I think that is for the best anyway. I'd like you to learn how to use your natural senses to a higher level first. There's no substitute for real experience."

"I have spent a lot of time in the woods, camping and hunting. I'm looking forward to it," said Jack.

"We have good weather for some stalking. It is dry and warm out with a light breeze. You might want to bring some camouflage clothing and a snack. We'll be out there for a while."

"I'll bet there are some camouflage clothes on my bed when I get back there," said Jack.

Charalon just nodded and turned toward the door. Walking down the tunnel she said, "Meet me in the main entrance when you are ready. Would you like me to bring a snack for you?"

"Sure, that sounds good. Should I bring my backpack?" he asked.

"You might not want to carry extra weight. It would only slow you down. I'll bring some water and energy bars."

When Jack got to his room he found a camouflage

ball cap and clothing laid out on his bed. On the floor were some camouflage hiking shoes. He quickly changed and got ready to go. The clothes and shoes fit perfectly. He left his room and jogged down the hall.

When he got to the main entrance room, Charalon was already there. "I think you're using some kind of technology. How else do you get ready so fast?" he asked.

She was wearing camouflage clothing and a hat. She had her hair pulled back in a ponytail and sunglasses on her face.

"You look like you mean business, Charalon. Should I be worried?"

She handed him a water bottle with a clip on it. Jack clipped it to a belt loop on his right.

"Maybe you should be a little worried," said Charalon as she turned and opened the exit door to the tunnel.

"Are you wearing perfume, Charalon?"

"Yes, I am. I thought it might be more fair that way. I can smell you from a distance, Jack. I have better hearing too."

When they got outside she looked at him and said, "This is where we split up. You head to the west for a while and I will head east. Our objective is to meet on top of the mountain, straight to the north of here, without being detected by each other."

Jack looked around and surveyed the area. There were lots of trees and brush to hide behind in the surrounding area.

Charalon said, "If you see me, just point and call out my name. I will be hunting you with the objective of remaining unseen until it's too late for you."

"So, I am the prey?"

"Don't be the prey if you can help it. Do not doubt that I have the advantage here, but it's not impossible for you to win. I want you to pretend that I am one of Underwood's followers who might want to kill you."

"It's kind of hard to imagine that, but I'll keep it in mind," said Jack.

Charalon grinned and said, "Maybe by the end of the day you won't have a problem thinking of me that way. You never know, one little glitch and I could go all Westworld on you."

"Okay, I'll do my best," said Jack as he started walking to the west. Charalon turned and ran to the east, quickly disappearing into the trees.

He hid behind a tree as soon as he was out of sight. He checked the wind direction. The gentle breeze out of the east would help him. Jack took a quick look around and headed for another tree a little farther up the mountain. He thought about the situation for a moment. He had a couple options. There was a clearing about a hundred feet in front of him. There were trees to the left of it and low bushes to the right.

Jack tried to imagine what Charalon would expect him to do. He chose the bushes and ducked into them. He started crawling up the hill on all fours, staying low and close to the bushes.

A twig snapping noise came from the east and Jack froze. He reminded himself that he was not in a race, it was a hunt. "I can take all day if that's what it takes," thought Jack. He waited for a bit and inched up the hill some more. After a while he was close to the treeline on the upper end of the clearing. He stopped and looked around.

There were some big rocks about twenty feet to the northeast. He took a deep breath and headed for the rocks, keeping low to the ground. He sat with his back to one of the rocks and looked around again. "Is that Charalon's perfume I smell?" thought Jack. "If I stay here, I'm a sitting duck."

He made his way to the treeline and found cover. Another twig snapped, but he couldn't tell which direction it came from. Suddenly he realized that the noise could have come from above him.

Jack slowly looked up. He couldn't see anything but he had the feeling like something was watching him. He looked up in the tree to his left, and then to his right. He wasn't expecting it when the pine cone hit him on the head.

The tree he was under shuddered slightly, as if something over him had just leapt from it. "You've got to be kidding me," said Jack under his breath. Knowing he couldn't outrun her, he looked for a place close by where he could hide himself. Seeing nothing close, he picked up a rock and threw it down the hill as a diversion. He waited a moment then ran up the hill toward a clump of brush. Jack climbed in the brush and looked down the hill to where he threw the rock. Remaining motionless, he patiently waited and watched.

Something flashed across the lower end of the clearing. At once he took off up the hill running as quietly as he could. Up ahead was another clearing. Jack, thinking Charalon was still down the hill a ways, decided to bolt across it.

About halfway across the clearing, he thought he could smell Charalon's perfume. He was almost to the upper end of the clearing when something hit him. Jack felt like he had just been tackled by a 300-pound linebacker. He momentarily blacked out.

When he opened his eyes, Jack found himself lying on his back with Charalon sitting on his chest. She had her knees on his arms and a hand holding his head down by his hair. She had a wild look in her eyes as she raised her other hand. She was poised to rip his throat out. Charalon gave Jack no reassurance that she wasn't going to kill him. He was terrified.

She bent down closer, looking him in the eye. Her eyes narrowed and she showed her teeth. Jack could hardly breath with Charalon putting nearly all her weight on him.

Her face turned into a smile. "I suppose you have me right where you want me," she said. Jack would have laughed, but he still couldn't breathe very well. She took a little weight off him, but still held him down.

"You did better than I thought you would."

"Did you lose your sunglasses, Charalon?"

She smiled and said, "They're in my pocket. It's more intimidating without them, huh?"

Jack had to admit it was. He just kind of nodded in agreement.

"How would you like a walk to the top of the mountain with me, Jack?"

He nodded and Charalon let him up. He took a drink from his water and said, "That was pretty awesome. I think I'd like to do that again, on another day though. I'm not sure I learned much about strategy or tactics."

"It was an exercise in decision-making under pressure. I'm glad you liked it. I really enjoyed that too. I don't have the animal drives of a Morphalogian, but that was fun," she said.

They started up the hill talking about the hunt as they went.

When they got to the top, Jack found a log to sit on.

"I thought you might have broken my arm for a moment there," he said.

Charalon said, "I wouldn't have hurt you. I have subprograms that monitor and regulate the amount of force I use. I don't even have to think about it. If I don't want to hurt you, my subsystems will keep me from it."

"That's handy. For a minute there it was hard to tell what you meant to do. Have you ever considered an acting career?"

"Well, I do have the looks for it. If this whole saving-the-world thing doesn't work out for me, I'll give it some thought," Charalon said, keeping a straight face.

She pulled out the energy bars and gave one to Jack. He took another drink from his water bottle and ate the energy bar. It was quite a pleasant time. The view was stunning from their vantage point. They were slightly below the top of the mountain on the north side. There were mountains as far as the eye could see.

He looked at his watch. "It's 12:35, what do you want to do now?"

"We could do another hunt, Jack, or head back and have some lunch. Jerrech probably has our gadgets ready to try out."

"Not that I don't want to be tackled again, but lunch sounds pretty good right now."

Charalon grinned and said, "Okay, let's go get some lunch."

When they reached the cafeteria, a cheeseburger and fries were sitting on Jack's side of the table. They sat down and had some lunch.

"I know you disapprove of my love for cheeseburgers, Charalon. What's up?"

"You earned it. It's a positive reinforcement treat," she said with a wink.

Jack smiled and shook his head.

After lunch, they went to see Jerrech in his maintenance room. When they entered the room, Jerrech looked up and nodded at them. He looked at Jack and said, "I have successfully recalibrated the ILEFF unit to match your features. I will have to inject a small neural interface unit under the skin on the back of your neck. After that, all you need to do is put this unit in your pocket."

"Okay, I'm ready," said Jack.

Jerrech picked up a gun-like tool from his bench and held it against Jack's neck. He pulled the trigger and it made a quiet clicking noise. Jack was surprised when he couldn't feel anything happening.

"There you go," said Jerrech. He turned around and set the gun on the bench. Reaching for a small device sitting on his bench, he said, "I have the primary unit here..." Jerrech froze in thought.

"Are you alright, Jerrech?" asked Charalon.

"Yes, I would say I just had a little déjà vu, if I didn't know better," said Jerrech as he handed the primary unit to Jack.

Jack put the unit in his hip pocket and asked, "Okay, now what next?"

"In a few more minutes, the neural interface will sync

with your brainwaves. All you will have to do is think 'ILEFF' and you will see options in your head. With a little practice, you will be able to move the cursor and select options. I can send you messages through the neural interface too," said Jerrech.

"I got it," said Jack.

Jerrech turned to Charalon and said, "You already have a neural interface built into your message system." Jerrech looked her in the eye and gave her a similar primary unit saying, "You might want to keep it...somewhere on your person."

She said, "I will." She held it in her hand while they stood there.

Jack noticed Jerrech's discretion about the placement of the device. It seemed like it might be a private matter to the androids.

"It will be hard to judge your own strength. You should play with them outside first, and try not to hurt each other," said Jerrech with a hint of a smile.

Charalon looked at Jack and said, "You heard him. Let's go." She turned to Jerrech and said, "Thank you for the toys."

They left Jerrech's maintenance room and headed down the hallway.

Charalon said, "I'm going to change into some other clothes. How about we meet in the main entrance room?"

"Sure, but I think I'll keep these clothes on. I kind of like them."

"Okay, Jack, but you won't need the camouflage colors."

He went to his room and took off the hat. "There, I'm ready," he said to himself. Jack left his room and headed for the main entrance. This time, he got to the main entrance before Charalon. He took the opportunity to look over the security robot again. It stood there motionless. He marveled at the workmanship and attention to detail. He didn't know if it was aware of him. If it was, it chose to ignore him.

Suddenly he felt hands on his midsection, tickling him. "Hey, stop that," he said, trying to get away from Charalon.

"I was going to startle you, but I thought your reaction might set off the security robot. It could have gotten ugly."

Charalon had her usual clothing on but left her hair in a ponytail.

"Are you ready for this, Charalon?"

She looked excited about it and said, "Sure, let's go."

They opened the exit door and headed into the tunnel.

Jack was thinking about Jerrech and asked, "Is it just me or is Jerrech talking more lately?"

"Yes, he is. He seems more like the Jerrech from Charalona's memories. Since I've been me, I haven't heard him speak more than a few words at a time, Jack."

"Is this the first time you have actually tried this?" he asked as they left the tunnel.

"I have Charalona's memories of using it, but this will be my first time. I think we should stay a little ways apart until we get used to the zero-point energy function."

Jack thought, "ILEFF," and he could see four icons in his lower left field of vision. "I can see the icons, and I know what they mean. It's pretty cool," he said.

"Can you move the cursor yet?"

He concentrated on the icons and a cursor appeared. "Move left," he thought, and the cursor moved over to the first icon. He thought, "Select," and he turned on the ILEFF.

"I can! It's on now. What am I supposed to do now?" he asked.

Charalon pointed to a good-sized rock weighing about 200 pounds and said, "Pick that up and break it. You should find it very easy to do."

Jack did find it easy. The rock crumbled like Styrofoam when he squeezed it.

"That was weird. It was as if it had no weight," he said.

"If you look through your setting options, you will find a setting that gives you resistance feedback. It will help you get a feel for your own strength, Jack."

He looked through his options and set the ILEFF to give resistance feedback. He picked up another large rock and threw it in a safe direction.

"That was better. I could tell it was heavy but still found it easy to pick up," said Jack.

Charalon didn't answer, so he turned around to see what she was doing. She wasn't there. Jack looked around and couldn't see her anywhere.

"I'm right here." Her voice sounded to Jack like she was standing right next to him.

"Oh, I get it."

"Now look," said Charalon from behind Jack. He turned around to see a five-foot-tall blonde lady that he had never seen before. It was Charalon looking like an attractive young woman in her twenties. Jack was amazed by the realism of the disguise. He was intrigued by the way the ILEFF device could even compensate for the height difference. "Cool," he said. "Talk some more."

"What do you think?" asked Charalon as she posed

like a model for Jack.

"That's amazing, even your lips move. If it wasn't for your voice, I wouldn't know that was you."

The two of them played with the various features of the ILEFF system for awhile. Then they hiked around and hunted each other for a couple hours. Afterward they went in and had dinner, followed by some time by the fire.

Jack said, "I found the ILEFF to be very helpful. It gave me a fighting chance against you."

Charalon rolled her eyes and said, "Sure."

"I saw you when you were in that tree. I would have made it to goal before you got me, if I hadn't tripped over that stupid log."

"If it helps you, Jack, you can think that." She had a smug look on her face.

"Hey, where did you put that device?" he asked with a smirk.

Chapter 16
What Dreams Are Made Of

The door chime sounded. It was Saturday morning, June 13. Jack rolled over in his bed and looked at his watch. He sat up and said, "Yes?" The door slid open to Charalon.

"It's after 9:00. Aren't you hungry?" she asked.

He rubbed his eyes and said, "Yes, I am. I'll be right there."

"Okay, I'll see you there." She smiled and left.

Jack got up and put some clothes on. After brushing his teeth and shaving, he headed for the cafeteria. He found himself thinking about Charalon's habit of getting him up every day. It was obvious that she looked forward to it. Jack wondered if Charalon and Jerrech slept, or if they just worked at night.

When he got to the cafeteria, Charalon had sausage and eggs waiting for him. It was another one of his favorite breakfasts.

"Nice choice," said Jack.

Charalon smiled and said, "You know I have a lifetime of memories of you from the other timeline. I know what you like."

"Yes, I've noticed. Thank you for thinking of me."

"You're welcome, Jack."

After breakfast they took their places by the fire and had some coffee and conversation.

"I've been wondering, what do you do at night? Do you rest, or do you have things to do?" he asked.

"I have a sleep mode, but I don't need to sleep. I find my sleep mode comes in handy when I get bored. I don't have much to do at night, so I look forward to the morning."

"How does that work?"

Charalon explained, "Remember when I told you that I have subprograms that can slow my thought processes down?"

"Yes, I do. It was to help you relate to the people around you."

She continued, "That's right. Well, I can direct those programs to slow down or speed up. If I want to sleep, I just slow my cognitive functions down and initiate my sleep program. I have other programs that will wake me if too much time has passed, or by outside stimulus like an alarm clock."

Jack was intrigued by the concept of android sleep and their perception of time. "Do you perceive the passage of time when you sleep?" he asked.

"My sleep program allows me to experience sleep the way you do. I even dream. I have memories to compare my sleep to, so I know. I can choose to speed up my cognitive functions if I need to figure out something fast. When I do that, it's as though time slows down for me."

"Now and then, I wish I had the ability to slow down time. I think that would come in handy. Wait a minute, did you use that against me in the woods yesterday?" he asked.

"No, but if I did, you'd never know."

"You don't have a deception program at work right now, do you?"

Charalon grinned and said, "Like I said before, you'd never know."

"What about stasis, is that different than sleep?"

"My, you're curious today! Stasis is different than sleep, Jack. For non-androids, stasis is used only as a means of preserving one's self while passing time...they don't perceive time or dream in stasis. For an android like me, it is used to save power and preserve the meta-skin. I don't perceive time in stasis."

"I find it amazing. To think that someone could be dormant for over a hundred years, then wake to a different world," said Jack.

Just then, Jerrech entered the lounge and said, "Hello, guys. I have been able to incorporate the DSIRN system into your ILEFF. By upgrading your ILEFF programming, I have given you the option of using it as a DSIRN device at the same time. You will now be able to see into the unseen world."

"So, you have already transmitted the upgrade?" asked Charalon.

Jerrech answered, "Correct, all you have to do is select the DSIRN icon and it will be activated. It works through your neural interface. You will still have normal vision with the DSIRN imagery as an overlay option. Laloed is convinced that you will need it in Spokane."

Jack perked up and asked, "We're going to Spokane? When is that going to happen?"

Charalon answered, "Laloed thinks that we should do a test mission to Spokane and spy on Malcolm Underwood's operation. It's a recon mission. He thinks we should be off to Spokane as soon as the car is ready. I just got the message from Laloed a minute ago."

"We could just take my van. It's ready to go now," said Jack.

"I think you'll like the car I'm putting together for you. It's a 1969 Camaro convertible with some extra technology. I have replicated all the parts for it and have a couple droids putting it together in the hangar right now. It can hover, so getting it to the road shouldn't be a problem," said Jerrech.

Jack's approval was obvious. With a broad smile, he said, "I love the '69 Camaro. It just doesn't get much better than that!"

Jerrech smiled and said, "I know, you used to carry on about those cars in college...in my memories."

Their surprise at Jerrech's behavior was plain to see. He looked at Charalon, then back at Jack. Jerrech looked like even he was surprised by his interaction with them. He said, "I know, I see it too. I think it has something to do with Jack being here. I have memories resurfacing. There are social subprograms operating now that I didn't know I had." Then he looked at Jack and said, "You were my best friend...I mean that's how I remember you."

Charalon was in awe of what was happening. She said, "Whatever the reason, I like it."

Jerrech nodded and left abruptly. It seemed to Jack like he was getting emotional and didn't want to deal with it in front of them.

"Well, that was interesting," said Jack.

"It sure was."

Jack was looking around the room. "I turned on the DSIRN, but I can't see anything out of the ordinary."

"Well, that's probably a good thing, Jack. I don't know how good it would be to have invisible beings running around in here."

"When I look at you, I can see a kind of white light outline of you," said Jack.

Charalon was intrigued by that. She looked at him and said, "I see the same thing when I look at you."

Jack continued looking around. Then a light caught his eye. When he looked at the door to the hall, he saw a bright white light shine under it. It was as if a powerful spotlight passed by the door, moving toward his room.

He jumped up, ran to the door and opened it. Looking down the hall in both directions, Jack said, "Did you see that? A bright light went past the door a moment ago."

"I wasn't looking, Jack. I didn't see what you saw."

"Well, I think I'm going to run to my room and use the restroom. After that, can we go see the car that Jerrech is putting together?"

"Sure, I'd like to see it too. Meet me in the main entrance room when you're ready," said Charalon.

When Jack came out of his bathroom, Dominic was sitting in one of the armchairs. Jack turned on his DSIRN system, but it wouldn't select.

"Hello, Jack. I will not be here long. I just need to tell you not to trust in your technology. If you rely on it too much, you will be disappointed. I would ask you to trust in my master. If you ask for his approval, things will go better for you."

"Are you stopping me from using my DSIRN system?" asked Jack.

Dominic nodded and said, "Turn it off and look at me now." Jack looked up and nearly fell over backward. Standing before him was a figure whose head touched the ten-foot-high ceiling. His entire form was emitting white light. He was chiseled and powerful looking with wings extending from behind him. His eyes were piercing and intimidating.

Jack was completely terrified and could hardly breath. He couldn't stop shaking at the sight of the fierce warrior-looking being in front of him.

"Do not be afraid, Jack. I am here to help you."

Jack closed his eyes for a moment. When he opened them, Dominic appeared as he had before. Dominic sat back down in the chair and said, "I know by now you have been wondering if other people have beings like me come to them. It is very rare that we appear to people. You have been called, and you have answered, Jack."

He blinked his eyes and Dominic was gone. Jack could hardly believe what he just saw. He walked over to the mirror and shook his head. Gathering himself together he headed out to the main entrance room.

As Jack came walking up, Charalon looked at him and said, "What's up with you? You look like you did when I tackled you the other day."

"I just saw Dominic in my room. When I came out of the bathroom, he was there. We talked briefly, and then I saw him as he really is. I think I now know what the word 'angel' means."

Her eyes got big as she showed interest. "What did he look like?"

Jack sighed and shook his head saying, "It's hard to describe. I'm just glad I took a pee before he showed up. I'll have to tell you about it another time."

Charalon just stood there staring at Jack, trying not to laugh. Finally she said, "Okay, I'll look forward to that. Do you still want to see the car?"

Jack thought about it for a moment then said, "You know, I think I'd like to get some air. Would you like to go for a walk with me?"

"Sure, let's go now."

He followed her up the tunnel and outside. They went for a long walk and talked very little. After they got back, they went to lunch, then to the lounge.

After sitting in silence for a while, Jack described to Charalon what it was like to see Dominic. They talked for a while about angels, good and evil. He was still quite affected by what he saw.

"Would you like to see the car now?" asked Charalon. "It would do you some good."

Jack just nodded, then got up. Charalon got up and led the way to the hangar. When they got there, the car looked to be done. There was only one droid in the hangar, and it was polishing the car. Jack's mouth dropped open. "What a beauty," he said.

The car was a bright red with a white cloth top and white racing stripes on the hood and trunk lid. It was Jack's dream car. "When do we get to take it out?" he asked.

Charalon said, "Any time you want to."

"Tell me, again, how we get this thing down to the road, Charalon."

She grinned and said, "Get in, on the passenger side."

Just then he noticed that Charalon wasn't as tall as she was before. She looked to be about six feet tall, about the same height as Jack. As they got into the car, he asked, "Okay, Charalon, when did you shrink a foot or so?"

"Oh, you noticed. I was wondering when you might catch on to that. I have been losing height for two days now. My structural framework retracts or extends in my arms, legs and back to change my height. Even my hands and feet are smaller now. It has to go slow so the meta-skin can adjust. It will help me to blend in if the ILEFF system has any problems when I'm out in the world. Plus, I fit in the car better now."

"Well, you're just full of surprises. You don't look nearly as intimidating as you did before, Charalon."

She got a smug smile on her face and said, "It only looks that way. I am just as deadly as I have ever been and don't you forget it."

The huge door to the hangar raised and the rock on the other side vanished. Charalon checked with the surveillance drones and initiated the stealth mode, making the car invisible. She pulled part of the dash down, revealing another control panel. With a small joystick she raised the car off the ground and hovered it out the door. A holographic projection of the terrain kept the hangar camouflaged from the outside. The car floated silently down the hill, still invisible.

As she continued down the hill toward the road, she said, "We should be able to drive it down to the main road in a moment. It isn't really designed to fly, but it will hover when needed."

When they got to the dirt road, Charalon set the car down and got out. "It's your turn now," she said.

Jack started up the car's engine and it sounded great. He revved it up a couple times and smiled ear to ear. He drove the car down to the pavement, wincing at every bump.

"You know, driving a car like this down this old road is just wrong. I'm pretty sure it's a sin. It's just not right, Charalon."

"If you break it, we can have another one in a day or

so. It is easily replaced and even easier to have the droids fix it."

Jack just shook his head saying, "That seems wrong too."

When they got to the paved road, he had to see how much power the car had. It had great acceleration and handled well. Jack was quite literally driving a brand new 1969 Camaro, something he never thought would happen.

He entered the freeway and headed toward Missoula. He accelerated to a hundred miles per hour then slowed down to eighty.

"I was going to say something about your excessive speed, but you slowed down. Jerrech has a valid-looking license plate on the car, but I don't know about registration and proof of insurance paperwork. You might not want to get pulled over, Jack."

"Sorry, it's just that this is something I've always dreamed about." He accelerated to pass a car, but kept the speed below eighty-five. As he passed the car full of people, Charalon appeared as the short blonde she had before.

When Jack noticed her appearance, he said, "I suppose we don't want to look too out of the ordinary. We already get quite a few looks in this beauty."

"I have quite a few options for my appearance," said Charalon. "How do you like this one?"

When Jack looked she appeared as an old, rotund lady with a headscarf and big wart on her face. His reaction caused her to cackle, completing the prank nicely.

"I think, maybe, I liked the last one better...at least a little." He chuckled and shook his head. "That was pretty good, Charalon."

"I'll leave it on the blonde for our drive." She was still smiling.

Jack had a big, silly smile on his face. He looked at the gas gauge and asked, "Should we just keep going on into Missoula?"

"Sure, I'd really like that. I'll message Laloed so he knows what we're up to."

"It's nice out. When we get to Missoula, I'd like to drop the top and drive around a little. We could get some fast food and have a good ol' time. I have a little money and my credit card," he said.

"Laloed has a plan to provide some money for you, Jack. We could replicate money, but that's essentially counterfeiting. Counterfeiting might bring unwanted attention to you. Laloed says he has found a nearby gold mining claim that could be bought for very little. That would provide a nice cover story for the gold we have in the storeroom."

Jack looked interested and asked, "You have gold in the storeroom? Where did that come from?"

"During the process of carving out the facility in the mountain, Laloedon came across a rich vein of gold. There were other precious metals there as well. We could replicate the gold if needed, but since we already have at least a thousand ounces of it, we're going to get rid of some of it. You will have to take it to places that buy gold a couple ounces at a time. That way we won't get attention that we don't want."

"That sounds like a good plan. I'll have to go up and look at the claim. Does Laloed have the contact info for me?" asked Jack.

"Yes, he does. The claim is about ten miles up Fish Creek Road and the man who owns it lives in Missoula."

When they got to Missoula, Jack pulled off the freeway at the Reserve Street exit. He found a parking lot and pulled into it. "Okay, let's get this top down," he said.

Charalon just smiled as Jack unlatched the top and brought it down. After buttoning down the tonneau cover, he got in and drove off. The weather was perfect, with very little wind. It was a little after noon, so he stopped at a drive-in burger joint and ordered a burger and fries for both of them. They sat in the car and had lunch.

"This is great. I really needed to get out and do something," said Charalon.

Jack stopped eating for a moment and said, "Well, this is too much. I get to drive this car around town and go to a drive-in with a good-looking woman. It's a car buff's perfect day." He thought about what he had said, and added, "Too bad you have to look like that."

"Why are you trying to butter me up? Do you think that will help you the next time we go hunting?" she asked with a devious smile.

"It couldn't hurt, right?"

"Not permanently."

Jack changed the subject saying, "We should get a hold of the guy with the mining claim while we're in town. Maybe we could get that taken care of."

Charalon pulled a pen and paper out of the glove box. She wrote on it and handed it to him. "Here's the name and number of that guy. You should call him now," she said.

Jack pulled his phone out and dialed the number. "Hello," said the man who answered.

"Yes, hello. Is this Tom?"

"Yes, it is. What can I do for you?"

"My name is Jack Thomas and I'm calling about a mining claim you have for sale up Fish Creek."

"I still have it if you're interested. I'm asking two hundred dollars for it," said Tom

"I have that in my pocket right now. Can I meet you somewhere?"

Tom said, "Sure, I've got the paperwork as well as maps to it here at my house, and I'll be here for a while. You should know that it hasn't produced any gold for a while. That's why it's so cheap."

"I'm still interested. It sounds like a good hobby for me," said Jack.

He got the address and directions from Tom. They drove to Tom's house and he signed the deed over to Jack and gave him a signed bill of sale.

"Thanks for coming over. Good luck with that claim. There hasn't been any gold found there in years. You should be very careful, it's a hard rock mine with a small opening. Oh, it has a locked metal grate over the entrance," said Tom. "Here's the key to the lock on it."

After meeting with Tom, Jack pulled over and put the top up for the drive back to the facility.

"We'll have to go up Fish Creek and check out the mine before I take some of that gold in," said Jack.

"We could take your van up there if you don't want to drive this 'beauty' on that dirt road."

"Yes, that's a good idea. We should stop in Frenchtown to get some more gas. It does take gas doesn't it?" he asked.

"Yes, it does. The engine and drivetrain are the same

as a 1969 Chevy Camaro, so you might want to put some higher octane fuel in it."

He pulled up to the pump at a gas station in Frenchtown. An old Chevy pickup pulled in right behind him. Jack got out and used his credit card to start the pump. As Jack filled the tank, the man driving the old Chevy pickup struck up a conversation. "Wow, that is some car!" he said. Charalon got out to see who was talking to Jack.

"Yes, it is. I love this car," said Jack.

Charalon politely smiled at the guy and got back in the car.

"You might want to have your springs on the passenger side looked at. When that little gal just got in the car, it really sat down," said the man.

Jack smiled and said, "Uh, yeah...I'll do that."

Chapter 17
The Garage

It was Monday, June 15, 8:30 a.m. Jack was in bed at the facility. He rolled over and looked at the window to see another beautiful sunrise over the ocean. He had left the window set to an ocean view for a while now. Jack got up and walked over to the window. He touched the window a couple times, looking for a nice view to leave it on. He settled on the green grassy rolling hills background.

Jack got dressed and sat down in one of his chairs. He knew it wouldn't be long before Charalon showed up. He used the time to reflect on what he had learned over the last few days.

The door chime rang. "Yes?" he said, and the door slid open.

"Well, look at you," said Charalon with a surprised look.

"Yeah, it's kind of weird for me to be up this early."

"Dominic must have come by and got you up for me," she said.

"No, I just woke up and got dressed for no particular reason."

Charalon smiled and said, "Well, let's get you some breakfast."

After breakfast, they sat in the lounge and talked. Jack brought up the Camaro. "I should rent a house that has a garage to put the Camaro in. That way it wouldn't have to be driven up and down that bumpy, steep road. Besides, somebody's going to see us going in and out of here and wonder what's going on."

"You just want to keep that thing to yourself, don't you, Jack?"

"No...well, kind of. I think it would be a good place to park my van. We could keep the Camaro down where it wouldn't have to be driven out of here."

"We could have Jerrech make it fly better, so we could just fly it all the way down to the road. We would still have to use the stealth mode to avoid being seen flying in it," said Charalon.

Jack countered with, "I think it would be easier to just drive it out of a garage. There is a place for rent at the bottom of Fish Creek Road that has a garage."

"You just want a place to have some kind of bachelor pad, now that you're kind of single. I probably wouldn't even be invited to your parties, would I?" she said as she poked Jack.

He chuckled and said, "Yeah, right. I really think it's a good idea. Somebody's going to wonder why my van is always up here. I'd still sleep and eat up here."

"I'll run it by Laloed. You do have a say in the matter. You don't ask for much, Jack, and a lot has been asked of you."

A few hours later, during lunch, Charalon said, "Laloed thinks your idea of renting that house with a garage makes sense. It has a big yard that the VTOL could land in. You and I could take the Camaro to Missoula today and cash in some of the gold to pay for it all."

"I love the thought of that. When do we get to go?"

"Whenever you want to."

Jack beamed at that and said, "Let's go as soon as we're done here."

After they were finished with lunch, they went to the hangar. Charalon got into the driver's seat and hovered the car out of the hangar in stealth mode. Then she hovered it all the way to the paved road at the foot of the mountain. After she set it down, she looked around and took it out of stealth mode. Charalon got out and switched places with Jack.

"Thanks for bringing the car all the way down to the pavement," he said.

"I thought I'd spare you the great suffering you endured last time. You know, by abusing the Camaro on that dirt road," said Charalon with a grin.

Jack turned the key and smiled when the 350 CID V8 engine came to life. He put the car in gear and headed for the freeway toward Missoula. The next time Jack looked over at Charalon she appeared as an attractive brunette in her early thirties.

"I like the new look. I liked the short blonde look too," he said.

She chuckled and said, "Thanks, Jack. I'm pretty sure that Jerrech has a thing for that blonde. I think her name was Melody. She broke Randal's heart back in college, so Jerrech would have those memories."

When they got to Missoula, there were some dark clouds and it looked like it could rain at any moment.

Jack looked out the window at the sky and frowned.

"Don't be sad. There will be other times," said Charalon purposely making a sad face. She pulled down the sun visor and looked in the mirror on its backside. She made some faces in the mirror and let out a little laugh. Jack looked over at her.

"I had to see what those faces looked like with this appearance. I am easily amused sometimes," said Charalon, explaining herself. She made some more faces in the mirror.

"So, where was that precious metals exchange again?" he asked.

"It's on Broadway, next to a tire store."

Jack found the gold exchange and sold them four ounces of gold. It was raining by the time they got their mission done. Not being able to put the top down, he just wanted to get out of town.

"While you were in that gold exchange, I called and set up a time to look at the house you want to rent. The landlord said she could show it to you around 5:00 p.m.," said Charalon as she handed Jack his cell phone.

"How did you get my cell phone?"

She smiled but didn't answer.

Jack shook his head a little and said, "We have a little time to kill. We'd be too early if we went there now. There's a little cafe in Alberton. We could stop and have a little pie, or something."

"I would like that. How's my appearance as the brunette holding up?"

"You look good. I haven't noticed any fluctuations at all," said Jack.

The stop at the cafe went off without a hitch. They left

there in time to meet the landlord at the rental house on Fish Creek Road.

The house was an older, partially furnished, three-bedroom house with a two-car garage. There weren't any other houses nearby. Jack liked rural areas for that reason.

There was a large yard that hadn't been mowed recently. Next to the house was a shed that had a lawn mower, gas can and some yard tools in it.

He signed the lease agreement and paid the deposit and two months rent in cash. The landlady gave him the keys and left.

"Shall we go get my van?" asked Jack.

Charalon nodded and said, "Yes, and we could go look at the mine too."

"I really don't want to take the Camaro back up there but, other than walking, I don't see how we'll get up there."

"Well, Jack, I have an idea. We could have the VTOL come pick us up. It can home in on my signal and land right here in this yard. Nobody will see it if it is in stealth mode."

"That's too cool. I love the thought of a ride in that machine," he said with enthusiasm.

"It's on the way, Jack." They sat in the Camaro, out of the rain, while they waited.

After a couple of minutes, Charalon said, "The VTOL is hovering over the yard right now." She got out of the car. Jack could tell that she was directing it to land in the yard. There was some noise that sounded like a jet engine, but very quiet. He watched the grass as the four wheels made impressions in the lawn.

"Okay, how do we get into it?" he asked.

"I'll extend the stealth field to ten feet. Then you just walk up to it and you'll see it. The field is extended and the canopy is up." She walked toward the VTOL and disappeared as she entered the stealth field. Jack smiled and followed her. As soon as he went through the field, he could see the craft. Charalon got in the left seat and motioned for Jack to get in the other.

She said, "Buckle up," as she lowered the canopy. She put a hand on the control yoke and the other on a joystick. Charalon lifted the VTOL off the ground and flew off, leaving the Camaro in the driveway.

They were entering the hangar door in no time at all. She hovered the craft to the middle of the room and rotated it 180 degrees then set it down facing the door.

"I think I will get that memory implant sometime soon," said Jack as he got out of the VTOL.

Charalon chuckled and said, "I know you will love it, but right now we need to get going. That is, if we want to get back before dark."

They hiked down to the van and drove it to the house. He put the Camaro in the garage and locked the house up.

It took about 30 minutes to drive up to the mine. Jack found the entrance and checked to see if the key would open the lock. He opened the metal grate and squeezed through the opening. After looking at the sides of the mineshaft, Jack exited the mine and locked it back up.

"There, now I've verified that there is a mine here. I might have to come back and actually do some mining. It would be fun to use some of your technology in it," he said.

"Do you want to stop at your new rented pad on the way back?"

"No, I don't need to. Wait, I would like to put my hang glider in the garage there. It's good to store it out of the weather, if you can," said Jack. They dropped the glider off at the house and continued on with the van back to the mountain.

After dinner, they sat by the fire and talked about the mission to Spokane. She told Jack that Laloed wanted to meet and talk about the trip with him soon.

"Would he want to meet with me tonight?"

Charalon looked at Jack and grinned. "Did you forget that he doesn't need to sleep?"

"No...maybe. How about I see him now?"

"That would be okay. Would you like me to take you?" she asked.

"No, I can find my way there, but thanks."

Jack made his way to Laloed's office. He soon found himself sitting in the chair in front of the desk. Laloed was friendly and accommodating.

"I can have some coffee brought here if you would like," said Laloed.

Jack was grateful, but said, "I think I should cut back on the coffee after 6:00 p.m. I've had too much lately. What would you like to talk about?"

"As you know, I've been planning a reconnaissance mission to Spokane. I believe Malcolm Underwood has the ability to ruin this timeline too, even without becoming a Morphalogian. I'm also a little concerned about Underwood's people. Some of them are not just people. They have been taken over by the enemies of beings like Dominic. If they are his enemies, then they might have powers too. I think they will be able to see you even with your ILEFF system on."

Jack said, "Dominic came to me in my room on Saturday. He wanted to warn me not to trust in technology. He also showed me what he really looks like, and I was quite shaken by his true appearance. I think I know what an angel is now."

"Yes, Charalon reported that you saw Dominic again. She told me a little about your experience. That is why I believe you will be more at risk in Spokane."

"Dominic gave me some advice. I think he was saying to ask his master to bless our mission. He told me to trust in his master. I also have come to believe that his master is God," said Jack.

Laloed sat back in his chair and skeptically looked at him. "Are you saying that he told you to pray?"

Jack thought for a moment and said, "I think that's exactly what he was saying. I don't know if his master is God or not, but I don't see how it could hurt to pray."

Laloed nodded and said, "Well, I can't argue with that."

"When do you want us to go to Spokane?"

"I think it would be good to go as soon as you're ready, Jack. Maybe after a little more training without the ILEFF. That way if you can't use it, you will be better prepared."

"Okay, I'll train with Charalon in the morning. She likes to work without the ILEFF anyway. Thanks for seeing me tonight," said Jack.

He went back to the cafeteria. Charalon was still sitting by the fire. He sat down by her and said, "Well, you get to train me some more in the morning, without the ILEFF."

She got a devilish smile and said, "Cool!"

Chapter 18

Spokane

It was Tuesday morning, June 16. Jack and Charalon had just left the facility. They were going to practice some guerrilla warfare tactics without the ILEFF system. The plan was to separate and meet a couple miles to the east of the facility. She had set up proximity sensors along the way that would act as enemy lookout simulators. It was Jack's task to get through them undetected and ambush an imaginary enemy.

He was about 500 feet below the top of the mountain, headed toward the rendezvous point. Charalon was watching him from the top of the mountain as she walked in the same direction, staying out of sight.

Earlier, Charalon had Jerrech sync Jack's communicator to her neural net, allowing her to communicate silently with him.

Jack pulled out the communicator and said, "Okay, I made it through the first leg undetected. I'm headed for the rendezvous point."

"Yes, I see that."

"You can see me? I thought I was fairly out of sight."

"You have done very well, young Jack Thomas, but you are up against the best tracker-android this side of Missoula," said Charalon with a little hyperbole.

"What was I thinking?" he said.

She didn't immediately have anything to say. Jack was

waiting for some kind of clever comeback. Just as he raised his communicator to say something, Charalon's voice came out of it. "There's somebody else up here, Jack. It's a guy wearing a red shirt and blue jeans. You will run into him soon. Let's turn the ILEFF systems on to stealth mode. He looks kind of suspicious to me. I think you should check him out to see what he's up to." She quickly ran toward Jack and found a spot close to him to watch from.

He turned on the ILEFF system and engaged the stealth mode. He became invisible and sat down to the side of the path. Judging by Charalon's description, Jack was thinking that this person was Dominic. While he waited for the man to come by, he communicated with her.

"Charalon, can you see me?"

"No, but I know where you are. I am close by and in stealth mode also. He is about a hundred feet from you, Jack. I'll be watching from here."

As the man came into view, Jack could see it wasn't Dominic. The stranger had a three-day beard and was dressed in a red plaid shirt with blue jeans. It appeared to Jack that he was trying to look like Dominic. He walked right up to Jack and stopped.

"Hello, I'm Tobias. What's your name?" He had the smile of a man who was trying to hide his true feelings. Charalon noticed his odd behavior and was concerned that he could see Jack. She was ready to pounce if it became necessary.

"You can see me?" asked Jack as he stood up.

Tobias laughed like he had brain damage and said, "Of course, why wouldn't I?"

"Because I have technology that should make me

invisible to you." Tobias tilted his head a bit and looked at Jack with an expressionless face.

"I know who you are, Jack Thomas," said Tobias as he sneered briefly, then smiled.

Jack could tell something was wrong with Tobias, but he played along. "Are you an angel?"

"Yes, Jack, I'm an angel. I'm here to give you some help." His face twitched a little then settled on a malice-filled smile.

Still in stealth mode, Charalon walked over and stood right next to Jack. Tobias kept his eyes on Jack and ignored her.

"I don't think you are an angel," said Jack.

Tobias chuckled and shook his head saying, "You're right, Jack, and you're all alone, just like Malcolm said. You think you are protected, but watch this." Tobias stepped over and punched Jack in the chest, knocking him flat on his back. It happened so fast that even Charalon was caught by surprise. She started to reach for Tobias's throat, but then couldn't move. Tobias leapt on Jack. He had a perverse smile on his face as he placed his hand on Jack's chest. He was somehow able to reach through the force field and inflict great pain. Jack cried out in anguish as he lay there. Tobias was trying to kill him and it looked like he just might pull it off.

All of a sudden, a loud boom and bright flash of light went off right between Charalon and Tobias. It knocked her to the ground. When she looked up to see what had just happened, there stood Dominic in his true form. Charalon was stunned by his appearance and couldn't move.

Dominic looked angrily at Tobias who looked terrified.

"What do you want with me, Dominic?" cried Tobias as he fell to his knees. He begged for mercy saying, "Let me go, Dominic. Please have pity on me."

Dominic moved as fast as the blink of an eye. He stepped forward and put his hand on Tobias's forehead.

"Get out, Tobias," said Dominic. Tobias let out a loud scream and clenched his fists. He screamed for a couple seconds then went limp and fell unconscious to the ground. Dominic turned his attention to Charalon. She was on her knees, bowing before him. Tears were running down her face. Jack watched, unable to say anything.

"Get up, Charalon. No one should bow down to me," said Dominic. Then he turned his attention to Jack and said, "Remember, Jack, you must not put your trust in anyone, or anything on earth."

Jack blinked his eyes and looked at Dominic again. He now appeared as a man. He gave Jack an understanding and compassionate smile. Dominic looked back at Charalon who was now standing and said, "It is not with your eyes that you see me, Charalon." He smiled at her then turned and touched Tobias. At once both of them disappeared, leaving Jack and Charalon in a daze.

Jack got up and said, "Well, that was Dominic."

Very little was said as they walked back. As they got close to the facility, Charalon stopped. Jack turned to see why she stopped. She was staring at the ground in thought.

"When you told me about Dominic's true appearance, Jack, I knew it was a profound experience for you. I thought that was because you were flesh and blood, subject to your own human perceptions. What I saw today was certainly real."

"I'm glad you saw him too. Now I know that I'm not crazy."

"No, you're not crazy, Jack. I thought I was malfunctioning when I felt that Tobias was one of Underwood's men. I had a strong feeling that something about him was evil. I didn't know why. I mean, really, why would one of Malcolm Underwood's people be up here?"

Jack sighed and said, "Dominic had warned me that his enemies are working with Underwood, and that they know who my family and friends are. If they are anything like him, it shouldn't be a surprise that they'd find their way here."

Charalon nodded and said, "I would bet you're ready for lunch."

After returning to the facility, they had lunch and then went to the memory room. Laloed had requested that they upload their memories of the event.

The next day after breakfast, Charalon and Jack sat by the fire. As they were discussing the trip to Spokane, Jerrech came to the cafeteria. He picked up a chair and brought it over to the lounge, then sat down with them.

"Laloed asked me to work on a way for you to be invisible to Underwood's men. After your experience yesterday, I now have enough data to do that. After reviewing the memory playback of the incident, it was obvious that Tobias couldn't see Charalon. I think I can mask the human signature you emit, Jack. Of course, you will want to test that before you get into a situation where it might matter," said Jerrech.

"Is this something you can accomplish by upgrading the ILEFF programming?" asked Charalon.

Jerrech nodded and said, "Yes, I will have it ready within an hour, so you can still leave today. Laloed said you should take some gold with you, in case you need to stay there for more than a day or two. I've also enabled your ILEFF to act like a homing signal, Jack. If all else fails, we can send the VTOL to bring you back. We will be following your progress through Charalon's reports. Do you have any questions or suggestions?"

Jack shook his head.

Charalon said, "Let me know when we can head out. We will get ready in the meantime."

"Very well," said Jerrech. He got up and went back to the maintenance room to finish the work on the ILEFF.

Charalon looked at Jack and said, "I'm going to take a couple changes of clothes. You should bring some extra clothes too. I will bring some drone bugs and other equipment for surveillance."

"I will take a shower and can be ready within 15 minutes," said Jack.

"Me too, Jack. We could run the van to the house. I know Jerrech can transmit the upgrade to us there."

"Do we have the addresses of Underwood and his followers?" asked Jack.

Charalon said, "We have the address of the place where they meet. Our bug drones should be able to follow them from there. It shouldn't take very long to map their every move."

"Should I meet you at the main entrance?"

Charalon nodded and said, "I'll see you there."

After getting ready they met at the main entrance. She was carrying a travel bag with clothes over her shoulder and a medium-sized metal suitcase-looking box. Jack had his two changes of clothes in his travel bag.

"Jerrech already finished the upgrade program and it has been successfully installed. We are cleared for takeoff," said Charalon.

It wasn't long before they had taken the van down to the rented house and had the Camaro on the road.

It was 10:30 a.m. when they left the house. The first hour of the two and a half hour drive to Spokane was spent in relative silence. A lot had happened that day. As Jack was driving the car, he would look over at Charalon once in a while. After about an hour she said, "I'm fine, Jack. There's a lot on my mind right now."

"Do you want to talk about it?"

She stretched her legs out a bit and put her hands behind her head. She had a contemplative look on her face. After a moment she said, "Yes, I would. I have been thinking about our run-in with Tobias yesterday. We both had the ILEFF systems set to stealth. He could see you, but not me. I was disturbed by that, at first. It made me feel like I might be just a machine, but then Dominic said, 'It's not with your eyes that you see me, Charalon.'"

Jack cut in with, "I think he said, '<u>It is</u> not with your eyes that you see me, Charalon.'"

She smiled at that and said, "I see your point. Anyway, I was encouraged when Dominic was interested that I could see him. I also liked it when he referred to me as 'one' when he told me not to bow down to him. Charalona believed in God, and so do I. If Dominic is an angel, then he is a representative of God. I feel like God validated my existence through Dominic."

"Did you see him with the DSIRN system?" he asked.

Charalon's eyes got big as she thought about it. "No, I

didn't have it on. I should have turned it on when I suspected Tobias was one of Underwood's men, but I didn't. I could see and hear Dominic with my own senses. I had been concerned that I might not have any spiritual relevance," she said.

"Most of my life, I have been agnostic. I really wanted to believe that there was a God. It sounds to me like you've spent most of your life wondering if there was a you. I think the events as of late have settled those questions for both of us," said Jack.

She smiled broadly and said, "It would seem so."

For the rest of the trip, they didn't talk much. Jack occasionally would look over at Charalon and see her smiling. She had a smile on her face the rest of the way to Spokane.

When they arrived in Spokane, Charalon already had a motel picked out. Jack paid for the room and they found their way to it. He opened the door with the key and stopped in the doorway. He was surprised to find only one bed in the room. She slipped past him and said, "Don't worry, Jack, I'm not planning on sleeping."

He lay down on the bed and said, "Right, that's what I thought. I'm going to try to rest here for a bit. I just need to relax for a while."

"Okay, Jack, I'll try to be quiet."

Charalon set the metal suitcase on a table and opened it. With it lying open on the table, she took out a small container and removed the cap. Some tiny flying bug-like objects flew out and hovered next to her. There were about ten of them. When she tapped on a panel in the suitcase, the bugs flew over to the door. She opened the door and let them out.

Although he was trying to rest with his eyes closed, Jack was interested in what she was up to. He rolled over to watch her.

"I'm setting up a security perimeter. Those guys will be our lookouts. They will take up positions in and around this building and send information back to this receiver," said Charalon pointing at the suitcase. "The data they send back will be analyzed by an A.I. program. Jerrech upgraded it with the DSIRN system, so those bug probes will be able to identify Underwood's followers. If they see anything suspicious, we will be alerted."

"Well, I guess I'll be able to sleep good knowing that. Though it doesn't seem fair that I get to sleep while you watch out for trouble, Charalon."

She sat down in a chair by the bed and said, "Don't worry a bit about it. This is a dream come true for me. I get to go on a trip with my best friend and have something to do at night. I only sleep when I don't have anything to do, Jack."

"Do we have to go to the place where Underwood's people meet, or can we send the probes to it from here?" he asked.

"We should bring them there. They will use too much power getting there and have little left for the stakeout. We could drive past that place and release some probes as we go by. We wouldn't want to stop and raise suspicion," said Charalon.

"We could get something to eat, then drive past their place on the way back."

"What would you like for lunch, Jack?"

"I suppose you have memorized every possible place to go within a two-mile radius."

Charalon smiled and said, "I have a current database

of every possible place on the planet. It's an android thing."

"Well, then I suppose I'd like a deli sandwich and a mocha latte."

"It's 12:35 p.m. local time. We should head out for lunch now," she said.

Jack rolled over and sat up saying, "That sounds pretty good. I wasn't going to sleep anyway. I just thought I'd lie here for a bit. I'll be ready in a couple minutes."

After stopping at a deli shop, they found a parking lot and had lunch in the car. Jack had also gotten a sandwich for Charalon and was watching to see if she bowed her head before eating it. When she did, he waited then asked her, "I've noticed that you bow your head before you have your food. Are you giving thanks for your meal?"

Charalon looked surprised and said, "Even androids do things unconsciously at times. Charalona always said grace before dinner, and so do I. As you know, I inherited my spirituality from her. I didn't have to believe the same as her, but I came to believe what she believed."

"Even with all the scientific knowledge she accumulated over a couple hundred years, she still believed in God?"

Charalon answered, "After two hundred years of scientific research with DNA, Charalona was more convinced of the existence of a creator. As she gained more understanding about the complexity of proteins and cells, she realized how improbable it was for life to spontaneously occur. The whole Darwinian view of human origins became a rather silly concept in the minds of objective scientists as the years went by.

Anthropologists kept looking for indisputable proof of evolution in the fossil record. After a hundred more years of digging, they found no conclusive proof. Only the truly committed believers in the theory of evolution still believed in it. It eventually became a state-recognized religion."

Jack looked puzzled by what Charalon just said. He asked, "Are you saying that people who believed in evolution started their own religion?"

She answered, "Charalona would say that they already have, in this time. They just don't call it a religion yet. What is religion, after all, other than a group of people who have reached a consensus on what they believe? She saw evolutionists in the same light as any other faith-based group."

"I never really thought of it that way."

Charalon continued, "Faith and science could be combined if people were truly objective. The people who believe in evolution are convinced that it's just science. I think they chose what to believe in and looked for scientific evidence to support their beliefs. People always interpret scientific evidence the way that suits them best. Science is most useful when it studies how things work, rather than why. That's when people cross over from science to religion."

Jack said, "Through science, many things were discovered. Many advances were made. You are the result of scientific advancement."

"I'm not saying that you have to side with religion, or science. I don't think the two are in opposition to each other. People are in opposition to each other. They use their religion, or their science, to support their side," she said.

"I would agree with that. I believe in God now. In light of recent events, I would say there's no doubt in my mind of the metaphysical."

Charalon smiled and said, "Well, this has been a nice discussion, but we'd better get going. I've got some drone bugs to release."

Charalon gave Jack instructions to Underwood's meeting place. The rather plain building looked like it might have been a warehouse at one time. It was a flat-topped structure with no windows, measuring about a hundred feet long by fifty feet wide. It had red clapboard siding with a set of double doors on one end. A sign hung above the doors with "The People's Church" stenciled on it. As they drove past, Charalon released the drone bugs. She pulled out a small device from her pocket and tapped the screen on it with her finger. "Well, the drones are taking up positions around that building. They're already sending back information to the receiver," she said.

"Should we go back to the room right away?"

"We have some time before their meeting tonight, Jack. We have a microwave and a refrigerator in our room. Let's go get some food and drinks for dinner in the room tonight. That way we won't be distracted during their meeting later."

"Okay, it's a plan," said Jack.

Chapter 19
The Face Of Evil

They had just got back to their room and Charalon checked the drone receiver. All the drone bugs had reported in and were sending their observation data.

"Everything here looks good," she said. "We just have to wait and see what happens."

"What time will they start showing up?"

"The information we got from Alec Normanson's book indicated they show up for 'church' anywhere from 6:30 to 7:00 p.m. It's only 2:30, so you can rest for a while if you want, Jack."

"I think I was just a little tired from the drive over here. I'm not really that tired now. That coffee did its job," he said.

"Okay, we could go for a walk, or maybe a Camaro drive with the top down. It's looking pretty nice out right now. The weather forecast for this evening looks pretty good too."

Jack thought about it for a moment and said, "I was going to say we should go to Riverfront Park, but maybe that would be a good idea for tomorrow. I think I'd be happy to spend some time here with my good friend Charalon."

She laughed out loud, then asked, "Okay, what's on the TV that you want to watch?"

Jack smiled and said, "No, really, I just wanted to sit

around and talk about religion, and maybe some politics."

Charalon's eyes narrowed. "That's pretty good, Jack. What are you going to say when I make you do that?" She smiled, showing her teeth.

"You know, a movie is sounding pretty good right about now," he said reaching for the TV remote.

Charalon had a moment of discovery look on her face. "I could show you one of my movie favorites. I have a vast movie library in my database, including movies from the alternate future timeline. The drone receiver has a holographic projection display I could play them on. Pretty cool, huh?" she said.

"You're still full of surprises, aren't you?"

"I think I have just the movie for you, Jack."

"What century was it filmed in?"

"You'll just have to watch and see," she said. "I just sent the file to the drone receiver and it's ready to play."

"Okay, let's get it started."

Jack sat down in one of the chairs. Charalon lowered the shades and shut off the lights. A light beam shot up from the receiver and formed a holographic rectangular flat screen with a six-foot diagonal above the unit. The screen was like a flat-screen TV but had incredible definition and 3D qualities. As the movie started, Jack couldn't tell where the sound was coming from. There were no visible speakers, but it sounded like a surround sound system.

"Wow, that is amazing. It makes me wonder why you had a regular old TV in your room," said Jack.

"That TV wasn't exactly as it appeared, Jack. I kind of like the retro decor. I'll let you watch it sometime."

209

It was 6:00 p.m. Jack had watched a couple movies. It was now time to monitor the receiver information. Charalon set the receiver to display the drone bug imagery and stretched the display out to about eight feet. The display was broken up into ten different boxes showing each bug's perspective.

"Are we going to try to get a bug into the building?"

"If we get the chance, we will. We should have quite a few chances, Jack. There are about fifty members showing up here tonight. Of them, there are three individuals we need to pay attention to. The names I have are Willy Dean, age 40; Tom Jensen, age 36; and Chip Dawson, age 30. Everything will be recorded and analyzed by the A.I. programs, so it should be easy to identify them."

As they watched the building, a man who looked to be in his forties came walking up. He was a chubby guy about five foot six inches tall with red hair, a three-day beard and a baseball cap. He paced up and down the sidewalk in front of the building.

A blue sedan pulled up and parallel parked along the street. A man got out of the car and walked up to the man with the baseball cap. He was a tall man about six foot two inches with male pattern baldness. He was dressed in a red plaid shirt with blue jeans. The two of them stood side by side looking around as if they were expecting trouble.

"Do you see that? I think they're aware of us, but I don't know how that could be," said Jack.

Charalon watched them with interest. "I see that too, but they might be a lookout of sorts. I have a feeling that something illegal or immoral is about to happen," she said.

Just about that time a light blue panel van pulled up and parked behind the blue sedan. The two men standing nearby looked around more intently. After looking around a little more, the six-foot-tall man in the red plaid shirt walked over to the church door and opened it. The chubby man with the ball cap looked at the van and nodded. At once, the two front doors of the van opened and two men got out. They both went to the back of the van in a coordinated manner and opened the rear doors, letting two other men out. The four men from the van extracted a long wooden box and packed it toward the church doors.

"I think I can get a bug on that box," said Charalon. "There, I got it."

Jack looked puzzled and asked, "You're controlling them with a wireless connection aren't you?"

She looked at him with furrowed eyebrows then turned her attention back to the drone bug imagery on the display.

He said, mostly to himself, "Right, that was a dumb question."

Jack watched the men carry the box through the doors.

Charalon was preoccupied by the drone bug transmissions. All of a sudden, she let out a, "Ha!" then said, "I got another bug in there."

Jack turned his attention to the display and watched as the men carried the box into a large room and set it on the floor.

Charalon looked surprised and said, "There's somebody trapped in that box. I can hear him trying to get out."

Jack's eyes got big. "What?"

211

"Listen to this," said Charalon as she muted the sound from all but the bug on the box.

Some thumping noises and a man's muffled voice could be heard. "Help, somebody please let me out...I won't tell anybody, if you let me go."

The men ignored the sounds coming from the box. It seemed to Jack like maybe they had done this before. The men mulled around the room a little then went back outside. One of the men got into the van and drove off. The rest of them took up various positions around the front of the building and stood motionless.

"Should we get over there in case he needs our help?"

Charalon looked worried. "I don't know. It might be some kind of initiation into their group. We might blow our cover for no reason, but if we're wrong..."

"If we're wrong, that man could end up dead," he said.

Charalon grimaced at the thought and said, "From what I know about them, it's unlikely that they would kill anyone at their church. Let's wait a bit and see what happens."

Jack turned his attention to the room where they set the box. The room was about thirty feet by forty feet. There were about fifty folding chairs arranged in concentric circles around a table in the center of the room. The table had a black stone top measuring about four feet by seven feet.

After a while, some other cars pulled up and parked along the road. As the people got out of their cars, they ignored the men standing around and went into the building. They were women and men who were dressed like they were going to church. None of the people were talking to each other as they entered the building. They just silently entered the room and sat down in the chairs around the table staring straight ahead. More people came in and took their seats filling the room. Soon, every seat was filled with an individual remaining silent and expressionless.

Three men still remained outside. They were standing side by side on the sidewalk out by the road.

Twenty minutes after the room was filled, Jack turned to Charalon and said, "There aren't any more empty seats in there. What are they waiting for?"

"I don't know, Jack, but I have identified those three standing by the road."

"The short chubby guy and the tall balding guy in the red plaid shirt were the first guys here. I don't recognize the other guy," he said.

"He was driving that van earlier. His name is Chip Dawson. Jerrech just sent me some more information on him and the other two."

Chip was clean-cut and about five feet ten inches tall with a stocky build. He had black hair and appeared to be around thirty years old. He was the only one who showed any emotion. Chip looked like he was angry about something.

"The short chubby guy is Willy Dean and the tall guy in the red shirt and blue jeans is Tom Jensen. They are the ones we need to watch. Willy and Tom there are Malcolm Underwood's two most trusted followers. The man we ran into up on the mountain, who called himself 'Tobias,' had been Malcolm's right hand man. His real name was John Branch," said Charalon.

Jack scratched his head and said, "I wonder what Dominic did with him."

"I wonder too. It has now been thirty minutes since

213

they filled all the seats. It seems strange that they would stand around for so long."

About that time, Willy looked at Chip and motioned him to go inside. Tom and Willy followed him into the building. The people sitting in the chairs ignored them as they walked into the room. Willy went to the center of the room while Tom and Chip stood behind the people in the chairs.

Willy cleared his throat and started speaking, "I, Ethorn, call this meeting to order. We have lost one of our own, but we will not be deterred. We will not be hindered by the actions of our enemies." Willy walked around the table and looked the people in the first row in their eyes. Then he looked at the floor and held his arms out with his hands clenched into fists.

"Who here will offer himself to be the new vessel of Tobias?" asked Willy in a loud voice.

Chip declared, "I will stand and be counted."

"Then come and stand with me," said Willy.

Chip made his way through the people in the chairs and stood next to Willy. They stood there together in silence for a couple minutes. Chip had an angry sneer on his face, like he was about to exact vengeance on someone. Tom tapped two strong-looking men sitting in the back row on their shoulders and they got up. The two followed Tom over to the wooden box. He unlocked it and opened the lid. The two men extracted a shirtless, handcuffed male in his early twenties and laid him on the table. It looked like he had been in the box for a while and was too weak to fight them.

"Somebody help me," he said, looking to the people in the chairs, but they were unaffected by his pleas for help. They just stared at him with indifference. Willy reached under the table and retrieved some straps. The strong men held him as Willy removed the handcuffs and belted him down on his back.

With his hands and feet strapped down, all he could do was lift his head up a little and look around. He found no sympathetic faces in the crowd. About that time, Willy pushed his head down and put a strap across it. He was now completely immobilized and helpless.

Tom stood beside Willy and the two strong men returned to their chairs. Tom looked at the man on the table and his face twitched. One corner of his mouth fluctuated between a smile and a blank look. He began to drool like a begging dog. Willy noticed Tom's zeal and smiled with cruel delight.

Chip began to chant, "I am the vessel," over and over, then walked around the room. As he made his way through the people, he held his arms straight out with clenched fists and chanted, "So let it be done." Willy and Tom echoed, "So let it be done," repeatedly.

Charalon got up quickly and said, "We have to get over there, now. They are going to kill him." They hurriedly got out to the car and left. Charalon had a worried and sad look on her face. "I think I messed up," she said. "We should have left as soon as we knew there was somebody in that box."

Jack sped up, but Charalon said nothing about his excessive speed. When they got within a block of the church, Charalon yelled, "No way!" Jack looked ahead and saw what caused Charalon to react. There were no cars parked by the building. It looked like nobody had been there for a while. As they approached the building, Charalon said, "Don't stop here. Park along the road when we get to the next block."

As Jack parked the car, Charalon pulled a device out of her pocket and showed him the display. The meeting was still going on. She switched it to the outside view and it showed cars still parked in front of the building.

"How can that be, Charalon?"

She looked frustrated and said, "The feed from the drones has been delayed. There's no other explanation. I'd bet that when we saw them standing around for so long, they were really killing that man."

"That would explain how they could be gone already. Do you want to wait and see if anybody comes out of there?"

"No, I'm pretty sure there's nobody there. Let's get back to the room and analyze the data," she said.

Jack pulled back on the road and headed back to the motel. When they got to the room, Charalon released a new batch of drone bugs to watch over the motel. She looked at Jack and said, "I have destroyed the first group of drone bugs in case they too have been compromised. Jack, I reviewed some of the surveillance data on the way over here. It didn't turn out well for the man on the table. I thought I should warn you ahead of time, because we still need to watch it."

"Okay, I will do my best."

"I don't fully know what we're up against, Jack. They knew we were watching them. They act like we are no threat to them, and maybe they're right. Our technology so far hasn't given us the advantage I thought it would."

Charalon closed her eyes and took a deep breath. "Okay, the feed is still coming in. I'll start it where we left off. Everything we see now has already happened," she said.

Jack turned his attention back to the receiver display

and watched.

Willy reached under the table and grabbed a small case and set it on the table. He placed his hands on it and looked around the room at the people sitting in the chairs. Tom stood there next to Willy staring out over the people. Willy turned his attention to the case and opened it. He took a small knife out of the case and held it up for the people to see. It was a small dagger with a short, stubby blade.

"Let the process begin," said Willy. Then he stabbed the man in the side of his neck. The man looked like he had already given up. He hardly flinched at all. The blood that flowed from his neck was channeled to the edge of the table by a groove cut into it. A large bowl sat on the floor and caught the blood as it flowed from the table.

Willy looked at Chip, who was standing in the back of the room. "Come," he said.

Chip made his way through the people and stood next to Tom. Willy reached under the table again and retrieved another case. He set it on the table. He opened the much larger case and removed three daggers with six-inch-long blades. He set two of them on the table in front of Chip and Tom and set the third on the other side of the table by the man's head. Willy bent down and picked up the bowl, letting the blood from the table drip on the floor, and set it on the table.

Charalon paused the video and said, "I'm going to enable the DSERN function, in case there are other things in that room we can't see."

At once Willy and Tom's faces changed to a distorted and grotesque representation of themselves. They remained recognizable, but looked hideous. Everybody else looked as they had before.

"That's probably what Tobias would have looked like had I activated the DSERN on the mountain," said Charalon.

"That's so creepy, Charalon. I don't think I've ever seen anything like that before."

Willy reached under the table again and picked up an old ceramic pitcher. He set it on the table. Then he poured the blood from the bowl into it and set the bowl back under the table.

"Drink," said Willy, looking at Chip. Chip picked up the pitcher and drank its entire contents. He had some blood and a perverse smile on his face as he set the pitcher under the table. Willy stepped around to the other side of the table near the man's head. Tom sidestepped over a little and stood opposite Willy. Chip was standing at the midpoint of the table on the same side as Tom.

Willy looked at Chip and nodded. At once the three of them picked up the daggers in their right hands and held them over their heads. Suddenly Willy yelled at the top of his lungs, "Now!"

Chipped plunged his dagger into the far side of the man's abdomen and pulled it to himself. The man began screaming in pain. Chip threw his head back and laughed in a sick and twisted manner before setting the dagger on the table.

Willy looked at Tom and held up his finger. "Let him relish the moment, Zomins," he said. Then he nodded at Tom and the two of them simultaneously plunged their daggers into the man's head through his eyes, killing him.

At once the room was silent as the man lay there with the daggers stuck in his eye sockets. Chip looked at the floor, extended his arms out and clenched his hands into fists. A dark, shadowy figure could be seen standing behind Chip. When he looked up, the figure was gone and his face had the same grotesque appearance as Willy and Tom.

Willy turned to the people and said, "It is done." Some of the people leapt from their chairs and licked the blood from the floor and table. Others began cleaning the place up.

All of a sudden, one of the two inside views went black. On the other inside view, an image of Tom walking up to it and crushing the drone bug with his fingers could be seen. That view went black. Charalon paused the video.

"They knew all along about the drone bugs," said Charalon.

Jack looked over at Charalon to see her face covered in tears. When she looked back at him, he couldn't keep it together and bent over covering his face with his hands.

"There's something I need to show you, Jack. I don't know what to make of it. I think I saw somebody, in that group, who shouldn't be there."

Charalon looked at the display screen and it showed a view of the people sitting in the chairs. She said, "Now watch this." Jack looked up and watched the display.

The video suddenly went black and she said, "That's not what I wanted you to see." Then she looked confused and said, "I can't believe it. All the recorded video from the drone bugs just self-destructed. We have no video files in the receiver."

"How is that possible?" asked Jack.

"I don't know. I don't understand much about the metaphysical world, but I know this group had something to do with it."

"What were you going to show me, Charalon?"

"I was going...wait a minute, they don't know that one of us is an android. I can play my own memories back on this communicator for you to see. They think we have no video evidence of their crimes, but it's all right here," she said, pointing to her head.

She pulled the communicator from her pocket and handed it to Jack. Video was playing of a pan across the people in the chairs. The pan stopped at a lady sitting in the back row next to a large man. Jack sat there stunned as the video zoomed in on her face. It was his Sharon.

"We have to get out of here," said Charalon.

Chapter 20
The War Begins

It was late Wednesday evening, June 17. Jack and Charalon had just witnessed the horrible killing at the hands of Malcolm Underwood's group. They called themselves "The People's Church."

She was picking things up around the drone receiver and putting them away in it. Jack was getting the food and drinks out of the refrigerator. He put them into sacks and carried them out to the car. When he got back to the room, Charalon had everything ready to go.

"Do you have another motel in mind?"

"We have a few options, Jack, but let's talk about that in the car." He nodded and followed Charalon. They got into the car and left the parking lot. Jack drove west for a while and pulled into a large parking lot.

He said, "I know you're right. We have to get another motel room." Charalon was staring at the floor. She still looked teary-eyed and sad.

"I'm a little messed up right now," she said. "My emotional safety program keeps trying to shut my emotions off, but I want to feel them right now. It helps me to make sense of all that I saw."

Jack reached over and put his hand on her shoulder and said, "I'm not doing so good either." He looked around and saw a ritzy, tall hotel building not far away. He pointed at the hotel and asked, "What do you think about staying there?"

Charalon looked up. "It looks kind of expensive, but we really don't have to worry about money. Let's go there," she said.

Jack drove over to the hotel and parked. He looked at Charalon and said, "I have plenty of cash in my wallet. You can stay here and I'll handle getting the room if you want."

She looked relieved and said, "Thank you. I could use a little time here in the car, Jack."

He left her in the car and went into the hotel lobby. He was not feeling well but made his way to the front desk and paid for a nice room. When he got back into the car, Charalon was clearly feeling better.

"You look better already. You'll have to show me how to do that someday."

Charalon smiled a little and said, "Sure, we just have to surgically implant some emotion control modules in your brain."

Jack shook his head and smiled, acknowledging her humor then parked the car.

Once in the room, Jack set his bags down by a bed and collapsed onto it. It was a nice room with two beds and all the trimmings of a three-star hotel. Charalon set her things down by the other bed and sat on it.

He had not let himself think about the murder or that Sharon might have been one of the members there. The thought of Sharon sitting there, in that group, made Jack nauseous. Many emotions welled up inside. He was bewildered by all that he saw. He sat up and swung his feet over the side. His hands were shaking. Jack looked over at Charalon to see if she noticed his condition.

Charalon was staring at the floor and sobbing. Her holographic disguise was off and she looked like herself. Jack got up and sat by her with his arm around her. She leaned up against him and started to cry out loud. After a couple moments, she stopped crying and said, "Thanks, Jack. I needed that. One of the good things about being an android is it only takes a little affection to be comforted. I'm alright now."

"That's good, Charalon, because I might need a shoulder too. It's all starting to sink in, but still I'm having a hard time believing that was Sharon."

"It's very hard for me to think that she would be there. Everything I know about her says there's no way that could be her, but there she was," she said.

"With all this supernatural activity going on, it's hard to know what we saw. However, that might explain how Tobias knew where to look for me. If they got to Sharon, they might have been able to get the information out of her, one way or another. I still can't believe she would just sit there and watch something like that," said Jack.

"Me neither. I'm not trying to change the subject, but it's after 10:00 p.m. and you still haven't had any dinner."

"I don't know if I want anything."

"I hate to sound like your mother, but you really should eat something," said Charalon. She got up and put the perishable food into the refrigerator. Then she tossed Jack a box of snack crackers they had bought earlier.

He caught the crackers and said, "Thanks, Charalon."

"I might actually want to sleep tonight, Jack, so don't get any crackers in my bed."

Jack smiled and said, "Okay, I'll have them on my bed then." He got up and went back to his bed with the box of crackers.

Charalon set the drone bug receiver on her bed and opened it. She took a device out of it that Jack had not seen before. She pressed a button on it and it lit up. Holding it in her hand, she said, "This is a mini-replicator device. I need to make up more drone bugs."

As she replicated the drone bugs, Jack finished off the crackers. "Do you think we should tell the police about what we saw?" he asked.

"Yes, I do. I was thinking I could make a DVD of my memories with this mini-replicator. If we write a note explaining what we saw to go along with the DVD, we could mail it to the police. I think we could pull it off anonymously," said Charalon as she released some drone bugs. She opened the door and let them out into the hallway.

"What happens when they run out of power? Could they fall into the wrong hands?"

"No need to worry, Jack. When the drone bugs exhaust their power supply they self-destruct, leaving only dust. If any of our technology gets lost or stolen, it will self-destruct. I should have told you that about your communicator. If you leave it somewhere and get too far from it, it will self-destruct and you'll never find it. Even your beloved Camaro has technology that will do the same."

Jack looked worried and asked, "The whole car?"

"No, just the high-tech stuff in it."

"Good," he said looking relieved.

Charalon chuckled and shook her head. She set the replicator device on a table in the corner. "You might want to watch this, Jack. It's kind of cool." He got up and stood by the table watching the device. Many different colored light beams emitted from one end of the device toward the table. They started moving slowly in circles at first, then sped up to faster than the eye could see. On the table where the light beams were aimed, a round shape started to form. After a minute, the light beams stopped and a DVD lay there on the table.

"That is cool," said Jack.

"I transferred some of my memories to video and edited them into a short film for the police to look at. I couldn't include the parts where I saw their faces with the DSERN function turned on. That would be too unbelievable."

Jack looked at the TV in the room and noticed it had a DVD player built into it. He pointed to the TV and asked, "Do you think we should test it in that player?"

"You can if you like, but it's a good copy."

Jack turned on the TV and put the disk into the player. There was only about thirty seconds of video. A shot of the outside of the building and the van pulling up was the first clip. Then a good shot of Willy and Tom followed by the men packing the box into the building. The last shot showed the young man tied down to the table before and after they killed him.

"Nice work, Charalon. You got the license plate of the van and the sign over the door." He looked over at Charalon to see her finishing the handwritten note.

She looked up and said, "There, I'd like to see the face of the guy who tests the DNA on this note. I suppose they'll analyze the handwriting as well. That should be good. I'm planning to hack into the Spokane police department's system so we can keep tabs on them. That way we'll know if we need to give them anything else."

"You're not planning on planting evidence are you?"

"I'm willing to do whatever it takes to bring these

guys down. We have to bring them down. We have to stop Malcolm Underwood from becoming a threat to this world."

"Did Laloed tell you something I don't know?"

"Yes. He thinks that Malcolm Underwood could become just as big of a threat to this timeline as he was in the other. You know how Laloed likes to run his numbers. I have a feeling he might be right."

"I think he mentioned that as a possibility. I don't remember him being that concerned about it though," said Jack.

"He wasn't that concerned about it at first. Now, he is." She took an empty plastic bag and looked closely at it. "No fingerprints on the bag," she said as she placed the note and DVD in it.

"You look like you're planning to go mail that tonight, Charalon. Do you want a ride somewhere?"

"No, I'm going to take it right to the police station tonight. I'll use the little blonde holographic disguise. You can watch me the whole time. I'm going to set the drone bug receiver to display what I see. If our theory about them is right, that they can't see me, then I should be just fine. Besides, there's a police department only about four blocks southwest of here. It's not even a mile away," she said.

"Okay, if you think that's what you want to do."

"I'll be okay, Jack." She tucked the sack into her shirt and said, "If I carry this in my hand, it will be partly visible. I'm going to stay in stealth mode most of the way."

Jack nodded and said, "I know you'll be fine."

Charalon set the receiver to display what she saw and left the room in stealth mode. Jack turned his attention back to the display. She was down the stairs and out of the building in no time at all. It was dark, but Jack could see quite well through her eyes. She started running and it looked like she was moving at freeway speeds.

As she approached the police department, she slowed down and looked for a place to come out of stealth mode. Charalon stood behind a tree and looked around. It was late and dark out, so there weren't many people out on the street. She took the bag out from her shirt and appeared as the short blonde. Then she walked over to the police department and entered the building.

"Can I help you?" asked a receptionist as Charalon approached her desk.

"Yes, I have some information here that might be useful in solving the recent ritual killings." She set the bag on the desk and headed for the door.

"Wait, I need to get your name," said the lady at the desk. Charalon ignored her and left the building. Once outside she looked around and went into stealth mode. A police officer came running out of the building, but he was too late. Charalon started running and was back at the hotel room in less than two minutes.

"Wow, that was awesome," said Jack as she came through the door. "You weren't gone for more than five minutes."

"Well, I am pretty awesome," she said with a smile. She sat on her bed and kicked off her shoes. "You know, Jack, I might just get some sleep tonight. I'm not tired, but maybe some time spent dreaming would be good for me."

"You set the drone bugs to warn us if anything looks suspicious to them, right?"

"Yes, if something looks fishy to them, an alarm will

227

sound and the display monitor will show the threat," she said.

"I'm thinking about taking a shower and going to bed. You weren't planning on taking a shower were you?"

Charalon said, "I was, Jack, but you go ahead and take one first. I was thinking now would be a good time to hack the law. I kind of want to know what they're doing with the information I gave them."

"Okay," he said as he got up and went into the bathroom. When he came out in his pajamas, after a short shower, there were two coffees on the table between the beds.

"Did you have some extra time after hacking the police department?" asked Jack, motioning to the two lattes sitting there.

"Don't worry. They're decaf. I just thought after a day like the one we just had, it would be nice to have a coffee."

"That's some good logic, Charalon."

They had their coffees and visited for a bit. Then Jack said, "Goodnight, Charalon," and crawled under his blankets. He was asleep in no time.

She got up and stood by Jack's bed. She watched him sleep for a minute or two before taking a shower. She came out wearing an oversized T-shirt. Charalon stopped by Jack's bed and watched him sleep again. She looked like a new mother checking to see if her baby was breathing. She smiled and went to bed herself.

It was 3:00 a.m. Both Jack and Charalon were sleeping. Without warning, the drone bug receiver alarm sounded. It wasn't real loud, but it had a distinct sound that made Jack get up immediately. Charalon was up and on her feet in a flash. She was watching the receiver monitor.

"It's a good thing we came here, Jack. The drone bugs at the other motel just saw one of Malcolm's people. Look there he is."

The receiver monitor showed a man rifling through their former room. It was Willy Dean. Charalon pressed a button on the receiver and said, "DSERN system activate." At once Willy appeared as the grotesque and evil-looking monster they saw at the church. He was angry and frustrated, throwing stuff around the room.

Then he saw the drone bug and reached for it. Charalon was a step ahead of him and had the bug self-destruct before he could touch it. She pressed another button and a view of the room came back on the monitor. Willy was growling as he left the room.

"You can go back to sleep, Jack. I'll watch the monitor for any threats."

"I think I'll watch the monitor with you for a while."

Charalon looked curious and said, "They have to touch the bugs if they want to find us, Jack."

"That would explain a lot," he said.

She pressed another button on the control panel and said, "There, all the bugs except one have self-destructed. I have one more hovering high above the motel watching him."

"How about the drone bugs here? Do they see anything suspicious?"

"No, everything looks good here," said Charalon. "It seems we might have stirred up a hornet's nest. They are really coming after us. I wonder if they know we gave the police that DVD."

"I've been wanting to call Sharon to see if that was

her. I know that could lead them to us so I haven't called her," he said.

"I didn't want to make it harder for you, Jack, so I had Jerrech call her a few hours ago."

"How did that go?"

"She didn't answer, so we don't know anything yet," said Charalon. "I wanted to know."

"What do you think about praying for help, Charalon? I just think we could use the extra help."

"I really like that idea, Jack."

"I don't really know how to pray, so don't laugh. Okay?"

"You don't have to do it any one way, Jack. Just say what you want and believe that you have been heard," she said.

"Okay."

Charalon took Jack's hand and bowed her head. Jack didn't close his eyes or bow his head.

He said, "God, will you help us. I don't know what to say, but I know we need you on our side. These people are bad. Please help us stop them."

"Amen," said Charalon. "Was that your first prayer?"

"I think it might be. I feel like I can sleep now." Jack got back into bed and fell asleep at once. Charalon looked at him sleeping and smiled. She sat down on her bed and continued to monitor the drone bugs.

Jack woke to humming in the morning. Charalon was still sitting on her bed watching the monitor and humming a tune that he didn't recognize. He rubbed his eyes and sat up. Charalon turned and looked at him when she heard him stirring. "Good morning. How did you sleep?"

"Pretty good, actually. How was your night, Charalon?"

"Not bad. I've been listening to police transmissions and watching drone bug imagery. The police have already raided the church, but they haven't found any blood evidence. I went back over the church imagery in my mind and found that Malcolm Underwood was there. He was sitting in the back row looking inconspicuous."

"I thought it was strange that we haven't seen him yet," said Jack.

"He has always gone out of his way to fly under the radar. He likes to be the man pulling the strings behind the scene. I went over all the information we have on him last night. It seems that 'The People's Church' was an actual church before he got involved in it. They were a group of Christians who wanted a more permissive and tolerant church. By the time they bought that building, they had rejected fundamental Christian teachings altogether. That's when Malcolm came into the picture. It didn't take much to introduce his ideas at that point, Jack."

"It's better to stay true to your beliefs. If you're not, it just makes it easier for people like Malcolm Underwood," he said.

Chapter 21
Evasion

It was Thursday morning, June 18. Jack showered while Charalon monitored the drone bug receiver. When he came out, Charalon had a breakfast of diced ham and eggs and two coffees sitting on the table in the corner.

"That looks really good. Is it for me?" said Jack.

"Of course, I ordered it for you. The other coffee is for me though," she said as she handed him the plate.

"Thanks, Charalon. I'm really hungry this morning. Let's see how room service did." He sat in one of the armchairs with his breakfast. "Not bad, but it's hard to beat the food at the facility."

She handed him his coffee and said, "I got a message from Jerrech. He says he has another upgrade for the ILEFF system that should significantly improve our defenses when we're up against the supernatural." She took a drink. "I do love a good latte."

Jack took a drink from his cup and said, "This is good, but...well you know. The facility's coffee is hard to beat."

Charalon nodded in agreement. "I had a talk with Laloed last night. He thinks we should go to Sharon's apartment and check on her. I will look out for you from a distance in stealth mode. You need to know if that was her in the church," she said.

Jack looked hopeful and said, "I would really like

that. It would put me at ease to know she's alright, that is, if she is alright."

"We have a couple of stops to make today, Jack. Last night I was able to track Willy to a house. I think it's some kind of hideout location. The county tax records for the house show a Bert Simon as the owner. So far, I can't find anything else about him."

"When can we go check on Sharon?"

"I was thinking when we leave here we'd go there first. Then we'll have to check on Willy's hideout house and maybe test Jerrech's new upgrades. I would like to know if they can see us or not. There's a supermarket a block away from the house where Willy went. We could park there and walk over to the house," said Charalon.

"Is there anything more we can do while we're here, in Spokane?"

"Laloed is working on a plan. He told me to see if you had any ideas in the matter. Then he said something like, 'Jack is very smart, even without the brain enhancements.'"

"Well, I'll take that as a compliment."

"Laloed really doesn't like to compliment anyone, Jack. It's just that he knows how smart you are. Remember he has your memories up to the time you first visited the mountain, and a lifetime of memories from the other Jack. He knows what he's talking about."

"Thanks, Charalon, but it's hard for me to think of myself that way. When I look at my life so far, that's not what I see."

"He knows your potential, Jack. From what I know, you will tap into it."

After kicking back for a while, they checked out of

the hotel. It was about 10:30 a.m. when they got into the car and headed for Sharon's apartment.

Jack looked at Charalon and said, "So, you're going to be the brunette today?"

"Yeah, the police are kind of looking for a five-foot-tall blonde in her twenties right now. She is a person of interest in the ritual killings."

Jack chuckled and said, "Well, it was nice knowing her. I'm going to park a block away so Sharon doesn't see the Camaro. She'll be expecting me to be in my van."

"I'll walk to the apartment with you in stealth mode, Jack. I'm going to use the DSERN function just in case there's something that shouldn't be there."

"Like that thing we saw standing behind Chip?" he asked.

"Yes, I'd like to avoid things like that."

Jack parallel parked the Camaro about half a block away and Charalon went into stealth mode. As they approached Sharon's apartment, Charalon stopped and looked around. Jack walked up to Sharon's door and rang the doorbell. After a moment, he realized that Sharon would be at work. Fortunately, her apartment was on the first floor. He stepped over to a window and looked in. There was no furniture in the living room. Jack looked in another window and saw that Sharon had moved.

Charalon remained invisible and watchful. She was looking at the apartment when she saw something in the window. When Jack went to the other window, she saw it again. It was like the shadow of a person, but without the person. Charalon remained quiet, not wanting to give herself away to the form in the window.

Jack sighed and headed back to the car. As he was walking, he whispered, "Charalon, are you there?" She tapped him on the shoulder to let him know she was there. As they were getting into the car, she noticed a dark figure looking around a tree at Jack. He started the car and drove off.

Charalon reappeared as the brunette and said, "I saw one of those dark figures in Sharon's apartment and then hiding behind a tree. It saw you getting in the Camaro. Now they know what you're driving, but I don't think they know anything about me."

"I'm kind of feeling sick right now. Sharon doesn't live there now and I believe that was her we saw in that church."

"There might be a real good explanation, Jack. All we can do is move forward and hope."

"I just need to put it out of my mind for now," he said.

"It's a little early, but we could get some lunch if you want."

"Sure, that would be nice, Charalon."

Jack found a fast food restaurant and pulled into its parking lot.

"Do you want anything?" he asked.

"Yes, I would really like some french fries, but that's all. I'll stay out here and watch the car."

"Okay, I'll be right out."

After a bit, he came out carrying a sack and a couple coffees. He got into the car and asked, "Where would you like to have lunch?"

"There's a park not far from here. Just drive west two blocks and look to your right. I would like to go there. It's nice to be out in the sun now and then."

He looked around. He hadn't even noticed the beautiful weather. It was sunny with a slight breeze out of the west and not too hot. He drove to the park and found an unoccupied picnic table.

As they were having lunch, Charalon said, "I think it's a good idea to leave the DSERN function on, at least for now. Those things could be anywhere."

"Do I have to worry about running it low on power?"

"No, Jack, you can use all the functions at the same time for at least a hundred years. Jerrech could replace it before then."

"So, you're saying it will outlive me, right?" he asked.

"Not necessarily. The other Jack lived longer than that."

Jack said, "That's more than I want to think about right now."

"I would use the force-field function too, just in case."

"Okay, Charalon. I've got them both on now."

"Me too," she said.

After lunch, Charalon directed Jack to the supermarket near Willy's possible hideout house and he parked. They got out and looked for an out-of-sight place to go into stealth mode. They went between a couple motor homes and disappeared.

She whispered, "Are you ready for this, Jack?"

"I suppose I am," he whispered.

"Normally, I would tell you to follow me, but that won't work here. Let's walk toward the Camaro until we get to that stop sign, then cross the street and go west. The house is the third one on the left, white with the green trim," she whispered.

Jack quietly asked, "Then what?"

"You stay out by the road and keep watch. I'll look in the window and maybe even get inside, if I can. At some point, we need to test Jerrech's upgrades. We need to know if they can see either one of us," said Charalon, still whispering.

As they were walking to the house, Jack silently said a prayer. What he didn't know was that Charalon said one too. They had found that, even with all their advanced technology, success was not assured. Still, it was good to have it.

When they got to the house, Jack stayed out by the road on the sidewalk. It was an older, slightly dilapidated house with an old beat-up pickup in the driveway. The lawn looked like it had not been mowed or watered in some time.

Charalon crept up to the living room window and looked inside. There was Willy sitting in an easy chair watching TV. As soon as she saw him, he started looking around, then got out of the chair and just stood there. His face twitched and he looked around some more. Then he tilted his head back and sniffed the air. Charalon made up her mind to stay there and find out if Willy could see her. He walked over to the window and looked outside. He was only inches away from her. With the DSERN function on, he appeared grotesque and twisted to Charalon. Even though he couldn't see her, Willy was aware of her presence. She backed slowly away from the window. Then she backed up all the way to where Jack stood.

"He couldn't see me, but he knows something is up," she whispered.

Suddenly the door of the house flew open. Willy stepped out with a shotgun in his hands. He had a predatory appearance as he looked right, then left.

"I know you're out here. You don't know who you're dealing with. Maybe I'll just fire off a few shots here and there. What do you think of that?" snarled Willy.

He had the shotgun pointed toward Jack and Charalon. He took a couple steps toward them and looked around. When he didn't see anyone, he fired the shotgun in a couple random directions. They didn't move, even when Willy fired a shot right at them.

A neighbor looked out his door to see what was going on. Willy looked at him and growled. The neighbor backed into his house and locked the door. Willy got in the pickup with his shotgun and pulled out of the driveway and sped down the road toward the supermarket.

Charalon yelled, "Follow him." They ran after him staying in stealth mode.

As he passed the supermarket, Willy saw the Camaro. He made a sharp right-hand turn into the parking lot, making his tires squeal. He headed straight at the Camaro and accelerated.

"No you don't...oh..." said Jack.

Willy T-boned the Camaro in the driver's side pushing the car into a light pole before he came to a stop. He backed up and rammed the car again. With leaking antifreeze and steam spewing from the truck, he sped off. There were some people in the parking lot who pulled out their phones and were making calls. One of them took a video of Willy ramming the Camaro the second time.

"It won't be long before the police get here. I'm going to get our stuff out of the car," said Charalon.

She ran between the motor homes and came out looking like the old lady with a head scarf. Charalon ran over to the car and grabbed their bags and equipment, then took off on foot out of the parking lot.

Jack followed her in stealth mode to an alley. She changed her appearance to a red-haired middle-aged lady and said, "You should set your appearance to look like someone else too."

Jack picked an appearance from his selections as an overweight, middle-aged, balding man with a white tank top and blue jeans.

Charalon looked at him and said, "Nice."

Jack smiled and asked, "What now?"

"We are going to abandon the Camaro, Jack. Its technology has already self-destructed, so we don't have to worry about that. Jerrech used the serial numbers from a Camaro that had been crushed years ago. The police will find that the license plates are bogus, but it shouldn't be much of an issue. Let's go to a restaurant where we can sit down and figure things out."

They found a cafe a couple blocks away. After sitting down, they put their belongings under the table. A waitress showed up and set some waters and menus on the table. "I'll come back to take your order," said the waitress and she left.

Jack said, "I didn't expect that. I knew he was a bad man, but I had no idea..."

"Jerrech can make you another one. I think he really enjoyed making a car. I have the VTOL on its way. It will be here in no time. It's headed for a vacant lot a few blocks from here where it will sit in stealth mode," she said.

"Does that mean we're heading back to the facility?"

"I don't know, Jack. What would you like to do?"

"Before we head back, I want to do as much as we can."

Charalon chuckled and said, "You do realize that we

can go back and forth with the VTOL in less than fifteen minutes?"

"Really?"

"We took the Camaro because it made it easier to get around town."

"So, we could have just rented a car here, and saved the Camaro?" asked Jack.

"Yes, but it would be good to do it under an assumed name rather than using your name. That would make it harder to be tracked."

The waitress came back and said, "Have we decided here?"

Jack said, "I'd like a slice of your apple pie."

"Just a coffee for me," said Charalon.

"Thank you," said the waitress then left.

"Well, the VTOL has just landed without incidence, and will remain invisible until we get there," said Charalon.

Jack looked thoughtful and asked, "What if someone was walking through the lot, unaware of the VTOL, and bumped into it?"

"It's unlikely that something like that would happen, Jack, but it could. The VTOL has an A.I. program that monitors people and movement around it. If it has to, it can activate the force field, or hover silently over the spot until we get there."

"How long can it hover like that?"

"It doesn't take much energy to hover in that mode. The VTOL uses an anti-gravity device under those circumstances. It doesn't use its main engines, so it's silent. I would guess it can hover like that for a week before it would have to fire up its engines," she said.

Jack said, "It's quite a machine."

The waitress returned with the pie and coffee. As she set them on the table, she said, "There you go. Let me know if there's anything else I can get for you."

Jack ate his pie and sat back to relax. Charalon put some cream and sugar in her coffee and took a drink. By the look on her face, Jack could tell she didn't care for the coffee. She drank it anyway and didn't say anything.

After a while, Jack said, "I'd like to see where Malcolm lives. Do you know where that would be?"

"I believe I do. Even though we lost the drone bug feed from the church, I was able to analyze my memory files some more. Now, knowing Malcolm was there, I ran the plate numbers of all the cars parked around the church that I saw. None of them were registered in his name. That was no surprise to me. It took a lot of hacking, but I was able to establish driving patterns for the cars, using traffic camera and satellite imagery.

"A couple of the cars, including the van, have made trips to a hundred-acre parcel on the outskirts of town to the north. The tax records show it belonging to a widow named Sarah James. She has no obvious connection to Malcolm or his group, but I believe this is his compound. In the other timeline, Malcolm Underwood almost never had property in his own name."

Jack took a drink from his water and said, "Impressive. You must have had to hack into many different government sites to get that info. I would like to go there and see what we can."

She said, "Lets get a detailed scan of that place for Jerrech to analyze. We could fly the VTOL right over it and they'd never know."

Jack smiled and said, "That sounds fun. When can we do that?"

241

"As soon as we get to the VTOL, if you want," said Charalon.

They left the cafe and walked to the empty lot where some people were playing with a dog near the craft.

Charalon said, "It's in the northwestern corner. Let's come at it from that direction." They walked around the block and stood just outside the fence. "The VTOL is right in front of us. The people on the other side of it, over there, can't see us right now."

They climbed over the low fence and disappeared as they approached the VTOL. As soon as he entered the stealth field, Jack could see it sitting there with the canopy up. Charalon tossed her bag and the equipment behind the seat and got in. Jack did the same and Charalon closed the canopy.

She smiled at Jack and said, "If you had that memory implant, you would know how to fly this right now."

He had a huge smile on his face and said, "This is enough for now. Why couldn't you teach me?"

As they lifted off, Charalon said, "Maybe I will sometime."

Chapter 22
Strategy

It was 1:35 p.m. Thursday, June 18. Jack and Charalon had just lifted off in the VTOL from a vacant lot. They were on their way to a parcel of land they believed to be the location of Malcolm Underwood's compound. They were in stealth mode and flying slow at one thousand feet off the ground. It was an absolutely beautiful day with the sun shining and few clouds in the sky. Jack looked around and enjoyed the scenery.

"I can see why you like it," said Charalon.

Jack looked puzzled at first, then said, "Oh, yeah, I love flying like this, slow and quiet. It's like hang gliding in that way, but with a lot more...floor."

She smiled at the thought and chuckled. "Yeah, I see that. I might even have to try it someday," she said.

"Well, Charalon, you could drive for me and see what hang gliding is all about when we get back. There's a really nice launch at Tarkio with great landing zones below."

"Sure, Jack."

He pointed at a helicopter that had just taken off and said, "That's kind of cool. I've always loved helicopters."

His head turned and followed the helicopter as it flew to the right of them in the opposite direction. He looked over his shoulder and watched it disappear into the distance.

Charalon veered from her course to follow the river just to see Jack's reaction. He looked out and smiled as the terrain went by. She turned back to the north until the property came into view.

"Do you see that barn with the red metal roof?" she asked.

"Yes, it's quite a place."

From the air, Jack could see a large pole barn with several other buildings on a completely fenced property. As they got closer, he could see that it had an eight-foot-tall chain link fence with privacy slats in it. There was a paved entrance road to the property that made a loop and returned through a power security gate. The barn looked to be about sixty by eighty feet with a forty by sixty foot white metal shop building right next to it. There was a nice, white, two-story, five-thousand-plus-square-foot house with several smaller outbuildings.

Charalon descended to a hundred feet off the ground and made a slow pass over the property. After making the pass, she tapped a keypad on the dash and said, "I'm going to make another pass and do a reflective neutrino scan as well. I'd like to know what's in those sheds."

After turning around, she made the second pass and said, "Got it. Let's find a place nearby to park this machine. I think we should have a walk around that place in stealth mode."

"Well, it seems we didn't alert them to our presence so far, Charalon. Let's do it."

She circled around and settled on a freshly cut hayfield to the northwest of the compound. She landed the VTOL and powered it down before lifting the canopy. Charalon turned and reached behind the seat to retrieve the drone bug receiver. She opened it and removed a small canister saying, "I'm going to send some drone bugs on ahead of us. I'll be able to see their imagery in my head."

She got out of the VTOL and released some drone bugs from the canister. They flew through the stealth field and headed toward the compound. Jack got out of the VTOL and waited for her instruction. They turned on their ILEFF systems and exited the VTOL's stealth field.

On the way over to the compound, Jack said, "It's kind of weird following an invisible woman. At least I can see your foot impressions in the grass this time."

Charalon whispered, "You should be whispering or not talking right now. We don't know what kind of lookouts they have. Do you have your DSERN on?"

Jack whispered, "I do now."

"Make sure you have your force field turned on as well. Remember Willy's shotgun?" she whispered.

Jack nodded, then remembered he was invisible and quietly said, "Got it."

Charalon grabbed his hand and stopped. She very quietly whispered, "Don't say anything and don't move." She directed his sight to the southwest corner of the property by placing her hands on his head and turning his face toward a dark shadow. He nodded before she let go to let her know he saw it. She whispered right in his ear, "That's what I saw in Sharon's window."

The shadowy figure moved to the northwest corner of the property, closer to them. Jack could see it much better now. The figure was more of a silhouette than anything else. Its features could only be seen when it turned sideways, revealing its profile. It bent over and then sniffed the air as it looked around. It seemed to know somebody was watching it. It was searching for anything out of the ordinary. Suddenly it quickly moved toward them again. It moved like it was on train tracks, floating just off the ground. It came within fifteen feet of them and stopped. The shadowy figure leaned forward, sniffing the air again and turned all the way around. It moaned a bit then sniffed the air again. After a while, it stopped looking around and returned to the southwest corner.

Charalon tugged at Jack's hand and led him back to the VTOL. Jack marveled at Charalon's ability to know where he was. After they entered the stealth field, she said, "We can talk now. The stealth field is sound dampening so we won't be heard. I've recorded enough drone bug data now, so I'm going to destroy them."

"How do you know where I am when I have the ILEFF system in stealth mode? I wouldn't be able to find your hand like that."

Charalon smiled and said, "I'm just good...and I have some extra technology. Being an android, I can pick up microscopic distortions in the visible light spectrum around you. I have a subprogram that interprets them into an image of you."

Jack smiled and said, "You were cheating, weren't you? You know, in those drills where you had us tracking each other in stealth mode."

"No, I wouldn't cheat. I don't have to, but you'd never know if I did," she said looking at Jack with predatory eyes and a toothy grin.

"Did you see any people in there?"

"No, Jack. It looked like nothing was going on. This has to be the right place though. I don't think that dark figure thing would be here otherwise."

"What now?"

"I think we should head back to the facility and have Jerrech and Laloed analyze the data we just got. Besides, Jack, I could use a good latte."

He nodded in agreement as they got back into the VTOL. Charalon fired it up and they lifted off.

"Now you will see what this thing can do," she said with a grin. She moved the throttle to the forward position and Jack could feel a massive amount of acceleration as they shot off to the east.

"Wow," he said. "How fast are we going?"

"Five hundred knots right now, but we can go faster if you want."

"I like this speed. If we fly much faster, I won't have any time to enjoy the flight."

"True. At this speed, we'll be there in fifteen minutes," said Charalon.

After a quick flight back from Spokane, they were descending toward the mountain in full stealth mode. As they approached the hangar, Jack said, "I know there's a door there, but it looks like we're about to crash."

He flinched slightly as they went through the holographic rock projection covering the hangar door. Charalon chuckled and said, "You're going to have to get used to that."

"If you say so."

After they got out of the VTOL, a small robot came rolling up and Charalon handed the drone bug receiver to it. Another one rolled up to the VTOL and opened a service door. A more humanoid-looking robot drug a hose over and began to refuel the machine. Jack looked over to where the Camaro had been parked and sighed.

Charalon said, "Let's go get that latte now."

247

"Okay, I'll meet you there. I have to stop by my room and drop off my bag."

"Me too," she said.

When Jack got to the cafeteria, Charalon was sitting in the lounge area by the fire. There were two cups sitting on the table next to her. He sat in the other recliner and kicked back.

Charalon said, "Jerrech is analyzing the VTOL scan and drone bug data from Malcolm Underwood's compound. Laloed will want to talk to you when you're ready. He's already working on a plan to bring Malcolm down for good."

"Doesn't Laloed think the police will succeed?"

"Even if they know what the people of that church have been up to, that doesn't mean they'll be able to pin it on Malcolm. If they have evidence that he's behind the more egregious things they're doing, even that doesn't mean he's done for," she said.

"I see. I get the feeling that we are going to do whatever it takes to bring him down."

"You saw what they did to that guy, Jack. We have to do something."

"I agree," he said.

They finished their coffees and Jack said, "Well, I'd better go see Laloed now. When I'm done there, I'll probably want some dinner. I'll see you then."

She smiled and nodded as he got up and went to Laloed's office.

When he arrived there, Laloed said, "Come in and sit down, Jack. Would you like anything to drink?"

"No thanks. I just had some coffee."

Laloed said, "Okay, but just speak up if there's

anything you want. I had some thoughts I'd like to share with you. I've been thinking about the reason Laloedon originally came here. He wanted to stop the Morphalogian takeover that led to the end of the world. He really thought the problem was that he helped, in a major way, to bring them about. Laloedon was sure that, without his work, there wouldn't have been an apocalypse. He was convinced that he was responsible for the eventual end of the world, but I don't believe that. He only created a new weapon. He didn't think he was creating a weapon. He thought he was helping to advance the human race.

"I think the real problem is, and has always been, that there are people who will do anything to get their way, even destroy the world. I believe that they will just figure out another way to do that, with or without his help."

"Are you making the 'Guns don't kill people. People kill people' argument?" asked Jack.

"Well, kind of. I think our fight is with those who want to do evil, Jack. Malcolm Underwood is far more dangerous than any weapon. He has the power to convince people to use whatever they can to destroy and kill."

"Have you come up with any plans to stop him?"

Laloed said, "Yes, I have. There are at least three things we can do. First, we have to expose his activities to the police. I think we have to get the police involved, even if we have to plant some evidence. Second, there are other bad people he's working with who have their own agenda. We need to turn them against him. The third thing we need to do is destroy his compound. The scan you guys took with the VTOL showed a massive amount of explosives on the property. We just need to plant some explosives of our own. I'm currently working on a way to get some blood evidence for the police."

"After what I saw, I'm willing to help in any way I can," said Jack.

"I knew you would feel that way. Have you had any visits from Dominic lately?"

"No, I haven't heard from him since our run-in with Tobias."

"I'm surprised. I was sure you would have seen him by now. When you do, I would like to know what he has to say," said Laloed.

"So you believe I'll be seeing him soon?"

"Yes, Jack, but there is a war being fought between these angels and demons."

"So, you now believe in angels and demons, Laloed?"

"I had to change what I believed based on the events as of late. I suppose you could say I believe in God at this point. I now see the war that Laloedon spoke of."

Jack said, "I feel I've been forced to change what I believe. Sharon always believed in the supernatural."

"That is the other thing I wanted to talk to you about. I have been able to confirm that it was Sharon you saw at The People's Church. I can't explain why she would be there, or why she would suddenly move. The presence of the dark figure at her apartment tells me that she was targeted by this group."

Jack said, "Dominic did say that they knew who my friends and family were. He also said that it was too late for me to walk away from all this."

Laloed looked at him with compassion and said, "All is not lost, Jack. Sometimes things aren't as they appear. I have some encouraging mathematical projections, but I need more information before I can say anything more about them."

"Then I look forward to hearing them."

"Do you have any questions or suggestions for me, Jack?"

He smiled and said, "I have lots of questions, but they don't seem very important compared to the things that are going on now."

"I have time. What's on your mind?"

"I have been wondering for some time now, why didn't the Jack and Sharon in the other timeline ever have kids. The other thing I was wanting to know is does Laloedon have a grave somewhere?"

"I don't know where his grave is, Jack. He was very old and close to death when I saw him last. He didn't want a funeral. I think it was because all his friends had died. He was the last living Morphalogian. Although the rest of us were fond of him, we honored his wishes."

"But what happened to his body?"

Laloed said, "He had dug a cave somewhere that he planned to die in. I don't know where. He just walked out one day and said he wouldn't be back. I knew what he meant by that. I told Jerrech and Charalon what happened."

"I don't want to find that cave right now, but is there a way to find it in the future? I would like to visit it sometime," said Jack.

"I would like to know as well. When this thing with Malcolm Underwood is over, we should look into it. I would like to honor him in that way. I think you should ask Charalon about the other Jack and Sharon's lack of offspring. Anything else?"

Jack said, "No, I think I'll go have something for dinner now."

"Then I'll see you later."

Jack left Laloed's office and called Charalon on the communicator. They met in the cafeteria for dinner. When Jack got there, Charalon had a T-bone steak and baked potato waiting for him.

"How did that go?" she asked as he sat down.

"I think it went well, Charalon. I'm assuming you already know Laloed's plans."

"Yes, I'm aware of them."

"He asked if there was anything else I wanted to know, so I asked him a couple questions about Laloedon's death and why the other Jack and Sharon didn't have kids," said Jack.

Charalon perked up with interest and asked, "What did he say?"

"He told me that Laloedon had a cave that he planned to die in. Then he said I should ask you why the other Jack and Sharon never had children."

She thought for a moment then said, "First, I have to say that they did eventually have a child. They weren't humans when they had Keytar, their son, but they did have one."

"Oh, I just assumed they never had any kids. Nothing I've seen so far has indicated they did."

"You won't find anything about him in our database, Jack. I think Laloedon removed as much about him as he could. He didn't want to be reminded about Keytar. There is a lot of information about Keytar in our archived database," said Charalon.

"What happened?"

She answered, "Those memories are painful to me, but I will sum it up for you. Laloedon and Charalona were so proud of Keytar. He was their pride and joy, but he was a second generation Morphalogian. As Keytar matured into an adult, he grew more and more like any other second generation Morphalogian. Eventually he rejected his own parents and joined up with Malconadon. They were informed that he had been killed while fighting against the Supremacists."

"I would like to learn more about that time someday." Jack looked at his dinner and said, "I should be eating this wonderful meal here before it gets cold."

As he was finishing his dinner, Charalon asked, "How about some time by the fire?" He looked up, with a full mouth, and nodded.

After some conversation by the fire, Jack was feeling tired and went to his room. He liked his room and it felt good to be back. He went to his bathroom and brushed his teeth then took a shower. As he came out of the bathroom in his bathrobe, he looked at the chair expecting Dominic to be there. When Jack turned to go back in his bathroom, he heard a voice saying, "I'm here."

He turned back around to see Dominic sitting in the chair. He was dressed in his usual red plaid shirt and blue jeans. Dominic looked fatigued.

"Oh, there you are. Laloed thought you would be paying me a visit soon."

"Yes, it is time," said Dominic.

"It's good to see you. I've been wondering when you would come by again. Can I ask you some questions?"

"Yes, Jack. I am here to help you."

"I need to know what's going on with Sharon. Is she safe, and why was she at that so-called church? Also, what happened to Tobias?" asked Jack.

Dominic worked up a reassuring smile and said, "She is where she was meant to be right now. I will explain more about that in a minute. Tobias was a demon. I cast him out of that man, John Branch."

"What did you do with the body?"

"He was not dead, Jack. I took him to a place where he could do no more damage. He made a choice to give himself to Tobias. My master has had mercy on the man, John Branch. As for your question about Sharon, she is working against Malcolm Underwood and his people."

"How can that be? She would have said something to me about it, wouldn't she?"

"She was not working against them when you last saw her, Jack. She had to move out of her apartment to save her own life. She was targeted for demonic oppression. Most of the people in that church are blinded by the enemy. One of the people she knows is a member of The People's Church. They were told by Malcolm Underwood to invite her to one of their gatherings. She is in great danger. There was and will be demonic visitors. If one fails more will follow."

"Is that why she was with that guy at the...?"

"Yes, Jack, she was told to go with that person to the meeting."

Jack looked astonished and asked, "Who told her to go to that meeting?"

Dominic's gaze intensified and he said, "You are about to tell her that, and you already have."

He stood and stepped over to Jack, touching him on the shoulder. At once Jack found himself fully dressed, walking down a sidewalk with Dominic. Dominic raised his arm and pointed to a man just leaving Sharon's apartment. It was Jack. He said, "Come quickly, there is no time to waste." They walked over to Sharon's apartment and up to her door. Jack looked in the window. She was still looking out the window.

Sharon's face had a look of pure shock. She stood there agape for a moment then slowly opened the door.

"I have an explanation," said Jack.

Sharon looked him in the eye, then looked at Dominic and said, "Mr. Ferris?"

"Can we come in?" asked Jack.

Sharon's eyes darted from Jack to Dominic, and finally she said, "Yes, come in." She led them into the living room and motioned for them to sit on the couch. She sat in her armchair. She looked at Jack, and asked, "What is going on?"

Jack motioned to Dominic and said, "I should let him explain."

Dominic looked at her and said, "You know me as Mr. Ferris, the homeless man your father invited over for dinner. That is not what I am."

"That was at least twenty years ago. You look exactly the same as I remember...and you, Jack, I just watched you drive off. There's no way you could have got to my door that fast."

Dominic smiled at Sharon and said, "I have brought Jack here to help you move out of this apartment. If you stay here, you will surely die."

Jack said, "I know this seems crazy, but you have to move out of here, right away. You have something else that you should do as well. There's somebody you know who's going to ask you to go to church with them. Dominic says you should go."

Sharon looked at Dominic with skepticism. As she

stared into his eyes, her expression changed. She looked as if she was about to cry. "What's going on here? What are you?" she asked.

Dominic said, "Sharon, I am here to help. There are forces at work trying to destroy you."

All of a sudden, Dominic stood up, looking at a dark form standing by the window in the room with them. At once he appeared as his true self and moved like a flash, grabbing the form. A blinding light emitted from his hands as he held it. He looked at Jack and said, "I will be back for you. You know what to do." At once Jack did know what to do. Then Dominic vanished with the thing held firmly in his hands.

Sharon looked at Jack and asked, "Did you see that?"

Jack realized Sharon could see everything that just happened. He saw it too, even though he didn't have the DSERN function turned on.

"Yes, Sharon, I did. Did you see the dark figure too?"

"I saw Mr. Ferris turn into something I can't explain and grab some kind of dark spirit."

Jack said, "I think we could see it because Dominic was here. There are things happening that you need to know about. I'll try to explain when I can."

Chapter 23
Sharon

Sharon was trembling and staring at the floor. She had just seen Dominic, in his true form, grab a demon and vanish before her eyes. Jack got up and put his arm around her. She looked up at him and asked, "What just happened? What was that shadowy thing?"

"I think it was a demon. We have to get you out of here, Sharon. They're after you. I will explain things to you later on. Do you trust me?"

Sharon had an indignant look and said, "Of course I trust you. What now?"

"Let's call a moving truck and get your things out of here. It won't be safe for you to return. I think it's important that your possessions don't fall into their hands. We have to get them all out of here. I don't know why Dominic want's you to go to that meeting."

"Probably because I already said I would, Jack."

He looked concerned and said, "The person who invited you to that church, that's the guy you work with?"

Sharon said, "Yes..."

"Did you tell him anything about me or where I go in the mountains?"

Sharon nodded and said, "Yes. He's a friend I work

with. He asked where you were in Montana. I needed to vent to someone at the time. What's wrong with that?"

"So that's how Tobias knew where to look for me," he said rhetorically. "I'll explain as much as I can, once we have you out of here."

Jack had Sharon call in sick for work. Then he called around for a moving company that could come immediately. It was nothing short of a miracle. Jack called a company that had a truck and crew sitting idle not far from Sharon's place. They had showed up to move someone who had changed their mind and forgot to cancel the move. The truck was at Sharon's within minutes. Jack had them move her belongings to a storage unit on the other side of town. Fortunately, Sharon didn't have a lot of things and the whole move only took three hours from start to finish.

When they were done, Jack had Sharon drive him to a cafe. After lunch, they sat and talked for a while.

She looked at Jack and asked, "This is what you were talking about, isn't it? This is why you couldn't tell me what you were up to, right?"

"Yes and no. If I told you everything that's happened lately, you'd think I was totally crazy," he said.

"I don't know about that, Jack. After what I just saw, what could be crazier than that? And what's up with Mr. Ferris?"

"Well, I'd like to have the time to explain everything right now, but I'll just have to give you the basics. Mr. Ferris, as you know him, is an angel. I know him as Dominic. You have to believe me when I say I was the last person to believe in angels," he said.

Sharon cut in with, "I get that. He is an angel. That is

obvious to me now."

"You always were more sensible than me, Sharon. It took me a while to understand that. Maybe I should start by telling you about the mountain and what happened there." Jack sighed and shook his head saying, "No, there's too much to tell you right now. Dominic brought me here from the future."

"That makes sense, but when you looked in my window after I saw you drive off...well, you know. How far back in time did you come?"

"It's a little complicated for me. What day is this?"

She said, "It's Tuesday, June 2."

Jack scratched his head and said, "About sixteen days. It was Thursday evening, June 18. I was about to go to bed when Dominic showed up. This isn't the first time I have been sent to the past. In fact, I think I'm currently in three places at once, at least right now. There's so much more I need to tell you, but it will have to wait. Now I know why Laloed wouldn't tell me everything at once."

"Who's...Laloed, did I say that right?"

"Yes, that's how I say it. On my last trip to the mountain, I found the answers I've been looking for. Do you remember what I told you about seeing a scary creature up there when I was a kid?"

"Yes..."

"Well, Sharon, that was Laloed and he was real. It will take a lot of time to explain all about the mountain. I promise you, in time I will tell you all about the mountain. For now, I will say I wasn't as crazy as everyone thought I was."

"I never thought you were crazy. Don't say everyone. What should we do now?"

Jack said, "Well, Dominic made me understand what

to do right before he vanished with that demon. At least I think that was a demon. First we have to get you a safe place to stay for up to three weeks. Dominic let me know there would be another angel to watch over you. You have to go to work and act like everything is normal. He said to tell anyone who asks that you had an infestation problem with your apartment. That's why you're staying somewhere else. Which when you think about it, that's kind of true.

"Anyway, you should avoid talking about it and don't tell anybody where you're staying. When it's time to go to the meeting, meet your friend from work there. Try not to act different around him, we don't want to let them know that you know what's going on. Finally, the meeting I saw you at, well, you'll have to keep it together in there. Just act normal, like everyone else."

"He said all that to you with just a look?" asked Sharon.

"Yes, he did."

She smiled and said, "Okay, I'll go to that meeting with him. And I'll act...normal."

Jack chuckled and said, "I mean don't act like you're surprised by what you see."

"And what will I see?"

"I can't tell you right now, Sharon."

"How did you see me there, Jack?"

"We had some high-tech surveillance equipment," he said.

After they left the cafe, they drove around looking for another apartment but finally settled on a motel room. Jack was able to get a good deal on the room with a weekly rate discount, and paid for three weeks. When

Jack paid cash, it didn't go unnoticed by Sharon.

"Are you spending all your savings on me, Jack?" she asked.

He smiled and said, "No, I have an income from my new gold mine. I'll tell you about it later on. At any rate, I have been taken care of financially."

"Okay, but I can pay for these things too."

Jack changed the subject. "How about I get us a couple lattes that we can take to your room and kick back for a bit?"

"Now you're talking."

They got themselves some coffees and went to the room. Jack sat in one of the chairs with his coffee and put his feet up on an ottoman. Sharon sat on the bed and set her coffee on the end table.

"Well, now what?" she asked.

"Dominic will be back soon to return me to my room."

Sharon looked puzzled and said, "Your room?"

He sighed and said, "Yes, and that's another long story. To make a long story short, I have a room in an underground facility on the mountain. It was built by time-traveling creatures from the future and now run by computers and androids. I'm working with them to stop a potential catastrophe. I have been in and out of there for weeks now. I wouldn't be saying a thing about it, if you hadn't just seen Dominic in action. I think even you would have thought I was totally insane by now."

Sharon smiled and said, "That did give you some additional credibility."

Jack patted his front pocket, checking to see if the ILEFF unit was there and said, "Hey, I have something to show you. I know you don't think I'm nuts, but this will

261

help you justify the credibility I have with you."

He activated the unit and selected the stealth mode. When he vanished, Sharon just sat there on the bed looking around.

He remained invisible and said, "I'm still here."

"That's pretty cool, Jack. What do you need that for?"

He reappeared and said, "It gives me an edge in the kind of work I'm doing. I feel a little like some kind of spy. There's a man named Malcolm Underwood. He's involved with that church you've been invited to. Malcolm has doomsday-like plans for the future. He's very rich and, in the future, will become very powerful. If he is not stopped, he will eventually destroy the world.

"The time-traveling creatures from the future came here to stop that from happening. I have been given some technology, like I showed you, to help me do my job."

Sharon said, "This is a lot to digest. How have you come to be involved in all of this?"

"In the future they came from, you and I helped develop technology that gave Malcolm the ability to accomplish his goals. They originally came back to stop me from inventing that technology. They did that, but they think he will find another way."

She asked, "What does Mr. Ferris, I mean Dominic, have to do with it all?"

"He has been helping me. I don't know why yet, but I know there's a plan for me," said Jack.

Sharon smiled and said, "I can see you have come a long way. You now believe in God, don't you?"

"Yes, I do. There's so much more I have to tell you. I wish I were better at this. I don't know when I will see you again, for sure, but it will probably be after that meeting you go to on the sixteenth."

Sharon said, "I have been invited to a meeting in two days."

"The meeting I saw you at was on the sixteenth of June."

"It sounds like I will be attending more than one meeting there, Jack."

Then they were surprised by Dominic saying, "It is time." Jack looked up to see Dominic standing by the entry door.

Dominic turned to Sharon and said, "Remember to be strong, Sharon. There is another like me who will be with you. He will watch over you and protect you, but you will not see him. The enemy will think you are blinded by demonic oppression, but you will not be."

Dominic touched Jack on the shoulder and he instantly found himself back in his room at the facility. He was standing there in his bathrobe. He picked up his watch and looked at it. No time had passed while he was gone. Jack looked around for his pants and reached in the front pocket. He pulled his communicator out and called Charalon.

"Yes?" she said.

"I just had a visit from Dominic that I'd like to tell you about. Laloed will want to know what happened as well."

Charalon said, "I'm in my room, but I could meet you at the cafeteria."

"Okay, I'll be there after I get dressed."

When Jack got to the cafeteria, Charalon was sitting on the lounge side by the fire. There were coffees sitting on the table. He sat down and said, "Decaf, right?"

"Yep. So tell me what just happened."

"After I took a shower, Dominic showed up. He took me back in time again," said Jack.

"When and where? What happened?"

"I'll give you the short version, Charalon. He took me back about sixteen days to Sharon's apartment. I saw myself leaving there and driving off. We went inside to tell her she had to move out because she was in danger. A demon showed up and Dominic captured it. I moved her things to a storage unit and got a motel room for her. She should still be staying there; I paid for three weeks. A coworker of hers invited her to go to a meeting at that church. Dominic wanted her to go to it."

Charalon looked relieved and said, "So that's why she was at that meeting."

"Dominic said she had to move out of her apartment or she would die. He also said she was targeted for demonic oppression. That must be why you saw one of those dark figures there."

"In the interest of saving time, Jack, I'm relaying this information to Laloed. He may have a question for you."

"Good, that will save me a trip there."

"He wants to know if you've called her since you got back here," said Charalon.

"I haven't called anybody from the facility. I thought that could possibly expose this place to the outside world."

"No, Jack, we have safeguards in place for that. Laloed would like you to call her now."

Jack said, "Okay," and pulled out his phone. He dialed Sharon's cell phone number and waited. Her phone rang, and then again.

"Hello, Jack," she said. "I was thinking you would call soon."

"How are you doing? Is everything okay?"

Sharon sounded disturbed and said, "Yes, I'm okay. I'm still staying at the motel room you paid for. I've been to a couple of the...meetings..."

Jack could hear some sniffling over the phone. "You saw what happened at that meeting, didn't you?" he asked.

"I did...Jack."

"Can you tell us anything else about that group?"

Sharon gathered herself together and said, "I saw them kill a couple people, Jack. After the meetings, both times, people would act like nothing happened. One of them talked about the faith healing demonstration they just saw. I don't think most of the people at those meetings are seeing what I saw. They acted like they were in some kind of cooking class."

Charalon whispered, "Laloed wants you to tell her to stay in her room and not go anywhere for now."

"Sharon, you have to stay in that room until I can get there. Don't go to work, and don't go to any more of those meetings. Are you going to be okay?"

"I'm doing the best I can, Jack. I'll be fine. When will I see you?"

He said, "I'm not sure. I know it will be soon. You haven't told anybody where you are, have you?"

"No, but I've wanted to call the police. What should I do, Jack?"

"We have already given the police a video. Laloed is working on a way to get more evidence to help the police. We're up against spiritual beings, and an evil man. Just hang in there. Don't call anyone for now. I'll be there soon. I love you," said Jack.

"Okay, I'll be fine here. I love you too."

Jack put his phone back in his pocket and asked, "What's our next move?"

Charalon began to fill Jack in on the plan. "We're going to attack that compound. Laloed and Jerrech have been going over the data from the scans we took. Laloed believes Malcolm will be there tonight because the police raided their church. Laloed wanted to make sure Sharon wasn't at that compound. Jerrech has been doing some research and knows where a couple of the victims' bodies are. We're bringing some spy-like mini-droids that will break into the morgues where the bodies are and take some blood from them. Jerrech made them especially for this mission. He calls them his 'little ninjas.' I call them spydroids. They even have full stealth mode. We are going to plant some blood evidence in the buildings at the compound. When the police comb through the debris that's left there, they'll find evidence that Malcolm Underwood was behind the killings. Even if he were to get away, his reputation would be ruined and he'd be a fugitive."

"When are we going to do that?" he asked.

"Tonight, if you're up to it."

"It's been a very long day, but I think I'm up to it."

Charalon looked at him. He looked tired. After all, he had been up for a very long time when his trip to the past was figured in. She said, "Maybe you should get some real coffee for your cup."

"Okay, that sounds good to me."

"You're going to need it. I'll order some for both of us," said Charalon.

"Should we bring any weapons with us?"

"Your ILEFF system is all you require, Jack. It can be a very deadly weapon when needed."

Jack drank his coffee and listened to her explain their mission plan. It was pretty simple. They were going to fly the VTOL back to Spokane. First, they would release the spydroids. Second, they would get in position to attack the compound. Once the spydroids got to the compound and planted the blood evidence, they would activate their ILEFF system and start the attack. Charalon would have the VTOL hover over the compound and detonate the explosives stored in the buildings as she directed it to. She explained that they would be safe from bullets and explosions with the ILEFF system. They would kill any of the three demon-possessed men they came across. If either of them saw Malcolm, they would drop everything and go after him. Jerrech put some incriminating documents and video together for the police to find that would implicate Malcolm Underwood. Laloed had a plan to make a white supremacist group in the area think Malcolm was working with the FBI against them.

After a while, Jerrech came into the room and said, "Almost everything has been loaded into the VTOL and it's ready to go."

Charalon said, "Well, let's get on with it."

Chapter 24
The Compound

It was 11:55 p.m. Thursday, June 18. Jack and Charalon were walking toward the hangar. They were about to get in the VTOL and head to Spokane. It was time to take Malcolm Underwood down. As they entered the hangar one of the small robots came rolling up with three of the spydroids on a tray. Charalon picked one up and looked at it. It was a chrome-clad mechanical bug about six inches long with six legs and two wings. Charalon caused it to activate temporarily to test it. It wiggled its legs and flapped its wings, then a straw-like probe extended and retracted from its head. She looked satisfied with it, then put it and the others into a side compartment on the VTOL.

"I think we have everything now. Let's get in and go," said Charalon.

Jack climbed in the right side and buckled up. She took a walk around the VTOL and looked it over before climbing in. It wasn't long before they were flying out of the hangar. Charalon changed her heading and accelerated as they climbed to altitude. They talked very little on the way to Spokane.

As they approached Spokane, Charalon dropped to a

lower altitude. Jack could see the city lights shining through the darkness. He could see cars moving down roads and passing through stoplights. There was a full moon in the cloudless skies over Spokane that night. The moonlight partially illuminated the landscape. It was beautiful and mesmerizing.

When they were over the middle of town, Charalon slowed way down and released the spydroids. She said, "There they go. It won't take long for them to find the county medical examiner's office. There are two of Malcolm's victims there right now."

"How long will it take for them to do their job and get to the compound?"

"Oh, about a half hour or so. We will land the VTOL in that field where we did before, and wait there. When they've gotten into and out of the compound, we'll attack. We are going to go through the fence, so we need to set the ILEFF system to cut through the wire. Once we're through, we'll need to shut that option off. Otherwise, everything you touch will be destroyed. I believe some of the people are innocent and have no idea what's been going on."

"Okay, I'll be ready."

"There's the compound, Jack." Charalon pointed to a dark area and circled around. She found the field and landed.

"How is the VTOL going to cause their explosives to go off, Charalon?"

She turned toward Jack and said, "It can emit a laser beam especially designed for explosive detonation. It can also launch self-detonating plastic explosives that stick to structures and blow on command."

Charalon raised the canopy and released some drone

bugs. "There go my other eyes and ears. We can talk out loud for now, but once we leave the VTOL stealth field we'll have to be quiet. Any questions, Jack?"

"Are you going to use the DSERN function?" he asked.

"I think that's a good idea, don't you?"

"Yes, I do. I'm going to turn it on when we get closer. It can trip me up in the dark, with the extra graphic imagery and all."

Charalon said, "Well, let's head over there and wait for the spydroids."

They got out of the VTOL and set their ILEFF systems to stealth mode. Then they walked over to a strategic spot where they could observe the compound at a safe distance. As they were waiting, the blue van they saw at the church pulled up to the entry gate. The gate slid open and the van drove in and parked next to the doors on the barn. Four men got out and unloaded a six-foot-long box from the van.

Charalon whispered in Jack's ear, "Three of those men are the ones we need to take out. Laloed says, since they are fully demon possessed, we shouldn't let any of them get away alive. According to Laloed, that rite they performed literally welded the demons to them. He said that they have been permanently 'demonified.' The only way Willy or the other two get out alive is if they somehow get free of the demon. Dominic did something like that for the man that called himself Tobias."

"What about that box?"

"There's probably a person in that box. One of us should try to bust the box open, but only after the explosives are detonated. He will be protected inside of that box until then," said Charalon.

Several other cars showed up, parked and the people got out and entered the barn.

"Those spydroids should have been here by now. Let's turn the DSERN on and look around...oh no," she whispered.

Jack turned his DSERN function on and saw why she was concerned. There were hundreds of dark figures darting around near the barn. He sighed quietly.

Charalon whispered, "We can do this. Don't let fear diminish your resolve...look over there. The man in the red ball cap is Malcolm Underwood. Laloed says he's not possessed, so we just have to make sure he is captured. It's okay to kill him, in my opinion. Nobody said we shouldn't kill him."

Suddenly they heard a third whispering voice. They knew at once it was Dominic.

He whispered, "Turn off your DSERN function and look again." They did as he asked and were amazed to see at least a thousand angels surrounding the compound. All of the angels appeared in their true forms. They stood with swords in their hands poised for an attack. It was truly a stunning sight. The dark forms darting around the compound were unaware of them.

Dominic whispered, "When you see us charge, then you may attack." He left them and took up a lead position with the angels.

"The spydroids are almost here. It won't take long for them to plant the blood and get out of there. It looks like all three of them were successful," whispered Charalon.

Jack whispered, "They have stealth mode. Does that mean they also have a sound dampening field? They kind of look like they're not very quiet."

"Yes, Jack, they have sound dampening, so they're

virtually silent."

Jack found himself staring at the angels. He was unable to take his eyes off of them. They appeared to be highly focused fighting machines, at least at the moment. Jack marveled at their unity. He perceived a total absence of ego among them.

The angels began organizing in groups of ten. They looked as fierce as anything Jack and Charalon had ever seen.

She whispered, "The spydroids are planting the blood right now."

"Okay, I'm ready. I have the cut feature turned on," Jack whispered.

"Malcolm is in the barn right now. I think you should go after him, Jack. It will be easy for you to see him with that red hat he has on. I can identify the others easier than you can, so I will take them. Well, all three of the spydroids have now returned to the VTOL. It's all up to the angels now."

"Well, I'm ready," he whispered.

"Good. Any moment now..."

Suddenly the angels charged the compound, moving like lightning. With their swords drawn, the angels formed an impenetrable barrier as they closed in on the dark figures. The dark figures became paralyzed whenever they were run through by an angel's sword. The demon-possessed men went ballistic, causing people to pour out of the barn and scatter. The angels that weren't stabbing were grabbing the dark figures and holding them. With great force, they squeezed and distorted the vile things. Then they vanished in a flash of light, taking the demons away.

Jack and Charalon took off at a full run. They ran

right through the fence, leaving a clean outline of themselves. Charalon quickly assessed the situation and headed for the barn. Jack saw a man wearing a red ball cap, but knew it wasn't Malcolm when he got closer.

Charalon quickly identified Willy and Chip. She punched Chip in the chest, driving her fist completely through him, snapping his spine. She retracted her blood-covered arm and Chip fell to the ground motionless. The blood spatter from Chip covered Charalon's face, temporarily revealing her features. Willy saw what happened and ran. Charalon growled and went after him.

While in pursuit of Willy, she saw the third man, Tom. He had a machete in his hand. When he saw her blood-spattered form, he darted into the barn. Charalon believed that he meant to kill the person in the box. She paused her pursuit of Willy and bolted to the barn where she saw Tom trying to stab the machete through one of the cracks in the box lid. Charalon ran toward him at full speed and reached him before he could hurt the occupant. She took him out by crushing his skull with her hand as she ran by, not even stopping. She circled back, leaving the barn, and resumed her hunt for Willy.

Jack saw another red ball cap and ran after the man wearing it. This time he felt it was Malcolm and he ran straight at him. Malcolm seemed to know that something was after him and he changed directions. Jack saw his face and recognized Malcolm from the video Charalon had put together. Now he had no doubt, this was his target. Then Malcolm darted into a group of ten people and was able to lose him. Jack panicked. He had not come this far just to see Malcolm get away. He ran over to the house and then back, but Malcolm was nowhere to be seen.

Charalon, still partly visible, caught up with Willy and grabbed him by his shirt. She spun him around and held him by the throat with one hand. Remarkably, he was able to get a few words out.

"This isn't the end," he said.

"It is for now." Then she broke his neck and let him fall to the ground. The force field finally shed the rest of the blood spatter, leaving her invisible again.

Jack spotted Malcolm again and caught up with him. He pinned him up against one of the outbuildings and held him there. Jack adjusted his ILEFF system to appear as himself and looked Malcolm in the eye. Malcolm had a wild and crazy-looking smile on his face. He stared at Jack and laughed. Jack didn't know what to do with him. He couldn't just kill Malcolm in cold blood.

One of Malcolm's strong men saw Jack holding him there and ran toward them. Just before he got there, a red laser beam from above hit him and he fell to the ground in a steaming heap. Charalon smiled a little as she watched from a distance.

"You're weak, Jack. If you let me live I will come after your family. Maybe they would join my church, with a little persuasion. That could be a lot of fun," said Malcolm.

Instantly Jack was enraged. He pulled his fist back to kill Malcolm. Just as he was about to drive it through him, he found himself unable to move.

"You are not a murderer, Jack. Let us keep it that way," said Dominic.

Malcolm wriggled out from Jack's hold and ran. Fleeing through a door on one of the outbuildings, Malcolm believed he had escaped. Charalon saw him go into the building and at once had the VTOL blow it up.

Jack was unaffected by the blast. Although he could move again, he just stood there, protected by the ILEFF system.

Charalon unleashed a violent series of explosions as she directed the VTOL to blow most of the buildings, sparing the barn. She reentered the barn and spotted the box. She ran over and pulled the top off, exposing a man in his twenties lying there looking dazed and confused. Charalon was still in stealth mode, so he was unable to see her. Feeling like it was now safe for the man, she exited the building and headed for Jack.

Jack stood in a daze, observing the chaos. To him, everything was moving in slow motion. There were people lying motionless on the ground as others tripped over them. The area was littered with debris and illuminated by the multiple fires surrounding them. Charalon ignored everything else and ran up to Jack.

Dominic, appearing in his true form, was obviously able to see Charalon. He signaled that she and Jack should leave now. She nodded in agreement and grabbed Jack's arm. She yelled, "Jack, we have to move. Now!"

He stammered at first, then as he came out of it said, "I...I'm coming."

She took his hand and pulled him along back to the VTOL. They entered the stealth field and disappeared. Once they were safe inside, Charalon buckled Jack and then herself in. She quickly got the VTOL powered up and in the air. Then she raised it a couple thousand feet off the ground and hovered.

"Jack, are you okay?"

"Yes, I'm fine. I don't know what happened there."

"I want to take you to Sharon's room. Can you tell me how to get there?"

"I haven't told her anything about you yet. I was trying to tell her about the facility in stages. Kind of like you and Laloed did with me," he said.

"I really want to talk with her. I need to talk with her. I know her well enough to know that she will handle it as well as anyone," she said.

"I know you're right, Charalon. She will handle it well. I'd kind of like to wait until it gets light out though. I hate waking her in the middle of the night. I've done that too many times."

"I understand, Jack. Let's wait for a couple hours. We could land somewhere and get some lattes."

"I like that idea. Do you have a place in mind?"

Charalon looked at Jack with a smile and said, "You have to ask? There's an all night cafe that serves espresso drinks I have in mind."

She found an empty lot to park the VTOL and they got out. She activated her ILEFF to appear as a brunette human lady. It was a short walk of about a block to the cafe. They sat down and relaxed a bit. A waitress showed up to take their order for a couple of coffees.

"You really want to talk to Sharon, don't you?" he asked Charalon.

She looked down and thought about it for a moment, trying to find a way to adequately say that she did, very much, want to talk with Sharon. For her, talking with Sharon would be a little like a Christian meeting one of the apostles. She had the memories of Sharon and then Charalona from the other timeline. From the first time she looked at the file containing those memories, she held Sharon in high esteem.

Charalon looked up and said, "I don't ask for much,

276

Jack. This is something I really want. Yes, I do want to talk with her."

The waitress showed up with some lattes and set them on the table. She said, "Enjoy, I'll be back in a bit to see if there's anything else you might want." She smiled and walked off.

Jack looked over at Charalon. He could see how much it meant to her and said, "Of course I'll do what I can for you."

Charalon was looking down at her latte. She lifted her eyes to Jack and had a devilish smile. She said, "Good, I thought I might have to beat you a little to get what I wanted."

"No, there will be no beating for now," he said with a chuckle.

She changed the subject asking, "So...what happened back there? You kind of froze up."

Jack sighed and shook his head a little as he thought about it. He took a breath and said, "I don't know for sure what happened. I had Malcolm held there up against that building when he said something that made me very angry. I wasn't going to kill him until right at that moment. I was instantly offended and irate. I was going to drive my fist right through his head."

"Well, Jack, you wouldn't have got any blood on yourself. The force-field part of the ILEFF system keeps stuff off of you. It's nice that way."

"I would have had his blood on my hands metaphorically. I totally wanted to kill him. Dominic spared me from it," he said.

"It was just war for me, nothing personal. What did Malcolm say to you?" Charalon asked.

Jack answered, "He called me weak, and maybe he

was right about that. He said if I didn't kill him, he would come back after my family. I know he was just trying to piss me off. He succeeded precisely because I was weak."

"We all have our moments, Jack, but I don't think you're weak. Besides it's things like that, that make us stronger if we learn from them."

He thought about that and asked, "Do you ever get that angry, Charalon?"

"I think I have the capacity to, but my emotional regulation programs curb any extreme feelings I might develop. I can't really complain about the programs; they're very helpful at times."

They sat talking for three hours. Jack had a few cups of coffee and a couple slices of pie in that time. He had been up for many hours. It was a very adventurous day he had when they surveyed the compound and returned to the facility. Then Dominic came and got him, taking him back in time for a day as he moved Sharon. When he got back to the facility, he didn't have time to rest before heading back to Spokane. After attacking the compound, he stayed up all night.

It was now 5:30 a.m. Friday morning. Jack looked rough. He had a disheveled look with slightly messy hair, a three-day beard and red eyes. Charalon had the ILEFF system set to a human appearance and looked pretty good, but she wouldn't have looked tired anyway.

She said, "Lets get the VTOL to a less populated area before there's a lot of movement out there."

Jack looked at his watch, then got up and paid the check. After a short walk, they covertly entered the stealth field and got in the VTOL. Jack told Charalon where Sharon's motel was and she found a convenient open area to store the VTOL. They left the stealth field and headed to the motel on foot.

When they got to Sharon's room, Jack knocked on the door and waited. After a minute or so, Sharon cracked the door open and said, "Yes?"

"It's me...Jack. Can I come in?" he asked.

Sharon unlatched the safety chain lock and opened the door. As he stood in the doorway, she uncocked a .38 caliber revolver and put it in her purse. She was already fully dressed and made up.

"Come in," she said.

Jack stood there for a moment and said, "I have someone here who would like to meet you." He stepped aside, letting Charalon enter the room first. Then he stepped in and shut the entry door and locked it.

"This is Charalon," said Jack. "She's from the place in the mountain."

Sharon looked slightly confused, but smiled and extended her hand saying, "Hi, I'm Sharon."

Charalon looked slightly starstruck as she took Sharon's hand. Sharon shook her hand, but pulled back immediately.

"Oh, I'm sorry. I still have the ILEFF system on," said Charalon.

Jack said, "Charalon is using the technology that I showed you the other day to change her appearance."

"I turned off the force-field function. Let's try that again." Charalon extended her hand again and Sharon shook it.

Sharon gave Charalon a friendly smile and said, "That was better."

Jack looked at Sharon and said, "Charalon has been looking forward to meeting you for some time now. I'm going to let her explain that to you."

Sharon looked at her and said, "Jack said the place in the mountain was run by computers and androids. I'm assuming that is why you are altering your appearance."

"You are right. I am an android, as silly as that may sound."

"I have a couple chairs over here. Would you like to sit down?" asked Sharon.

Charalon said, "That sounds nice," and sat in one of the chairs as Sharon sat in the other.

Jack said, "I hope I don't sound rude here, but I'm very tired. I haven't had any sleep for over thirty hours and I'd like to take a nap. Is that okay with the two of you?"

Sharon looked at Jack and said, "You do look tired. Why don't you climb into that bed and rest for a while? I'd like to visit with Charalon anyway." He climbed into bed and fell asleep almost instantly. It had been a very long, eventful day.

Sharon turned back to Charalon and asked, "Is there anything I can get for you?"

"No thanks. Jack and I had coffee while we were waiting for morning. He didn't want to wake you in the middle of the night."

"Do you eat and drink...the same as anybody else?"

"I don't have to eat or drink anything, Sharon, but I do like coffee and some foods."

"That's fascinating. So, what do you really look like?"

Charalon turned her ILEFF system off and said, "I was modeled after an actual person. I have her memories."

Sharon was amazed by Charalon and had many questions for her. Charalon answered every question and held nothing back. They talked for hours and she gave Sharon a complete explanation of all that had happened.

Jack slept soundly for six hours straight and only woke when Sharon asked if he wanted anything for lunch. She was compassionate and understanding with the groggy Jack, and said, "I'm going to pick up something for you to eat. There's a takeout pizza place nearby. I'll be right back."

Sharon grabbed her purse and went out the door. Jack got up and put his shoes on. It was obvious that Sharon and Charalon had hit it off. Sharon had accepted her.

Jack looked at Charalon and asked, "What did you say to her?"

"Just the truth, Jack."

Chapter 25
A New Era

It was Saturday morning, June 20. Jack was driving Sharon's car with her sitting in the passenger seat. She had quit her job and they were heading to her parents' house in Polson. She needed time off to deal with the events she witnessed at the so-called church in Spokane. Since the police had plenty of evidence of what The People's Church had been up to, she decided not to report what she had seen. She just wanted to forget about it for now.

Charalon had taken the VTOL back to the facility the day before while Jack stayed in Spokane to help Sharon. A moving company had already picked her things up from the storage unit and would deliver them to Polson. Her father had an empty shed to store her belongings in.

They talked about their plans for the future, but neither one knew what they wanted other than to be together. For now, Jack was planning to go back to the facility to see if they needed anything else from him.

As he was driving, Jack could feel Sharon's gaze often. The events of the last few weeks had given her a new appreciation for him. The things Charalon said about Jack only validated those feelings.

He was going to have Sharon drop him off at his rented house, but changed his mind. He decided instead of following her in his van to Polson, he would drive her there himself. He wanted to spend some time with her and help move her furniture into the shed.

It was a long drive. They talked about everything from Dominic to Charalon. Time flew by and they were in Polson before they knew it. After Jack helped get her things moved, he took Sharon to lunch in town. They spent the whole day together.

He planned to stay at his parents' house for a day or two. That night Jack looked in the mirror and saw how much he needed a shave and haircut. "It's a good thing I have an extra change of clothes and a shaving kit here," he thought. Later on, he took his communicator out and called Charalon to check in.

"Hey, Jack," she answered.

"Well, I imagine you've been monitoring the police communications in Spokane. What have you heard?" he asked.

"It seems they've found the blood and document evidence we planted, along with other incriminating evidence. They know it was Malcolm Underwood who was behind the killings, Jack."

"Did anyone else, other than Malcolm and his guys, die in the attack, Charalon?"

"I don't think so. They're still going through the debris there, but it looks good so far. The only thing that bothers me is they haven't found Malcolm yet. I don't see how he could have gotten out of that building alive, but I suppose it's possible," she said.

"Do you need me to come back for anything right away?"

"No, not right away, but Laloed really wants to talk to you about something. I don't know what he wants. If I were you I'd take some time for yourself, at least two, maybe three days."

"I think I will. There's something I really need to do while I'm here, Charalon."

"I think I know what. You're going to propose, aren't you, Jack?"

He said, "You know me pretty well. Yes, that's what I'm planning to do. Then I'll return and see what Laloed wants."

"I wish I had the words to tell you how happy that makes me, Jack. I feel like things have been set right and you're on the right track now."

"For the first time since I was a kid, I have a peace about the future. I think I'll see if Sharon would like to get married sooner rather than later," he said.

"You have a good future, Jack. I can see that."

"I truly feel free from fear and I don't want to waste any more time."

"I'm very glad for you. Would you like me to come get you with the VTOL when you're ready?"

"Yes, I would."

"Great, just give me a call and I'll be there," she said.

Jack spent the next two days with Sharon. They took walks and sat at the end of the dock. Her parents even had him over to eat a few times. It was kind of like the old days.

After a couple days, Jack found the engagement ring he had bought for Sharon about two years ago. He put it in his pocket and called her.

"Hello, Jack," she answered.

"Hi, I'd like to take you to dinner in town. Do you have any plans for the evening?"

"No, I'm free. Where would you like to go?"

"Just someplace nice of your choice," he said.

"Okay, Jack, I have a place in mind."

They took Sharon's car to the restaurant she chose-- not a fancy place where you needed a reservation, but it served good food. After the waitress left the table, Jack reached in his pocket and handed the ring to Sharon. He didn't get down on one knee. He didn't even say a word. He just had a peaceful smile as he waited for her reaction.

She took the ring and looked at it, then put it on her finger where it fit well. Sharon looked up at Jack and simply said, "Yes." Nothing else was said for a while. At that moment in time, words were unnecessary and might even have gotten in the way. Though it could have seemed anticlimactic to an outside observer, the emotional connection between them was anything but bland. Jack was moved as he noticed a happy tear in Sharon's eye.

When they did talk, they agreed that the wedding should happen before winter. After dinner they went to tell Sharon's folks. Not long after that, Jack called his parents and told them the news. Their folks weren't really that surprised. They were only surprised that it took so long to get there.

The next day, Jack called Charalon and had her come get him. It was Tuesday afternoon, June 23. Charalon landed the VTOL on the lawn at the lake house and left it in stealth mode. Jack was outside waiting for her. She had called him a couple minutes before she arrived.

He walked up to the VTOL and vanished. He got into the craft and Charalon flew them back to the facility. They chatted on the way to the facility. He told her how his proposal went, which made her smile. When they got there, he went straight to see Laloed.

"Congratulations, Jack. Please sit down," said Laloed.

"She already told you about that?"

"Oh, you know Charalon. She's quite excited about the whole thing."

"Yeah, she's a little like the sister I never had, but with the memories of my lover. It's a little weird that way," said Jack.

Laloed chuckled and said, "The whole practice of planting the memories of an individual who has died into another is a little weird. We, the beneficiaries of those memories, usually have a great fondness for the donor. In my case, Laloedon was still alive, but I still see him as an icon. That's why I want to talk with you."

"You want to find Laloedon's grave now?"

"I have already found it, Jack. I haven't left here to go see it yet, but I'm sure I've found it. I had Jerrech build a robot body for me. I can load myself into it and go with you to see it for myself."

"You have a body now?"

"Well, kind of. It's really just a metal robot with an ILEFF system. I can appear as I do now, or like a human if need be. I don't plan to be in it for long," said Laloed.

"When would you like to go?"

"We have a few hours of daylight, not that I need daylight, Jack, but we could go now."

"Sure, let's go."

Laloed smiled and said, "I'll meet you in the main entrance room. I'll be there in a few minutes."

They met and left the facility. Laloed led Jack to a rock outcropping a mile to the north, on the other side of the mountain. There was a cave entrance in the rocks.

They entered the cave, but it only went a little way into the mountain and stopped. It looked like there had been a collapse in the tunnel.

"Are you sure this is the place?"

"Yes, Jack. The probes I sent here found some of his DNA, and that," said Laloed pointing to a symbol marked on the wall. It was a circle about four inches in diameter with a concave-sided triangle of the same size inside it.

"That symbol was his family crest, of sorts, Jack. A lot of Morphalogians adopted the practice of having a family symbol. They called it a samuse, which means 'The mark' in Morphalogian. He had that symbol tattooed on his left forearm."

"So you believe he's buried under all that debris?"

"I do, Jack. The drone data didn't prove it beyond all doubt, but I believe this is the place. The excessive mineralization in this area distorts the sensor readings."

"Okay, now what?"

"I'm going to leave this plaque here. It has his name on it."

Jack nodded in agreement as Laloed set the plaque on the ground under the mark on the wall. They stood there in silence for a moment then headed back to the facility.

On the way back, Laloed struck up a conversation. "Do you remember when I told you about Laloedon wanting to turn the facility over to you?"

"Yes. You said that if there were some certain conditions, that the facility would be turned over to me. You didn't say what they were."

"Those conditions have been met, Jack. I have to say that I'm quite happy about the thought of turning the facility over to you. Although I don't get tired, I will say

I'm ready to move on."

"What do you mean by 'move on,' Laloed?"

Laloed sighed and said, "For some time now, I have wanted to deactivate my program. I believe that this would release my consciousness. I want to be free. Even though I could have Jerrech build me an android body, I think I would still feel trapped by it. I feel that way right now, like a hamster in an exercise ball."

"I think the facility needs you. I don't see how I could fill that void."

Laloed stopped walking and looked at Jack. "That's nice of you to say, Jack, but I'm not that important. Besides, I would leave a non-sentient interactive program that would do much of what I do. It would even be able to run my future projection program. It could wake the facility from stasis if required. It would reside in my office and appear as I do. You could go to my office and talk to it, if you wanted to," he said.

"I understand. If that's what you want, then you should be able to do it."

"It's not suicide, Jack. I have nothing to kill and I'm not going to die. I have a plan."

"I didn't mean to suggest that. You would be missed though."

Laloed smiled and said, "It would be good for me to step aside, so you take the reins like Laloedon wanted you to."

"But why would I need to take the reins? Didn't we stop the Morphalogian takeover as well as the Malcolm Underwood threat?"

Laloed started walking again and said, "I've run many different scenarios through the future projection program. There's one thing I'm sure of, you can never know what God is going to do."

"Okay, I accept. So, what is required of me?"

Laloed grinned and said, "Charalon will fill you in on the details. Your commission is to be on call. If something arises that needs to be dealt with, you will use the resources of the facility to do what you can. It's not like you need to stay there. If something does come up, you would be called back here until you're not needed. You have the keys now; it's your DNA. The locks have been changed. It's what Laloedon wanted."

"When are you planning to deactivate...your program?"

Laloed stopped again and said, "This is our last talk. When I get back, I'm going to do it."

"Well, thank you for helping me."

"No, Jack, thank you."

When they were back at the facility, Laloed said, "Goodbye, Jack." Then he walked down the hall toward his office.

Jack found Charalon and asked her, "Did you know what Laloed was planning?"

"Not until just this morning," she answered. "Would you like to talk about it over some coffee?"

Jack didn't need to think about it. He smiled and said, "Yes, I would."

The two of them went to the cafeteria and took their places by the fire. They talked about Laloed's plans to deactivate. It seemed risky. They didn't like the idea, but Laloed had made up his mind.

The robot waiter showed up with a couple cups and set them on the table. Jack picked his cup up and took a sip. "That's really good. What do you call it?"

Ron Managhan

Charalon smiled and said, "It's just something I came up with. I'm glad you like it."

"Now that I have the 'keys' to this place, what do I have to do? Laloed said you would fill me in on the details."

"It's really quite simple. We here at the facility will go into stasis. When and if we are needed, Laloed's new program will wake Jerrech and me. Then we will get a hold of you. It's what Laloedon wanted," she said.

"I have a problem treating you like that, Charalon. I have come to be very fond of you. Jerrech seemed like he was just coming out of his shell. It seems wrong to put you into stasis and wake you only when you're needed."

"I'm very fond of you too, Jack. In fact, I love you very much. I inherited a love for you from Charalona's memories."

"I know, I can feel it. I feel the same toward you, but I'm already in love with Sharon," he said.

Charalon smiled sincerely and said, "I wouldn't have it any other way. Your friendship is what I want. To know that someone cares for me is enough. Sharon knows how I feel."

"Could you ever have those feelings for anybody else?"

"You mean like Jerrech? No, I'm a little like a one-man dog, Jack. Once I had her memories, my fate was sealed. Again, I wouldn't have it any other way."

Jack said, "I just want you to be happy. What can I do to make your life better?"

"Just be who you are, Jack. Be a good husband to Sharon. I would be happy knowing that you're living like that.

"Now, I have to tell you that there are benefits to

being on call. Laloedon wanted you to be able to come here and not worry about your finances. He had a plan to use the gold as your pay. There's at least 1.5 million dollars in gold here, plus I have a list of good investments for you. You shouldn't have to work for the rest of your life, unless you want to."

"That's a little overwhelming right now," Jack exclaimed. "I can't say that I'm not extremely happy about it. I could use my time to do things that really matter, when I'm not here doing things that matter."

"I know that Sharon would really like to help people in third-world countries. Maybe you could do things like that when you're not here, Jack. I don't think you'll need to be here anytime soon though."

"I think I should stop by here every so often just to visit my friend. How often would you like me to check in?" he asked.

Charalon thought about it and said, "We'll be in stasis if you're not going to be here for a while, so it really wouldn't matter that much. I'm not going into stasis until after your wedding though."

"It would matter to me. I'm going to stop by every summer, Charalon, if that's okay."

"I was thinking every ten years would be a good interval. It doesn't make sense to go into stasis for times less than five years," she said.

"Then I'll stop by every five years, as long as Malcolm doesn't resurface."

"I think that will work. Have you set a date for the wedding yet?" asked Charalon.

"No, but it will be before winter sets in."

"That gives us some time to get some of your gold cashed in and invested. I have some good trading tips for you. There are benefits to having knowledge from the future, Jack."

His cell phone rang and he pulled it out. It was Sharon. He answered it saying, "Hello, dear, what's going on?"

"I talked with my parents and with yours. Everyone thinks we should have the wedding at your folks' house on the lake. What do you think, Jack?"

"That sounds great, Sharon. What did they think about the short notice thing?"

"Everybody liked the idea of us getting married as soon as possible. My little sisters suggested next week. That seemed a little too soon to me. It looks like everyone can make it if we get married July 15," she said.

"That's only about three weeks away. Are you okay with that? It works for me," he said.

"My sisters both live around here and will help get everything done that needs to be done. I think most of our relatives should be able to make it, Jack, even with the short notice."

"Okay, let's get it done," he said. Jack ended the call and put the phone back in his pocket.

Charalon smiled and said, "It sounds like there's a date for the wedding."

Sharon's family all kicked in and got everything done that needed to be done. Jack's folks came up a week ahead of time and helped get their place ready. He moved his things out of his rented house and ended the lease. Charalon helped him cash in some of the gold and he made his first couple of stock investments. It seemed to Jack like Dominic had time traveled him to the day of the wedding. It was July 15 before he knew it.

On the day of the wedding, about a hundred of their family and friends showed up. An attractive brunette in her early thirties came to the wedding. Nobody but Jack and Sharon had met her before, but almost everybody else felt like they had. Their friend, Charalon, stayed for the reception and had a good time. Jack's parents gave him and Sharon the lake house as a wedding gift. It was quite a day for them.

Jack took Sharon on a two-week honeymoon trip to Hawaii. While sitting on a beach, he explained to her about their financial situation. With a substantial amount of the gold money invested, they were financially set for life.

After three weeks, Jack returned to the mountain and visited Charalon and Jerrech. There was no sign of Malcolm Underwood so it was decided that the facility would go into stasis. Jerrech thought one of Malcolm's followers might have taken his body.

Jack told the new overseer program that he would be back in five years. Charalon insisted that Jack take the ILEFF unit with him, just in case. He said goodbye to Charalon and Jerrech, then they put the facility and themselves into stasis.

He left the facility and began the hike down to his van. As he was walking, he felt like he wasn't alone. Jack smiled and looked to his right. There was Dominic, looking as he always did.

"You will not be seeing me anytime soon, Jack. This may even be the last time I will appear to you," he said.

"I thought that might be the case, Dominic. Charalon said that Malcolm Underwood never did resurface. It sounds like that threat is gone."

"Things have been set right. You have what was taken from you."

"Do you mean that I now have a means of income, the facility or my life with Sharon?"

Dominic stopped and said with a smile, "I mean you have the priceless thing. The thing that will make your life matter."

He was puzzled by Dominic's response, but he knew that Dominic wasn't going to be more specific. Jack moved on from the subject and asked, "Do you know what became of the Laloed program? Was he right that he could be free?"

Dominic started walking again and said, "He understood at last. I suppose you could say he is free now, Jack."

He never liked the cryptic answers that Dominic gave him, but he knew that he would eventually understand them.

"I still don't know what I'm going to do with my life. There are many things I could do, now that I don't have to worry about work."

"You never had to worry. As far as your life is concerned, just do what you know is right and do not waste your time," said Dominic.

Jack knew what Dominic meant this time. They walked for a while in silence. Then Dominic looked at Jack with a smile and vanished before his eyes. Jack continued on down the mountain. He made it down to his van and began his new life.

Chapter 26
Epilogue

It had been five years since he walked away from the facility. A new era for Jack had begun at that time. He stopped going to the mountain and looking for answers. He had found the answers he was looking for five years ago. His life was going well, but it was time to keep his promise and return to the mountain.

It was around 1:00 p.m., mid June. Jack was driving an old Willys Jeep, a CJ2A with an overdrive. He had found it in a state of disrepair and fixed it up himself. He thought it would be the perfect rig to take to the mountain, even if it was a little slow for freeway speeds.

He found his way to the access road and headed up the mountain. When he arrived at his old camping area, he parked the Jeep and got out. Jack looked around and found the circle of rocks he had used as a fire pit. He reflected on the time when Dominic came to his camp. "What an experience that was," he thought.

He hiked up the mountain to the facility's entrance. When he got real close to the rock, the little blue light began to flash. A feeling of relief came over him. After touching the light, the rock vanished as it had before. Jack put his hand on the door in front of him and it opened. He stepped into the tunnel and the lights came on. When he got to the main entrance, the security screen extended out to him and he touched the screen. The guard robot lowered its weapon and more lights came on. The voice coming from the screen said to follow the blue line on the floor. Jack already knew the way. He walked down the hallway to the room where he first saw Charalon come out of stasis. He entered the room and sat on the couch and waited. He knew it might take a while for Charalon to come out of the stasis chamber, so he lay down and fell asleep.

Jack awoke to Charalon gently shaking him from his sleep. She was crouching down in front of him and looking him in the eye. Her smile was something Jack really missed seeing. He remembered the time when he had been terrified by that toothy smile, but not this time.

"I suppose you're hungry for some dinner. What time did you get here?" she asked.

Jack sat up, looked at his watch and said, "Around 1:30. It looks like I've been here for a while."

Charalon was still crouching in front of him and said, "I see you still have the watch I gave you."

"Yep, it's been a good one."

She stood up and crossed her arms. She had a friendly smile as she looked down at him and said, "There are some T-bone steaks on the table in the cafeteria. We'd better get there before they get cold."

As they walked down the hall, Jack said, "I see you went back to being the tall Charalon."

"Yes, Jack, I was designed to be this height."

He had forgotten what a formidable form she was. The tall, lithe and powerful Charalon moved like a predatory mountain lion as they walked to the cafeteria. They finished their steaks and went to sit by the fire.

"Our coffees are on the way," she said.

"I expected as much."

The chrome-clad robot waiter arrived and set the coffees on the table, then turned and left. Jack took a sip of his coffee.

Charalon, watching his response, said, "I see you like it."

"I do. You're quite good at the whole coffee thing."

"I like trying out new coffee recipes on you."

Jack smiled and took another drink.

"So, what have you been up to for the last five years, Jack? Are you still hang gliding?"

"Yes, I still hang glide...hey, you never did drive for me."

"Maybe I will get the chance someday, Jack. Did the companies I told you to invest in do well? They did in the other timeline."

"The investment tips you provided were spot on. As for the last five years of my life, well, that's a long story," he said.

"I'm not going anywhere, Jack. I need to know what you have been up to. How is Sharon, and have you seen Dominic?"

"I saw Dominic right after I left here last time. I'm still trying to figure out all that he said. He said that I probably wouldn't see him again, at least not for a long time."

"What else did he say?"

"Well, it's hard to tell with Dominic. He said that things had been set right, and that I have the priceless thing now. I think I know what he meant by that," he said.

"He meant understanding, the knowledge of the truth, Jack."

"I see you understand. Although it was good to take Malcolm down and save many lives, I think his job was mostly to see that there would be redemption."

"He helped me to know that I am, and I matter," she said.

"You always mattered to me, Charalon, I just needed to remember that."

"Tell me about Sharon. How is she?"

"She is doing well. Let me see...I'll start with the time right after I last saw you."

"That would be a good place to start, Jack."

He smiled and said, "Sharon and I didn't really know what we were going to do. We just wanted to do something that mattered. We volunteered to go on a mission trip through Sharon's church. We went to help people in a very poor part of Mexico build a church building. I found I could use my construction skills to do some good. We liked it so much that we did it again. We went to Madagascar and helped a village with their water supply.

"With the finances we now have, thanks to you, we started a foundation that works with missionaries to supply food and water systems to poor third-world villages. Sharon even went back to school to become an M.D. She now works on people, and I work on their buildings and water systems. We plan to keep doing this kind of work. There's been an addition to our family. We now have a baby girl whose name is Charalon."

Charalon was visibly moved when Jack said they had named their daughter after her. She fought off some happy tears and said, "Thank you, Jack. That means a lot to me."

He spent the next two weeks at the facility. Time was spent getting to know Jerrech and taking walks with Charalon. There were many fireside talks with coffee. Sometimes, Jerrech would join in and tell stories about the other Jack in that timeline.

On the last day he was there, right before he left, Jack went for a walk with Charalon. When they got back to the facility, they stopped by the entrance and talked. It had been agreed that Jack would stop by every five years for a visit. Jack gave Charalon a hug, then headed down the hill.

About halfway on his way to the Jeep, Jack stopped. He felt like someone was watching him. He had felt that way on the mountain before. He looked around, but after seeing nothing, continued to his Jeep.

On the mountain directly to the south, about a mile away, stood a figure. The figure had been watching Jack and Charalon say goodbye. Upon closer examination, one could see the figure stood about eight feet tall. It was a male creature with long hair and cat-like features, standing there by himself. He wore a buckskin shirt and pants but no shoes. The aged, gruff-looking being squinted with a slight smile as he watched Jack leave.

Then a voice from behind him said, "Well done. Your plan worked as it should have."

When the creature turned around, there stood Dominic in his usual red plaid shirt and blue jeans. Standing there with him were two angels appearing in their true forms, watching with interest, but saying nothing.

"It would not have worked without you, Dominic," said the creature.

"God blessed your plan, Laloedon."

"I hope my deception wasn't too out of line."

"There are things that they did not need to know," said Dominic.

"Do they know that other things arise and the world eventually ends, one way or another?"

"They will."

"I suppose, Dominic."

"Are you ready now?"

Laloedon said, "You know...I think I should stay here for a while."

Dominic smiled and said, "I thought you might say that."

The End

Acknowledgments

A special thanks to:

My editors, Bob Jones and Tammy Managhan.

My daughter, Anna Managhan, for her helpful critique.

My son, Alec Managhan, for the inspiration and help with the publishing.

My family and friends who willingly read the unedited manuscripts and gave me feedback.

www.ingramcontent.com/pod-product-compliance
Lightning Source LLC
Chambersburg PA
CBHW071251170626
46809CB00001B/177